HARSHA

HARSHA

The Fearless Warrior of Thanesar

Rajat Pillai

JAICO PUBLISHING HOUSE

Ahmedabad Bangalore Bhopal Chennai
Delhi Hyderabad Kolkata Lucknow Mumbai

DISCLAIMER

This is a work of fiction inspired by real events. No claim for complete accuracy is made through this work.

Published by Jaico Publishing House
A-2 Jash Chambers, 7-A Sir Phirozshah Mehta Road
Fort, Mumbai - 400 001
jaicopub@jaicobooks.com
www.jaicobooks.com

HARSHA: THE FEARLESS WARRIOR OF THANESAR
ISBN 978-93-91019-66-2

First Jaico Impression: 2022

Page design and layout by Inosoft Systems, Delhi

Nutech Photolithographers, New Delhi

To two friends, Muraleedharan and Mohan Kumar.
Hope they are in a good place and having a good time.

one

Battle-Hardened

It had rained intermittently in the past few days, but the thunderstorms before had done the damage. The Dharini River had breached its banks eight days back and the flooding was of a magnitude never seen before in these parts. Nearer the horizon one could see dunes with a few trees emerging out of the water, like miniature islands. Everywhere else, there was only murky water in varying depths. On the surface it was placid, concealing all the misery and debris below, like people who lead normal lives.

Two armies stood facing each other in knee-deep water. A face-off was imminent and unavoidable. Whether rain or sunshine, flood or drought, poverty or prosperity, human conflict is bereft of a sense of time, place and even reason. Here, the reason for conflict was a piece of land next to a narrow stretch of the river which gave a strategic advantage to the conqueror.

Mounted atop a white horse was Crown Prince Rajyavardhan of Sthaneshwar, commanding his army. His face resembled that of a child who had abruptly grown into an adult. Rajyavardhan's compassionate eyes, pleasant smile and beaming righteousness were overshadowed today by a look of controlled anxiety because his younger brother had accompanied him to the battlefield for the very first time. Murmuring a prayer for his own men and for those he was about to fight, he inspected the terrain ahead. Next to him, seated on a brown horse, was his maternal cousin Bhandi, 20 years old, the same age as Rajyavardhan but with a more rugged and mature look owing to his whiskers and beard. His sharp eyes were the only remarkable feature on a face and body covered by scars from burns sustained in his childhood.

"They neither have a battle formation nor seem to have a battle plan," Bhandi commented.

Rajyavardhan's eyes narrowed as he surveyed the battlefield, "We need to be cautious because they seem willing to give it all they have."

"We can handle that kind of difficulty! What do you say, Harsha?" remarked Bhandi.

A little behind them was the crown prince's younger brother Harshavardhan, fondly called Harsha. He was 17 and looked his age. His fair skin, sharp features, long straight hair and dark brown eyes made him a very attractive-looking young man. He had a distinct scar, a red birthmark on his left cheek. His lucky charm, a gold chain with a tiger-claw pendant, a gift from his father, dangled around his neck below the armour. His thoughts today oscillated between summoning his inner strength and a certain reluctance. This was the moment for which he had prepared for years, but he also wondered if he really belonged here.

"I am Prabhakarvardhan's son. I will not shy away from a difficult situation," said Harsha, concealing his anxiety.

King Prabhakar, the ruler of Sthaneshwar and the father of the princes, was convinced that his army chief Chakravarti was not required to accompany the princes for this particular mission. "Let them handle the situation. It will prepare them for the future," he had said, handing over the family sword Asi to his elder son, Rajyavardhan. The sword, made of iron alloy with a copper and gold-plated handle, and inscribed with the 108 names of Shiva, was a royal heirloom. Named after the mythical blade used to slay demons, it was a symbol of trust and responsibility passed on from one generation to the next.

Facing the brothers and their soldiers was the Malava army commanded by a veteran army general named Gyanabhatt. However, contrary to his name, he was known not for his knowledge but for his brutality. Just like his master, the ruthless King Devagupta of Malava, the bald general had a prominent scar that ran across his face. His men, positioned behind him, were anxious and in disarray. Their situation had turned precarious soon after they crossed the Dharini in large numbers and encroached on the bordering villages of the Sthaneshwar kingdom. The heavy rains and unexpected flood had cut them off from their kingdom, leaving them without supplies or reinforcements. They would have to manage for another couple of days before help arrived. In the meanwhile, the Sthaneshwar army was waiting to eliminate them and secure the banks of the Dharini before the floods receded.

The silence before the battle was unsettling.

"Attack! Finish them!" Gyanabhatt yelled, pulling at the reins, making his horse rear.

Instantly, his soldiers charged at the Sthaneshwar army.

Rajyavardhan and Bhandi raised their swords. "Har Har Mahadev!"

Rajyavardhan and Harsha stayed behind with a small contingent of soldiers while Bhandi and his men galloped into the enemy lines. A little later, as if nature wanted to join the action on the ground, it started to rain. The fighting in the waterlogged, rain-drenched battlefield was fierce. Gyanabhatt was armed with a sword in one hand and a heavy mace with sharp spikes in the other. His combat style was barbaric—he would swiftly move his horse around, stab a Sthaneshwar soldier with his sword and follow it up immediately with a blow to his face with the spiked mace.

"I have never seen so much brutality and blood in my life!" Harsha exclaimed. He took a deep breath, then exhaled slowly. He had not come to the battleground for its thrills but because it had been inculcated in his mind since childhood that this was his duty.

"Use your emotions, let them not use you," Rajyavardhan said.

Bhandi and his soldiers were slowly and steadily driving the rival army towards Rajyavardhan and Harsha. The stretches of deep water limited the space for battle.

Blazing a trail of mutilated dead soldiers, Gyanabhatt noticed a young cavalry soldier from Sthaneshwar galloping towards him. Harsha watched the young man too—good-looking, skilful with the sword; he seemed to be in his late teens. From this distance, Harsha saw the two warriors engaged in a fierce sword fight. It was a fight among equals, until Trivikram, the bearded rival deputy, mounted on a black stallion, spear in hand, joined in the fight to assist Gyanabhatt.

"Unfair!" murmured Rajyavardhan.

Taking advantage of the distraction, Gyanabhatt swung his mace at the Sthaneshwar cavalry soldier, taking him by surprise. The impact almost dislodged his jaw, leaving a blood-drenched mess. As the poor soldier crouched on his horse, Gyanabhatt's sword slashed his neck. The headless body clung to the horse. Gyanabhatt said something in a mocking manner to Trivikram and then signalled to another soldier to pass him a flag of Malava tied to a metal rod. The ruthless general dug the flag into the neck of the blood-drenched torso. The body fell off the horse, to the laughter of the Malava soldiers. This type of intimidation usually worked, petrifying young rival soldiers, often instilling enough fear to make them flee the battlefield.

"Bloodthirsty savages!" exclaimed Rajyavardhan as the brothers looked on in disbelief.

Harsha took out his bow and arrow, "This is unacceptable!" He took aim with the arrow, stretching the bow as far as possible. He was one of the better marksmen of Sthaneshwar, something that made his parents and the royal family proud. He took his time to get his aim right and was lethal in long-range shots.

The arrow traversed the battlefield, missed Gyanabhatt and killed the soldier right behind him. Harsha's next arrow followed immediately. Rajyavardhan's gaze followed the trajectory as it again missed the target and dug into Gyanabhatt's horse above its hind leg. The animal neighed loudly and, despite the obvious pain, raised its forelegs and wheeled around.

"You will not get your mark today because of the wind and rain," said Rajyavardhan.

Gyanabhatt saw Bhandi and his contingent driving his men from the right side. With the waterlogged portions of the terrain to their left, they had no option but to move towards Harsha and Rajyavardhan.

"He is making the mistake of abandoning his home territory and heading for us. It's your day today, Harsha, believe me. It was on our mother Queen Yashomati's insistence that I came here to support you, otherwise I trust your ability to handle this by yourself," said Rajyavardhan, as he placed his hand on his brother's shoulder. Harsha responded with a smile that was only half reassuring and his brother could see the strain in his eyes. Rajyavardhan knew that his brother had retained only a pale shadow of self-confidence from his adolescent years. Even a few years of people creating an illusory image, judging one against it and continued public banter can shake a person's confidence. At his age, it was difficult for Harsha to shrug off those numerous eyes that watched his every move carefully as fodder for laughter or gossip. It was harsh on a young man to be perceived as a failure even before he came into his own. Only time had the power to resolve that. Leaning forward, Rajyavardhan tightened the thick leather straps on Harsha's alloy-plated armour. He also adjusted his brother's bronze helmet. "Now it's perfect!" Harsha replaced his bow and pulled out his sword.

"Remember to be careful of stray arrows!" said Rajyavardhan.

Harsha replied, "You also take care."

"Do well! Let your enemies know that you are a warrior matching your father's stature. I'll cover you from here, just as mother instructed," Rajyavardhan said as he raised his sword to signal readiness for the attack.

"Har Har Mahadev!" Harsha gave out the war cry and along with his men, charged at the enemy heading towards them.

The soldiers led by Bhandi were steadily driving the Malava army from behind, who crashed into the group led by Harsha. Due to the rain, it was difficult to follow the proceedings from a distance. Gyanabhatt saw Harsha and recognised him as one of the faces from a life-size painting of the Vardhan family he had seen a year ago. His scarred face lit up. "They sent Prabhakarvardhan's 17-year-old into my territory to wage battle," he said to Trivikram. "I admire their confidence. They expect this lad to get out of here alive."

Gyanabhatt directed his horse towards Harsha. His cunning mind was already devising plans to capture the young man and negotiate with Rajyavardhan to cease battle till such time as the flood subsided and their reinforcements arrived. His master, King Devagupta, would spare his life for having persevered throughout the rainy season and still maintained their army encroachment on this side of the Dharini.

Followed closely on horseback by Trivikram, Gyanabhatt smashed his way through the heads of Sthaneshwar soldiers to reach Harsha. His horse was limping slightly since the arrow was still stuck near its hind leg, but Gyanabhatt did not pay attention to it. "Nice shiny sword! Looks like this young boy has got a new toy to play with," he yelled out to his deputy.

"Just that he selected the wrong place to play with it," Trivikram said with a sly smile.

Gyanabhatt's eyes opened wide and spit squirted from his mouth as he shouted, "This is not the play area that you think it is. You are stuck in the wrong place with the wrong kind of people now."

"You talk a lot! Come here and let's settle this," said Harsha.

From his position on the battlefield, Rajyavardhan watched with pride his brother's skill with weapons. Every now and then, when Gyanabhatt swung his mace in a surprise move, Harsha blocked it with equal might using his metal shield. Their horses moved back and forth as their swords clanged ferociously. Then Harsha made a surprise strike at Gyanabhatt's head. In that instant, the wily soldier moved backwards. Harsha had dislodged Gyanabhatt's sword from his hand, but Trivikram swiftly intervened and tried to spear Harsha. As the young prince quickly moved sideways to save himself, his shield fell out of his hand.

"Vicious barbarians!" Rajyavardhan swore. He was very far from Harsha and there were a thousand soldiers engaged in fierce battle between them. The plan of safely familiarising Harsha with a battlefield had gone haywire.

Gyanabhatt swung his mace at Harsha. As his horse moved forward, Harsha bent backwards to avoid the strike. Before he could realise what was happening, Harsha fell off his horse, dropping his sword in the process.

"This is getting out of hand!" exclaimed Rajyavardhan, reining in his mount.

Unarmed, Harsha sprang to his feet only to instantly realise that Gyanabhatt and Trivikram were charging towards him from opposite sides. Time froze. Harsha tried to control his nerves and think of his options. At a distance, Rajyavardhan was trying in vain to reach his brother.

Waving his mace, smiling from ear to ear, Gyanabhatt rode towards the hapless 17-year-old prince, whose skull he was about to smash to splinters. Harsha turned. He saw Trivikram at a little distance, galloping towards him with his spear.

Rajyavardhan and Bhandi too were trying to reach him from opposite sides. A stray arrow in his shoulder disoriented Rajyavardhan, but he pulled it out immediately, ripping a chunk of flesh along with it. Ahead of him, Harsha stood still, eyes focused on Gyanabhatt as he rushed towards him like a whirlwind, mace swinging. In a flash, Harsha bent backwards, almost reclining, saving himself from the mace in the nick of time. He quickly grabbed the arrow which protruded above the hind leg of Gyanabhatt's horse and pulled it out. The horse neighed in agony, reared and turned in an abrupt circle, throwing Gyanabhatt on the ground. Trivikram tried to stab Harsha with his spear but the young prince rolled away sideways and saved himself once again. He noticed that Gyanabhatt was about to get up from the ground and dashed towards him. Gyanabhatt knew that the situation was in his favour because he was still holding on to his mace. He pounced on Harsha and pinned him down with his spare arm and shoulder. Harsha gripped Gyanabhatt's wrist that held the mace.

"It's sad that you will die so young," growled Gyanabhatt.

Harsha grasped the arrowhead and pierced Gyanabhatt's throat, stabbing him thrice and crying out, "Die! Die! Die!"

Gyanabhatt's eyes widened, blood gushed out of his mouth. Harsha lay still for a few seconds, dazed by what he had just done. Then, he stood up and wiped the blood from his face. Trivikram saw Harsha standing over the dead body of his master, holding the mace. A rider rushed towards Harsha, spear in hand. Harsha grabbed it and, pulling his attacker down, hit him on the shoulder with the mace. Dropping the weapon, Harsha snatched his fallen sword and ran to mount his horse which was waiting a little way off. Confrontation was no longer an option for Trivikram. His army, already reduced to one-third its size, started to panic as the news of Gyanabhatt's death spread. Many soldiers started to flee the battlefield. The enemy seemed to be retreating but it was taking an unnaturally long time. Harsha wondered what was going on. Sporadic clashes continued, which came to an abrupt stop when the losing army fled the battlefield.

Something is not right, Harsha thought.

It was getting dark. The long day had finally come to an end. Harsha spotted Rajyavardhan at a distance and rode towards him.

"What happened? You told me to be careful of stray arrows and look at that wound."

Rajyavardhan said, “I forgot about my surroundings when you were in danger.”

“We need to take you to the physician in our camp now!” exclaimed Harsha.

“I think we have a bigger problem than that to handle. Trivikram’s men have taken Bhandi and eight of our soldiers captive before escaping.”

“Where will they escape to? With all this flooding around us, they have no option but to camp nearby under our watch.”

“You’re right. We are all stuck here for a while. They might ask for a negotiation tomorrow morning.”

Rajyavardhan and Harsha knew that with both parties being in a really tight situation, it was going to be an intense battle of wits—one party would want to buy time and the other would not want to lose any.

two

Difficult Conversations

Even a full moon was not able to counter the all-engulfing darkness. Outside their tent, Harsha stood looking towards the battlefield. Every once in a while, a slight breeze wafted in from that direction, bringing along the stench of rotting corpses. Rajyavardhan saw his brother standing outside, looking sad. He came up from behind, splashing through the water, and put an arm around Harsha's shoulders.

"The good part of today was that it was your first day in the battlefield and you fared well!"

When his younger brother turned to him, in the light of the flaming torch, Rajyavardhan saw that his eyes were red and moist.

"That sense of achievement is missing! I am just 17 and, in a moment of self-preservation, I acted rather violently. It's so strange; killing a person, ending his life with my own hands," said Harsha, his voice quivering.

Rajyavardhan tightened his arm around his brother's shoulders, "You are a warrior. This is your dharma."

"These people we killed in the battle have families and loved ones."

"Harsha! These men made a choice to be involved in this. If we did not eliminate them, they would encroach further into our kingdom, plunder our villages, attack our women and children. We need to keep aside remorse and protect our people."

Harsha sighed, "It's easier said than done."

"Most of them are mercenaries or henchmen of warlords, and even if they have families, these men knew what they were getting into when they stepped into our land to torment our people."

"As a young boy, I was fascinated by the tales of bravery and wars. In reality it is so grotesque."

"It is a dirty game, Harsha. Often, cowardly leaders satisfy their ego by declaring wars. Then they hide behind hapless soldiers who have nothing to do with the conflict. War is nothing but strangers with no real animosity killing each other."

"*Jyeshta-sri*! I don't feel victorious; instead, I feel very low."

"You seem to have inherited qualities from both our parents. Sometimes you are emotional and vulnerable like mother; not as much as her, but close. At other times, you are as mentally tough, calm and composed as father is."

"That is an exaggeration!" Harsha smiled. "I am not like mother."

They looked at the small dots of illumination from the fire torches lit by the Malava army far away.

"Harsha, Trivikram has asked for negotiations tomorrow morning."

"Now that he has taken Bhandi and some of our men hostage, he will be using that to his advantage. Let me meet him."

"No! Things can go really wrong during a negotiation. It can get dangerous for those present and also for Bhandi and his men."

Rajyavardhan, Bhandi and Harsha had grown up together inside Thanesara palace, a close team since childhood.

Harsha replied, “These are precisely my reasons for going. You are the crown prince and your life is precious. I will ensure nothing bad happens to Bhandi and our men. Please give me a chance. I need to learn all this someday.”

Reluctantly, Rajyavardhan agreed to let Harsha lead the negotiations the next day.

Harsha twisted and turned on his sleeping mat all night, wondering what stance his enemy would take and what his arguments would be. Lives were at stake. He could not go wrong or upset his rivals. The Malava king Devagupta was known to be ruthless and unforgiving. Should the line of argument and negotiation be diverted in that direction? To bring out the hidden fears in the minds of the rival soldiers. It started to rain abruptly. The thick fabric of the tent absorbed the water and the night breeze made it extremely cold inside the tent. But it was not the chill that kept Harsha awake but a thought. Was he being overconfident by taking up something that was beyond his age? Harsha knew, from the look on their faces over the years, that some of the soldiers believed he received opportunities and praise for his martial skills only because he was a prince. The perception started at the harvest festival celebrations. His brother had just finished addressing the assembled crowd when, suddenly, his father asked Harsha to address them. Jittery, he fumbled in front of everyone and what he said did not make much sense. A few months later, during an army exhibition, the horse Harsha had selected decided to throw him off in the middle of the event. The roar of laughter from the onlookers still haunted him. It had been two years since then and a lot had changed, except for the perception created by these events. Harsha had always been careful to not let the thought of 'entitlement' cross his mind while interacting with others, but it did not matter because people believed what they wanted to believe. It is an amusing story since the beginning of time involving two siblings—one capable and the other being an 'entitled' lost cause. According to common belief, Rajyavardhan was indeed the better warrior, tactician and strategist. Harsha was fine with that, but he craved some respect. Tonight, it was not even about respect. Harsha believed that he was good at negotiation. All he wanted was to save the lives of his cousin and of his men.

Early in the morning, as was agreed upon, an unarmed Harsha along with two advisers started walking towards a spot midway between the Malava and Sthaneshwar camps. They were trailed by a group of ten archers spread out with arrows loaded and bows stretched, splashing water as they walked. From the other side, Trivikram and his two advisers appeared, followed by ten Malava archers. Harsha looked at Trivikram and his men. They looked tired, worried and were dishevelled. A slight drizzle started as they walked towards each other. The presence of archers from both sides added to the tense situation at the negotiation spot.

Trivikram looked annoyed, "I was expecting to meet your elder brother. Frankly, I am a bit surprised that you have turned up. I hope you understand the seriousness of what we are going to discuss." His dialect of Sanskrit was very different from the way people talked in Sthaneshwar.

"I definitely understand. My brother was keen to go after all of you, complete the mission and return home. On the contrary, it is my belief that there is no requirement for more bloodshed and there is indeed scope for discussion," replied Harsha in a matter-of-fact way, creating both a small connect and a mild threat.

"I am surprised your brother wanted to come after us knowing that we have your cousin Bhandi and eight soldiers as hostages. Is he not worried that they will be beheaded before we are harmed?"

Harsha paused for a split second before speaking, "For us, Bhandi is like any other soldier. When these men took up this job, they were willing to sacrifice their life for their kingdom. It's a small sacrifice for a larger cause."

A sarcastic smile spread across Trivikram's face, "You expect me to believe that? I suggest that, as both of us are in such a tight situation, we don't play mind games with each other. Let's be transparent."

For a moment, Harsha's heart skipped a beat. He felt overwhelmed and exposed. Trivikram was sharper than he thought.

"So, you speak your mind then," remarked Harsha.

"I say, all of you must return to your capital. After a couple of days, when we feel safe, we will release the hostages."

Harsha shook his head, "That is not even an option. We are not going anywhere. How can we trust you to keep your word? Not acceptable!"

"So then, what are we discussing? You people are more in number and you might kill us, but our hostages will surely be executed before that."

"Trivikram, that is the easier path for sure, but I believe we can avoid that kind of bloodshed. Tell me, what do you want?"

"Let me make you a better offer. We want a stoppage to the battle for six days, after which we will peacefully release the hostages."

This was followed by a long pause because Harsha knew that this was the right moment to weaken his enemy's argument and show him logical gaps. He said, "This is what I call placing your own life and that of your men in the hands of fate. You are expecting the rains to subside, the floods to recede and reinforcements to arrive by then. This buying time for six days or ten days is not a good idea. What if the rains and floods continue?"

"Then I guess it will be a prolonged deadlock for both sides." The breeze blew around them and both sides were silent. Harsha started to speak, when suddenly, because of the drizzle, one of his soldiers lost his grip on his arrow. It flew past the negotiating group, barely missing Trivikram's face. All the archers around them aimed their loaded bows at their rivals in a show of aggression. An already tense situation reached a sudden boil.

"Hold it, everyone!" said Harsha raising his hand, "It was a mistake, not intentional."

Trivikram said, "Stop, everyone! You were saying something."

Harsha looked Trivikram in the eye and said compassionately, "Your food supplies and the morale of your men will not sustain for that long. At some point, our army will lose patience and eliminate you all even at the cost of losing the hostages. What if the reinforcements arrive? Your King Devagupta is famous for not letting any lapses go unpunished. The leader of the reinforcements will get the credit for salvaging the situation. Depending on Devagupta's mood, all of you will be beheaded or imprisoned for life to pacify his hurt ego."

"What are you trying to say?"

"I am saying that you and your men have two options. One is to get killed in the battlefield or to be beheaded by your master Devagupta. I don't have to tell you how savage he is."

Trivikram said with a nervous smile, "I don't think so."

"Hmm... You are hoping against the inevitable. However, I can think of a third option," said Harsha and paused.

"And what is that?" Trivikram seemed to be latching on to the young prince's words by now. Good sign, Harsha thought.

"We will allow you safe passage to the forest near Kannauj in exchange for our men handed over to us peacefully. That way you escape from us as well as the wrath of your King Devagupta. If any of you have families, our soldiers can assist with a gradual relocation. With so many dead bodies floating here in the battle zone, you will all be presumed dead. This is your chance to start life anew in a neutral territory than be slaves to a tyrant king for life."

"Oh really? That does not sound like a good option to me."

Harsha paused and said, "Choose wisely! All your other options lead to dead ends."

Harsha was starting to feel that this was going to move in the wrong direction with undesirable consequences. Then suddenly an adviser behind Trivikram spoke out of turn, "Wait a moment! I think we need to discuss this internally."

Another of his archers added, "Yes! Let's not make any hasty decisions now."

Harsha had managed to use the climate of fear in the Malava army against them. Their king Devagupta had used all the wrong values to create the driving principles of his army. Externally, they looked like a strong cohesive unit but internally, they were weak, with every man fending for himself.

Trivikram looked at both the men behind him, thought for a moment and said, "Let's disengage for now and we will communicate our decision to you later in the day."

Next morning, they released the eight soldiers. Rajyavardhan and Harsha kept their word and allowed them safe passage to the forests bordering Kannauj. Bhandi was released just before the last of the Malava soldiers left. There was elation in the Sthaneshwar camp at the well-deserved victory that had been earned by a combination of might and mind.

The following day, Rajyavardhan told Harsha, "Before we return to Thanesara palace, let's take a quick detour to a place where some people are awaiting us."

three

Training Ground

East of Indraprastha, on the road to Thanesara, the capital of Sthaneshwar, was the training academy for young army recruits—Prashikshan Kendra of the Yuva-Sena. Surrounded by pristine forest-covered hills and accessible from the main highway, this was the grooming place for hand-picked prodigies. Rajyavardhan, Harsha and Bhandi had stopped over with their soldiers in the morning to oversee the daily regimen of the trainees. 2,000 cadets between 15 and 17 years of age who possessed exceptional combat skills had been screened and selected by Bhandi and Rajyavardhan from across the kingdom's villages. The official age of joining the army was 18 years and this academy was the training ground for these recruits. These young men eventually joined the more elite battalions of the Sthaneshwar army as future leaders of various units.

On this overcast morning, Rajyavardhan, Harsha and Bhandi were seated on wooden chairs in the centre of a podium attached to the main structure of the Kendra. The trainees' accommodation could be seen at a distance covering the perimeter of the training ground. Though the fatigue of the battle was visible on their faces, the princes and Bhandi were glad to see the brimming enthusiasm of the young men. Medicinal paste made out of turmeric and herbs had caused stains on a cloth wrapped tightly around Rajyavardhan's arm where the arrow had wounded him. Harsha had nothing more than a scratch across his face and a few bruises.

On the ground in front of them were 2,000 trainees seated in 20 columns. They were happy to get this opportunity to interact with the princes. Rajyavardhan had just shared with them his experience of joining his father in battle campaigns against the tribal warlords of the west. He stressed on how preparation was the most important thing in a battle. Bhandi chose not to address the recruits since he was not very good at public speaking. For the past few days, he had been feeling upset, annoyed with himself for being captured by the retreating Malava army. His horse, galloping at full speed, had been hit on the face by an enemy spear, thus flinging Bhandi down on the ground. Though some of his soldiers nearby had rushed to help, it was unfortunate that they were in the path of the retreating Malava army. Rajyavardhan and Harsha had tried to pacify Bhandi by reiterating many times that it was bad luck, but it did not help.

Rajyavardhan ended his speech by saying, "The first time you step on to a battlefield, you will get to know things about yourself that you never knew. I have seen the hands and legs of the best army trainees turn cold in the battlefield. I have also seen meek trainees transform into brave warriors, driven by self-preservation and patriotism. So, understand yourself and select the stream that suits you. Foot soldiers, archers, horseback riders and those managing the supplies, all matter in a war. I wish you all the very best!"

Everyone cheered for Rajyavardhan. A senior cadet got up and said, "I thank our dear crown prince for these useful insights. Now, for the amusement of Crown Prince Rajyavardhan and Harshavardhan, we present to you a local boy who hails from a nearby village. The first time the trainees of this academy saw him during the early morning run outside the premises, they were really surprised. Presenting to you our own Prince Harsha!"

From behind the podium appeared a boy dressed in a prince's costume with a fake crown. Rajyavardhan and Harsha were surprised since he looked a lot like Harsha. He walked around the podium like a royal. The trainees were in splits, laughing till their stomachs ached. Even the princes started to laugh along with them. Bhandi was the only one who was not amused. The resemblance was uncanny in the royal costume, but at the end of the act, when the boy took off his crown and grinned, the similarity ended.

"What is your name?" asked Rajyavardhan.

"Badrinath, from Jantiya village."

"You look like a better version of me," Harsha commented.

"I wish the royal family would adopt me!" replied Badrinath.

The shape of his head and teeth were very different from Harsha's, but the eyes and nose were exactly like his. He could pass off as Harsha if he wore a headgear and kept his mouth closed.

The next item of entertainment was a show of acrobatics and jugglery by some trainees. Once the performers left the podium, the senior cadet stood up again to speak, "Now I will present to you a tribal boy from near my native village. His special skills and knowledge is the reason we invited him to be with us for the past ten days or so. We have learned a lot from him in these few days and we would like our princes to hear him too. Come here, Radheya."

A dark, lean, colourfully dressed tribal boy walked to the podium to greet the princes and Bhandi. Two trainees dragged a wooden desk to the podium; on it were some herbs, metal holders and a strange dark ball made of dry leaves tied with hemp. The boy's bright eyes widened as he started speaking in a loud voice, thoroughly enjoying all the attention, "Today, my friends, we talk about weaknesses in animals. Knowledge passed on from generation to generation in my tribe. Tricks you can use as a prank or for self-defence. Tricks that will make you remember this not-so-humble tribal boy Radheya."

"That's interesting!" commented Rajyavardhan.

"Now, all pay attention! If I ask you how to scare away a tiger and then suggest that you use fire... how to escape an attack of honeybees and suggest you jump into the nearest water body, what will you say?"

"We will say, Radheya, please don't waste our time," said Bhandi, who could not resist a sarcastic moment.

"Exactly! So today we will talk about some not-so-common ways to scare away animals. What do you do when you are faced with an elephant and in a tight situation?"

One of the trainees in the audience yelled, "Run in a zigzag pattern and hope the animal does not knock down a tree on top of you."

"That is common knowledge, but you are talking about escaping from the elephant. I am asking you, how will you scare away a tusker, if he is on a rampage?" asked Radheya.

Silence. Radheya went to the wooden desk, picked up the dark ball of wrapped dry herbs and held it up for everyone to see. "Tribes a little to the south, like the Saharitas, Koruwas and Jantiyas have hand-picked herbs and ingredients from the forests and created many versions of this for generations. I got one here to show it to you all. This is not the real thing since some ingredients are missing, but I made something up for a demonstration. Farmers come looking for it when elephants attack agricultural land and we tribals use it to prevent tuskers from attacking our huts." He lit the ball with a fire torch and threw it into an open space where it continued to fume vigorously, emitting a lot of smoke.

"This is not the complete prescribed mix. Even then, your eyes are becoming red because of this smoke. In an elephant, this will unleash uncontrolled madness. We have seen them with watery bloodshot eyes and leaking trunks running for cover when we unleash the fumes of this ball. It is made of crushed yellow cave stone, charcoal, long pepper and forest herbs."

"That's a good one, Radheya!" said Rajyavardhan, appreciatively.

The tribal boy was brimming with confidence, his outlandish accent no deterrent. "What if you are faced with a bear?"

"Drop down and pretend that you are dead," yelled a cadet from the back rows.

"Correct! What else?"

There was silence. Radheya was enjoying his time on the stage. He raised an eyebrow, almost teasing his elite audience. "Well, if it is a small-sized bear, you can scare it away by raising your hands and spreading your legs so that your body appears as big as possible. Whatever you do, don't yell at the bear and avoid eye contact. The animal will not attack you."

Bhandi interrupted, "I would not risk that. Running as fast as my feet can is a better option." Harsha smiled. Bhandi was slowly coming out of his shell.

"Now I will teach you how to play a prank on anybody who has a horse."

"Go on!" said Harsha. He was paying close attention to the session. The macabre sights of the battlefield were loosening their grip on his mind with the passage of days, and Harsha was surprised with himself. He believed that it had something to do with Rajyavardhan's comforting words and the perspective he so clearly elucidated.

From the wooden table Radheya picked up a green fruit and said, "This looks like a green mango, but is a bitter fruit. We call it Yama's fruit after the god of death and it grows on a wild tree which looks like oleander." He knew he had everyone's attention. "All that needs to be done is to smash it into pulp, mix it with water and let the horse have it in small quantities. In less than half a day, the animal will fall sick, very sick. Indigestion, vomiting, erratic behaviour—our tribe has observed various effects in different breeds of horses."

Interrupting Radheya came a bold voice from the corner of the podium, "What strange situation makes a lower caste tribal boy take centre stage in a gathering of noble Kshatriya warriors?"

It was Janardhan, the bald, bearded *mahakshapatalike,* head of the ministerial council of the kingdom. He had been King Prabhakar's trusted associate for two decades, a muscular, hirsute man, secretly nicknamed by the princes and Bhandi as 'the bear'.

Bhandi murmured, "We were just discussing that the best way to intimidate you is to stretch our arms and legs to appear as big as possible."

"What?" Janardhan did not understand and was annoyed, while Rajyavardhan and Harsha could not suppress their giggles.

"I repeat. What pearls of wisdom does this tribal boy have to offer you all? It's below the dignity of Kshatriyas to do this," commented Janardhan.

"I don't think we care about the source as long as it is useful knowledge," said Harsha.

Rajyavardhan added, "I agree with young Harsha. Nobody has a choice as to which family or community he is born into. However, everybody has a choice as to what kind of a person they want to become. Anyway, what brings you here, Chief Minister Janardhan?"

Even before he could answer, someone behind them spoke up in a rich baritone, "He is accompanying us. And I agree with my boys, we should not discriminate on the basis of caste or background."

The assembled group of 2,000 army trainees stood up in respect. King Prabhakarvardhan and Queen Yashomati had arrived unnoticed by the audience.

Prabhakarvardhan had a lean and tall body, a bushy moustache and long greying hair. His hooked nose, sharp eyes and chiselled face made him stand out. For a king, he wore very little gold on his body except for his crown; just his presence exuded respect and authority. The image of Surya, the sun god, adorned all his robes. His military excellence and conquests were folklore across Bharatvarsh, spoken about with admiration in the same breath as his good looks. Yashomati, his queen, was a glowing picture of grace, resembling the idol of Goddess Saraswati in the small temple inside Thanesara palace. Other than a few streaks of grey hair, she could easily pass off as Rajyavardhan and Harsha's elder sister.

She turned towards her elder son. "You are fine! I am so glad! I could not sleep at night," she said in a rush, looking anxious and relieved at the same time.

"We are surprised that you left the palace and came here," said Harsha.

Prabhakar smirked, "You know your mother. The moment she came to know that Rajyavardhan was injured, she panicked, crying with no end. I tried to tell her it's a minor injury, but she wanted to verify it with her own eyes and at once. So, here we are."

"What minor injury? Look at this. Must have been so painful and would have caused serious bleeding. Why do you need to take so much risk?" It was obvious to all that the queen was still finding it difficult to fight back her tears.

Rajyavardhan's eyes widened as he said, "It's not too deep, don't worry! It will heal in a few days. Anyway, I must tell you both that my little brother here made us really proud with his performance on and off the battlefield. I will tell you more later, but at this age, he is a master negotiator already."

Prabhakar hugged Harsha. "I am so glad! You are made for big things in life." Harsha's face lit up at his father's words. He did not care what the world thought about him as long as his family believed in his abilities.

"Are you hurt too, Harsha?" asked Yashomati.

"Nothing except for some scratches and bruises. Relax mother, and breathe easy," said Harsha as he put his hands on his mother's shoulders.

King Prabhakar walked towards Radheya who stood head bowed and hands clasped in respect. "You are a brilliant boy and it's nice of you to share your wisdom with the young army trainees here. My father used to say that when there is hunger in the house, every coin comes in handy. In the same way, when our motherland is in crisis, all of us, no matter what background we come from, need to come together."

The king turned towards his minister and said, "So, Janardhan! How about inviting all the young men here to join us in the capital for our daughter's wedding?" Janardhan frowned. "Well, I thought only the aristocratic families and influential..."

Prabhakar smirked as he turned towards the cadets, "Janardhan is always worried about anything that depletes the royal treasury. He is loyal to the kingdom and that is why he is obsessed with it. He does not understand when I tell him that money has no use when it is hoarded or used for buying material things or to lead an extravagant lifestyle. I believe that it is useless to have a loaded treasury if I cannot share my joy with my extended family, my subjects."

"I agree!" Yashomati added.

"These young men here are the future of our kingdom. How can I enjoy the occasion without them? I, Prabhakarvardhan, the head of the Pushyabhuti family and ruler of Sthaneshwar, invite all you young men for the wedding of my daughter Rajashri with Grihavarman, the Maukhari king of Kannauj, after 12 days. Please come and grace the occasion. Janardhan! Discuss the arrangements with me."

The king's announcement was followed by a loud cheer from the assembled trainees. Many people in the kingdom believed that Prabhakarvardhan was not worried about spending from the kingdom's treasury since the family had set aside excess gold from the exchequer for decades, to be used in case of natural disasters or epidemics. The location of this large gold storage was supposedly known only to the royal family.

"Let's leave for the palace today. I am looking forward to organising the arrangements for the grand wedding," said Harsha.

As they were preparing to leave the arena, a messenger arrived from Narana, the king of the Hunas. The Hunas were invaders from far-off lands, who for centuries had been invading and plundering the kingdoms of Bharatvarsh until King Prabhakarvardhan and his allies united to keep them under check. Narana had to sign a humiliating treaty limiting his powers and indirectly subordinating him to the ruler of Sthaneshwar. There was peace, but it was an uneasy one.

The messenger came straight to the point, "King Prabhakarvardhan, our king Narana has requested to be excused from joining you for your daughter's wedding due to personal reasons. He requests that, if it is possible, we discuss this a couple of lunar months later."

"No! I want to meet him and discuss something important. I am sure that he knows what this is about," instructed Prabhakar.

"It will be difficult..." Even before the messenger could complete his sentence, the king interrupted, "I have said what I have to say. You may leave now."

four

Prying Eyes

The Vardhan family was engrossed in their pleasant reunion at the Prashikshan Kendra.

Up on the slope of a nearby hill, concealed in the dense vegetation, two prying eyes watched their every move. Tall, lean, with long flowing hair, a large forehead, sharp features and dark skin, the man had a crippled hand and a few missing teeth. As he watched, he was taken aback by the arrival of the king and queen at the academy. He studied the expressions and gestures of the people on the podium. This was his competency; a sharper mind as compared to his brother's. His body was his weakness, and not just because of his lean frame. He had lost his left arm as punishment for a mistake; his hand repeatedly crushed between boulders on the instructions of his master. Yet, he did not resent his authority.

A thought crossed his mind and Vakul left his position to go to his twin brother positioned behind a row of trees. Vamsi was equally tall, with a similar face and hair, and wheatish skin, but he was muscular. In their circle of infamous people, his nickname was 'The Crusher'. In missions and brawls, he had earned the notorious reputation of killing his adversaries purely by crushing their skulls between his palms or against hard objects. He now squatted beside a rack above an open fire, which he had created to roast the birds he had caught that morning.

Vakul said, "Doesn't it occur to you that the smoke might catch their attention?"

"There is hardly any smoke. Down there, with all these trees in-between, those people can see nothing for sure."

The crippled brother looked at his twin's catch roasting on the fire. Some strange wild birds. He sat down next to it, took out his knife and started to cut his long dirty toenails.

"What is that disgusting smell? You're going to eat some dirty wild crow!" commented Vakul.

"It is a rare black bird. What is the harm in trying something different? How will you know how bad or good it is without trying?"

There was silence before Vamsi spoke again. "So, what did you see below?"

"The king and queen made a surprise visit to meet their princes. All overflowing with love and emotion!" Vakul giggled.

"Fake spectacle," said Vamsi. The twins did not know what family meant. They had been orphaned very early in life and had spent their childhood roaming from one town to another. Starting with small thefts, they had graduated to physical assault and robbery, until they were discovered by their master in a chance encounter.

"So, what now? Should we leave?" asked Vamsi.

"Not exactly! On second thoughts, it's actually a good time to try now. Take out your poison-tipped arrow and bow," replied Vakul.

"Are you serious?"

"We need to follow the master's orders!"

"To kill someone from the Vardhan family!" Vamsi exclaimed. "The most protected family in the whole of Bharatvarsh? Don't you think our master keeps pushing us for suicidal missions?"

"I think he has a plan for us, brother."

"I don't think so! We mean nothing to him," Vamsi retorted.

Vakul narrowed his eyes, "I sense some kind of resentment in your tone."

"We will talk some other day. Let's focus on the task ahead."

Abandoning their hideout among the dense trees, the twins rushed down the hillock and in no time, reached their black horses that they had tethered to a mid-sized sal tree.

Vakul said, "We need to only go so far that we can return here quickly after the job and flee."

Vamsi took out the poison-tipped arrow and his bow while Vakul took out his spear. They moved towards the boundary wall of the training ground, concealing themselves behind the vegetation till they reached a safe distance from where they could see King Prabhakar, Rajyavardhan, Harsha and Yashomati on the podium. As Vakul kept watch, Vamsi held his bow firmly and mounted the arrow.

"Vakul! Are you sure it is a good idea to do this now?"

"What better place can you think of than this?"

Vakul looked around while Vamsi took aim. They worked like professionals; composed, calm, with no signs of nervousness, afraid of nothing.

"What is taking you so much time?"

"Too long a range," Vamsi said in a hushed tone. "I am not sure if I can hit the target."

"What do you mean by you are..."

Vakul was suddenly distracted by a movement in the bushes behind them. As he watched, a young tribal woman appeared out of the vegetation, a blanket wrapped around her, a pot of water balanced on her hips. She froze on seeing the two men, trying to comprehend what appeared to be two miscreants taking aim at the royal family inside the Prashikshan Kendra. Vakul tapped Vamsi on his shoulder, then took out his knife and held it to his lips, signalling to the woman to keep quiet. She was petrified. Vamsi turned, looked at her and dropped his bow and arrow to take out his dagger. The twins signalled the trembling woman to walk away. Pointing their daggers at her, they followed her for some distance between the dense vegetation until they were far from the army training ground. Once they were in the denser portions of the forest, Vakul pinned the woman against a tree. Eyes red with anger, he placed his dagger against her neck while Vamsi dug his knife into her abdomen. The woman started to wail in fear.

"Just when we were about to cause some disruption, you had to barge in!" muttered Vamsi. She said something in her tribal language which the twins did not comprehend.

"She was witness to what we were about to do. In no time her tribe will know about it and tongues will start wagging. Before you know it, this will reach the army trainees and from them to the royal family," said Vakul.

"Let's just slice her tongue so that she keeps mum," growled Vamsi. The woman was terrified; she shivered as she watched the expressions of the savage twins, trying to figure out what they would eventually do.

"Are you naïve, brother? What is the use of just slicing out her tongue? She cannot write, but she can use gestures to let her people know what happened here," remarked Vakul.

By now she was sobbing uncontrollably. Her trembling hands dropped the pot of water, which crashed to the ground.

"All this crying and wailing is making my head rattle," said Vakul.

Vamsi commented, "Just like our childhood!"

"She sounds like mother. That makes me even more angry," remarked Vakul.

"Should we?"

"Do we have any other choice, Vamsi? This wandering bitch just ended up being in the wrong place at the wrong time." The woman's eyes darted nervously from one twin to the other.

"You will do it, or should I?"

"Totally up to you." Just then the blanket around the woman fell sideways, revealing her abdomen.

"She is pregnant!" exclaimed Vamsi. By now the woman, hands clasped, looked at the twins as if she was surrounded by wild predators who might just have some pity and spare her.

"Should we do this to her in this state?" asked Vamsi, glancing at his brother. The woman placed her hands on her swollen abdomen and continued to sob, gasping for breath every now and then.

"It will be morally wrong!"

"I agree, Vakul, it will be a very cruel thing to do."

"Poor thing!" said Vakul as he swung his dagger and sliced her throat in a flash. The woman gave out a low shriek; blood squirted on the twins, in a vicious spray. Vamsi quickly put his hand over her mouth. Her body collapsed, then arched as she winced in pain. Her eyes popped open; then she was cold and motionless.

"It had to be done," said Vakul, coldly.

"That's the way it is."

The twins took their time to wipe the blood from their faces in their regular relaxed manner before heading for their horses.

"Where to?" asked Vamsi.

"Thanesara palace, just like master instructed."

five

Royal Nest

The rising sun kissed her face, making it even more vibrant than before. Sleeping outstretched like a child on her vast bed surrounded by attendants fanning her with hand-held fans made of peacock feathers, she looked every bit as gorgeous as she was known to be. Fair, with a small face, slight build, dark brown hair and hazel eyes, Rajashri's beauty was famous across the kingdoms of Bharatvarsh. Today, when she opened her eyes, she found her father, mother and brothers standing before her.

"What brings you all here at this time in the morning?"

"It's the last day before your grand wedding," said her father, King Prabhakar. "Your mother and brothers have lined up a great schedule for you today."

"Everything has been elaborately planned," added Yashomati with a wide smile.

"Where is cousin Bhandi?" asked Rajashri.

Harsha replied, "He requested father to make him the main coordinator of the wedding arrangements. It is a busy day for him."

"That is what I love most about cousin Bhandi. He is always doing such nice things in the background, without wanting any credit for it," said Rajashri.

"He is like that! Now don't just laze around on your bed. Get up and let's show you around," said Rajyavardhan.

Harsha said, "First, we go to the royal bath."

Prabhakar, Rajyavardhan and Harsha waited outside, while Yashomati and Rajashri entered the princess's royal bath area.

"The water is lukewarm, sprinkled lavishly with petals and aromatic oils," said Yashomati.

Rajashri said, "This place is filled with the fragrance of incense fumes."

"If you'd like a relaxing oil massage, we have summoned the best lady for the job all the way from Kapilavastu," elaborated Yashomati.

"Ma, what is in those trays of gold?"

"All the accessories for your bath—sandalwood paste, turmeric paste, fresh butter, exotic and rare ayurvedic herbs. The choicest and the best available."

Rajashri said, "I will take a bath after my morning meal. Let's step out before my father and brothers become impatient waiting outside."

The family walked together around the royal palace, which had artificial water bodies, water dykes and well-maintained lush green gardens all around. The main structures inside the complex were made of burnt clay bricks and lime mortar. However, the section for the royal family consisted of red sandstone structures with domes and arches, designed by architects who were summoned from Paarshava, far west of the Indus River. This particular compound of the palace belonged to Rajashri. It was called the *Dhavala Griha* and everything was painted in white, her favourite colour. Even the teak doors and windows were inlaid with white ivory work and patterns studded with precious white stones. Today, everything had been cleaned and painted. The palace screamed opulence and grandeur.

Rajyavardhan said, "Tomorrow is her wedding day. Feels like yesterday when Harsha and I used to carry our baby sister on our shoulders to look at the cows, goats and hens of the barn and the horses in the stables next to it."

"There were evenings when she used to throw a tantrum that she wanted to sleep on a bed in the open between the cow shed and the hens," remarked Harsha.

"I remember helping Harsha to make a tree house for her, to satisfy her whims," added Rajyavardhan.

Prabhakarvardhan placed his hands affectionately on his daughter's shoulders. "Everybody had predicted that, with all this attention and love, she would grow up to be a spoilt girl. She surprised them all by being noble, well-behaved and soft-spoken."

"The soft-spoken bit is only with you to get things done her way," Harsha responded before the others could.

"Of course not! Tell the truth, brother!" retorted Rajashri, turning to her elder brother.

"I choose to remain mum," Rajyavardhan said with a teasing smile. Harsha patted his brother's shoulder and they shared a laugh at Rajashri's expense.

The Vardhans reached the royal kitchen where the aroma of spicy vegetables cooking in clarified butter filled the air. King Prabhakar said, "Look at the scale at which your brothers have arranged for the food. The best dairy products from Vrindavan, sweets from Mathura and Varanasi, juicy fruits, fresh vegetables, the finest grains, jaggery, honey from the Shivaliks and spices from down south."

Prabhakar had recently developed a major swelling in his neck, a lump that was palpable. Even though he tried to conceal his discomfort, it was obvious that he had difficulty while talking.

"The best cooks and sweet-makers from each of our neighbouring kingdoms have been commissioned for you today," added Yashomati.

"The next best thing we could have done was to cook the meals for you with our own hands, but considering how we both fare in cooking, we decided against it," remarked Harsha.

"That was a good decision. The last time you both made something for us, we all had an upset stomach," Rajashri retorted.

Rajashri had a morning meal of fresh fruits and flavoured milk with dry fruits and followed it up with a lavish bath that stretched till the afternoon. After this, the family sat down to a lavish multi-course lunch. The day was cloudy and overcast. They spent the afternoon in the garden while the court musicians and dancers entertained them. All around them, rows of carts loaded with flowers, ingredients in bulk for the royal feast and decorative items trundled in for unloading. Bhandi flitted around coordinating everything. Gardeners were busy curating the palace garden; attendants cleaned and refilled the palace pool. The cleaning staff concentrated on scrubbing every nook and cranny of the reception area. Some of the attendants had been given the responsibility of flying large kites to add to the festivities.

Amidst the hubbub all around, some attendants brought in four wooden boxes and placed them before the royal family.

"Look what Harsha found in the old storeroom," said Yashomati.

Rajashri opened the boxes and was overjoyed at their contents, "My wooden horse, my clay bullock cart and my miniature palace! I did not know they were still here. Look! My wooden acrobat."

"It's amazing how one's childhood shrinks into little boxes to find its resting place in the corners of storerooms and basements," said Prabhakar.

"Yes! It's like bygone times getting trapped inside the boxes," added Yashomati.

"I knew you would be overjoyed to see these again!" said Harsha, grinning.

"I sure am!" exclaimed Rajashri with a wide smile. There was a festive feel everywhere. Amidst all the noise of the celebration, it was as if on silent, soft steps, the angels of happiness roamed all around the palace complex spreading the rhythm of joy.

"This palace will lose its liveliness in your absence, Rajashri," said Yashomati, who had been in tears frequently during the afternoon.

"Don't worry, Ma! It's less than two days' travel between Thanesara and Kannauj. I will be here every other lunar month."

"In her absence we will console ourselves knowing that she is happy," added Rajyavardhan.

"I think we all must be happy that after marriage she is going into such an amazing family and will become the queen of a man like King Grihavarman of Kannauj," said Prabhakar.

"Grihavarman is a rare combination—wise, humble and calm," remarked Harsha.

Rajyavardhan added, "I totally agree! With such a strong standing army and a royal treasury loaded more than ours, he is neither aggressive nor arrogant."

"Also, so young and good-looking," blurted Rajashri.

"God! Look at her face. Glowing and blushing at the mention of him!" said Harsha as the whole family laughed aloud, their faces brimming with happiness, an air of revelry all around the palace.

In the evening, at the main gate, King Prabhakar, Rajyavardhan and Harsha stood welcoming the invited kings, vassals and warlords from the whole of Bharatvarsh. Army Chief Chakravarti and Chief Minister Janardhan assisted the royal family in the welcome. Chakravarti, with his long greying hair, intimidating moustache and muscular body, was a towering figure among them. They were joined by Prabhakar's long-time friend King Bhaskaravarman of Kamarupa. With his grey hair and flowing beard, he resembled the sculptures of Lord Brahma on temple walls. He had on a pleasant smile, as always.

"I feel so happy and honoured to stand beside you, Prabhakarvardhan, welcoming guests as if I am part of your family," said Bhaskar.

"This is our little girl's wedding. You are her favourite. You spoiled her with toys in her childhood and gifts in her adolescent years. It's your right to be here," said Prabhakar.

Chief Minister Janardhan commented, "King Prabhakar is courteous to all fellow kings, no matter how big or small the kingdom they rule." Bhaskar reigned over a small kingdom, but he was highly valued and influential inside the Vardhan palace.

"Janardhan! You have the skill of unintentionally getting entangled with your choice of words. Ignore him, Bhaskar, I am sure even he did not understand what he meant," intervened Prabhakar.

"I am sure he meant no harm. Anyway, do you know that along with her wedding gift, I also gave some advice to our girl Rajashri last evening?" asked Bhaskar.

"What was that?"

"She was anxious about getting married and I said that it's very simple. Prioritise your partner more than yourself and in all probability he will reciprocate. That's it!"

"Well said, my friend!" remarked Prabhakar as he placed his hands on his friend's shoulders.

The Hunas entered, led by their ruler Narana, bringing along with them their trademark pungent smell. All of them were well-built, muscular and had thick leather hides wrapped around their hairy upper bodies. There was something savage about their appearance, what with their long fingernails, unkempt beards and long dreadlocks. Narana had sharp features, penetrating eyes and a baritone. "My compliments, King Prabhakar!"

Prabhakar replied, "Welcome Narana, the Huna! I am glad that you and your chiefs are joining us on this occasion. We need to talk after my girl's wedding."

"Sure! I know what this is about and you must hear our side of the story."

Prabhakar replied, "You have known me for a long time. I always try to understand all the aspects of a situation."

"We respect you for that."

Narana and his chiefs were escorted by attendants to his accommodation inside the palace.

At that moment, behind the crowd of visiting dignitaries, appeared Shashank, the king of Gauda, related to the Vardhans. He was plump, with a bushy moustache and always wore a lot of gold chains and rings. He was 47 years old but, having married early, he had three daughters, the youngest being 16 years old.

"*Suswagatam*, Shashank!" Prabhakar greeted him. "You are reversing in age, it seems."

"Oh! After my illness, I take better care of myself. At our age, we do not have many years left, so I believe in making the most of it," replied Shashank.

"Where is Sharada, the future sunshine of our palace?" Prabhakar was referring to Shashank's daughter, engaged to be married to Harsha.

"Her closed chariot and convoy of guards is a little behind and will be here shortly," said Shashank.

"How was the journey, Shashank?"

"As usual it was tiresome due to the bumpy ride. The roads connecting our capital towns are a pain to travel, especially after the rains."

"We hope to comfort and rejuvenate you during your stay here," intervened Rajyavardhan.

"The arrangements are splendid and grand. It's a great time for a matrimonial alliance between the kingdoms of Sthaneshwar and Kannauj. Both kingdoms have witnessed three years of decent rains, overflowing foodgrain reserves and unprecedented trade," commented Shashank.

"How are things back home in Gauda?" asked Harsha.

"Floods are destroying the crops as usual. We live near the delta, where the great rivers meet the sea, and are at the receiving end of all the excess water. Every year the same story, crops getting destroyed and peasants seeking grants from the royal treasury to manage their livelihood," Shashank sighed. "It's made worse with fake coins circulating inside the kingdom."

"Somebody made fake replicas of your royal coin?" asked Prabhakar.

"Loads of them, with cheap metals! They are in circulation and the economy is in a mess because of all this. The rains have been even more unkind than in previous years, making it worse."

Prabhakar said, "Rajyavardhan and Harsha just drove out a Malava incursion into our territory. They inform me that even in our southern borders there is flooding. Also, Devagupta, who is focused on war campaigns more than promoting agriculture, is responsible for major mismanagement in those parts."

Shashank joked, "Please be considerate towards my barbaric lunatic cousin." Shashank and Devagupta's mothers were sisters.

Prabhakar smirked, "Ha! I will be if he stops being the kind of monster he is. Just recently, it seems he publicly executed some of his spies on various pretexts because they were caught unaware about this wedding until the official invitations went out."

Shashank said, "He is a savage just like his lineage and will not improve. That is why my father had severed all ties with Malava during his reign."

Prabhakar said, "When Devagupta sent a proposal for marriage with Rajashri, I assumed that he had moved ahead from his father's humiliating defeat at my hands and was looking for a fresh start. It was when his true intentions surfaced that I was furious. No wonder his own people have nicknamed Devagupta *Asura-gupta*, the devil king."

Shashank said, "Forget him, that nasty addict! My dear Rajyavardhan and Harsha, you both look exhausted."

Rajyavardhan said, "Since morning we have been doing our bit to make Rajashri feel special and have also been overseeing the preparations going on all around the complex."

Shashank looked around and exclaimed, "This palace is shining and in its full glory. The last time I saw it like this was when I came here after Rajyavardhan and Swaranya's wedding, to leave her here and for the closing rituals. When I was leaving,

I saw her standing there on that parapet with her attendants, shedding a few tears before starting her new life."

Rajyavardhan's face turned pale and Harsha could feel the sudden sense of grief in the air. Shashank's eldest daughter Swaranya had been married to Rajyavardhan—a match made in heaven, a marriage of eternal bliss, but short-lived. She died during her pregnancy a year into their marriage.

Prabhakar said, "I am sure that she is looking down on all of us now with a smile on her lovely face."

Janardhan excused himself for evening prayers. Army Chief Chakravarti left to supervise the security arrangements around the palace. A little later, a convoy of guards and a closed royal chariot arrived from Gauda. The door of the chariot opened and the mesmerising Sharada alighted, adorned in an elegant green silk *angavastram* and lavish jewellery. From the other side of the chariot appeared Shashank's youngest daughter, Gautami. She was the taller of the sisters, slightly dusky, with a very attractive face.

Shashank said, "Finally, my daughters are here!"

Sharada and Gautami folded their hands and bowed in front of Prabhakar, Rajyavardhan and Bhaskar. Harsha was beaming with joy at the sight of his betrothed.

"*Suswagatam*! Welcome to your future home, Sharada. Gautami, you have grown from a shy adolescent into a fine, attractive woman in the last year or so. How fast they grow up!" marvelled Prabhakar.

Bhaskar interrupted, "The last time I saw them was on the day of her engagement with Harsha in the Gauda palace. With every passing year they are becoming more and more beautiful. Harsha! You'd better marry Sharada quickly before she changes her mind."

Prabhakar commented, "Gautami is looking slightly unwell though."

"Yes, it's because of the travel. She just vomited at the outskirts of the city," remarked Shashank. Prabhakar signalled to the attendant who came at once with a team of physicians and escorted young Gautami to the healing room inside the palace.

"Harsha, please accompany Sharada to the women's section of the palace where mother is waiting to meet her," said Rajyavardhan.

Bhaskar added, "Well done, Rajyavardhan! Ensuring pretty elegantly and promptly that your brother gets some private moments with his girl."

Prabhakar smiled at Harsha, who accompanied Sharada from the main entrance to the palace gardens on the way to Yashomati's quarters. The gardens were a huge encirclement around Thanesara palace. This particular section had an underground tunnel which went all the way from the palace, around the water tank to the outside. There were three such secret tunnels to the outside known only to the royal family and close associates.

Harsha said, "We are meeting after half a year. I was so excited and looking forward to this." When she walked near him, Harsha could smell the scent of fresh jasmine in her hair. Her breath had the aromatic fragrance of the rare Arabian twig that Chakravarti had brought for the princes after his maiden voyage to Paarshava.

Sharada replied, "Prince Harsha, I am glad to know that."

"How was the journey?"

"Father must have told you. It was bumpy and tiring as usual."

Harsha pointed at a cloth bag she was carrying in her hand, "What is that?"

Sharada took out a ring with a rare garnet gemstone from the bag and gave it to Harsha, "It's very rare and supposed to bring good luck. Since you are interested in rare and exquisite things, I thought of gifting it to you."

Harsha wore the ring on his finger. "See! Fits perfectly. It's beautiful."

Sharada smiled.

"Lovely smile! You are looking more and more pretty as time passes by," said Harsha with a little hesitation. His hand touched hers momentarily and she withdrew.

"I don't know why everyone is saying that. Someday it will all fade away. You tell me, what have you been up to recently?"

"I was on a mission with Rajyavardhan to drive away an encroachment into our territory by Devagupta's army."

"Good!" There was a momentary silence.

"Princess Sharada, don't you want to ask more about the battle?"

"Battles are all the same. Blood and dead bodies. What is there to ask? You are here with me. That means nothing bad happened to you."

"Is something wrong, Princess Sharada?"

"No, Prince Harsha!"

"Do you realise that we run out of topics every time?"

"It happens! I think it might require some getting used to each other."

"In your presence, I become so overwhelmed that I lose track of what I am saying, mesmerised by your beauty."

"Prince Harsha! You load me with so much praise that it sometimes sounds a little too much."

"I am sorry but I am just smitten by you, Princess Sharada."

Just then a loud splashing sound was heard from somewhere near the rear wall of the palace.

Sharada wondered aloud, "What is that sound?"

"That is Chief Minister Janardhan's daily rejuvenation. In the late evening he drinks a cup of wine, then dives into the palace pool from the top of the palace wall."

"From the top of the wall? That is one tall wall. He must be an experienced diver."

Harsha replied, "Sure he is! Once he emerges from the pool, more copper cups of wine follow."

"Chief Minister Janardhan surely enjoys life to the fullest."

All through the evening, Harsha wondered why Sharada never seemed to be enthusiastic or forthcoming. He had seen his elder brother Rajyavardhan and wife Swaranya interact. They were so much in love with each other, having never-ending conversations, in awe of each other. Between him and Sharada there was no such 'magic'. Every time they met, he felt that her interest in him had further deteriorated. She was the first girl he was strongly attracted to of all the princesses he had met during social occasions. The first time they had talked, she had said that she always wanted a life partner who was 'special'. With her interest in him waning, he wondered what he should do to become special in her eyes. To not feel any love from the one you love is a despair only few other miseries can match. He just hoped she was open enough to talk about what was going through her mind.

six

Disruption

"Stop playing with your bow and arrow. It's time to get ready," Vakul instructed his brother. At the traveller's rest house, *Devimaya Yatri Niwas,* on the outskirts of Thanesara town, the twins had hired a room for two days. The town was bustling with people and activities, adorned with colours and lights as it prepared for Princess Rajashri's wedding. It was a matter of sheer luck that they were able to find a room.

The room had two mats, a pot of water, numerous cracks on the walls, cobwebs on the ceiling and a termite-infested wooden storage space built into one wall. Unmindful of the room's sorry state, the twins continued with their activities. Vamsi was aiming with his bow and arrow through the window at some birds on a nearby tree. He was not going to roast and eat them today because it was not any regular day. They had taken baths and groomed themselves after almost half a lunar month. Applying sandalwood oil on his armpits and navel, Vakul remarked, "Did you know that this Rajashri girl got a proposal from Devagupta of Malava initially?"

"The Vardhans have a long running enmity with Malava. That would have been good enough reason for them to have turned down the proposal," replied Vamsi.

"On the contrary, the word out there is that King Prabhakar was surprised, inquisitive and did not turn the proposal down immediately. It was when his spy service informed him of the underlying reason for the proposal that he was furious."

Vamsi shot the arrow out of the window and missed his target, "What was the reason?"

"Devagupta had organised a seven-day yagna, rituals and offerings in his palace. He was told by his trusted astrologer that doing this would make his dream of being the undisputed emperor of all Bharatvarsh a reality," said Vakul as he put on his tunic. "They had a surprise visitor on the second day of the ritual, their family guru Nalananda."

Vamsi interrupted, "I have heard of him. The lord of black magic, who stays for half the year in the Himalayas."

"Nalananda loathed the large-scale ritual. He looked at Devagupta's horoscope and announced that the only way he could realise his dream would be by marrying a princess born on the night of Mahashivratri. His clear prescription was to marry the girl on Saptami, consummate the marriage that night and the next day of Durgashtami, behead the new bride as a sacrifice at his family temple's altar," explained Vakul.

"So how is that related to the marriage proposal?"

Vakul smiled, "Isn't it obvious? Rajashri is the only princess in the whole of Bharatvarsh who fitted the requirement of being born on the night of Mahashivratri."

Vamsi kept his bow aside and his eyes widened, "So Devagupta wanted to marry Rajashri so that he could offer her as a human sacrifice on Durgashtami?"

"Yes! Had the Sthaneshwar spy service not got a hint of it, the groom for Rajashri today would have been Devagupta of Malava instead of Grihavarman of Kannauj."

Vamsi smirked, "And on the day of Durgashtami they would have butchered the pretty princess. That would have been an interesting spectacle." He put on his colourful tunic and ran his hands through his hair.

"Time to go! Take out the invitation scrolls," said Vakul.

His brother clumsily fumbled with his cloth sack and pulled out two scrolls from it.

"You think this will be cleared at the screening?" asked Vamsi.

"Look at the royal seal," Vakul said. "I don't think we should have a problem."

Later that evening, the twins managed to dupe the palace security with the fake scrolls. Once inside, they saw that the perimeter of the Thanesara palace wall was adorned with numerous small oil lamps. All the paths inside were carpeted with layers of scented flowers. The main podium was a massive structure made out of multiple smaller structures of wood merged seamlessly into each other. In the centre were a larger-than-life Shiva-Parvathi and two elephants with raised trunks on either side. Behind the podium was a row of poor farmers who were being given warm clothes, a tray of fruits and a sack of silver *Sri-Siladitya* coins by the state as a grant. On one side was a huge temporary wooden structure with a dome supported by pillars where hundreds of people could dine together. This was the largest structure ever constructed for a single event. Around 30 tall metallic poles had been fixed across the wedding ground, each with a large spoke-like crown from which hung hundreds of lanterns that seemed to illuminate the sky. A sea of people dressed in their best colourful dresses had come to witness the grand celebrations. The first eight rows around the main podium were for kings, vassals, warlords and noblemen from all around Bharatvarsh. The next rows belonged to Sthaneshwar's noblemen and their families. On the main podium was the handsome bridegroom Grihavarman, the Maukhari king of Kannauj, with his younger sister and cousins awaiting the bride's family.

King Prabhakar, Rajyavardhan and Harsha arrived to welcome the groom's family with garlands and trays of sandalwood and vermilion paste. A little later, the bride joined the others on the podium for the start of the rituals. Rajashri and Grihavarman's eyes lit up at the sight of each other. Vakul and Vamsi were engrossed in the proceedings. There was a tap on Vamsi's shoulder. He turned back to see a dark, well-built, almost giant-sized guard with a bushy moustache who said, "May I ask whether you hail from Magadha?"

Vakul replied, "No, we are here with the delegation from the kingdom of Kamarupa."

The guard's eyes narrowed. The man's Sanskrit was not Kamarupi. "That delegation is on the left side of the podium. What are you people doing here? If you don't mind, can I see your invitation scrolls?"

Vamsi handed the scrolls to the guard who glanced from the content of the scroll to the twins and back in rapid succession.

"Can you both please accompany me to the guard room?"

Vakul protested, "We are here to attend the ceremony. How can you ask us to come along with you in the midst of all this?"

"I insist!" The guard led the twins through the crowd towards the guard room.

"What if I disobey?" said Vamsi, trying to intimidate the guard who was much bigger than him. The guard was unperturbed and remarked, "People don't normally annoy me!"

Vakul evaluated the situation and muttered to his twin, "Let's go! I don't think we have a choice."

The twins walked, followed closely by the giant guard. Suddenly there was a commotion in the crowd, ripples of people moving helter-skelter. The fragrance of thousands of flowers was overtaken by a disgusting smell. People covered their faces with their shoulder cloths. The twins used the chaos to sneak away and disappear into the crowd from where they watched the proceedings. They saw a messenger from Malava arrive, followed by two soldiers carrying a long thin log of wood between them. On it were the decomposed heads of eight soldiers nailed to the wood at equal distances. The only reason they were recognisable as Sthaneshwar soldiers was because of their turbans. On the podium, King Prabhakar, Rajyavardhan, Harsha, the royal families of Sthaneshwar and Kannauj looked appalled. When the palace guards tried to intervene, Prabhakar signalled for them to stop.

Fearlessly, the messenger from Malava read out the message:

> "*Vandanam*! King Prabhakar of Sthaneshwar,
>
> I am conveying my best wishes to you on the wedding day of your daughter Rajashri. In the most humble manner, I had requested you for her hand in marriage. Instead, you believed some rumours and chose to fix her marriage with the incompetent Grihavarman of Kannauj. I might not be as good-looking as him, but let me tell you that one day I will be the most powerful king in the whole of Bharatvarsh. On this important day for your family, in front of your own people, I, Devagupta of Malava, declare that I will make Rajashri mine in the near future. I will then offer her as a sacrifice to my family deity on the day of Durgashtami. If you, your two sons or

Grihavarman have the strength to stop me, I challenge you to try. Once she is beheaded, I will take her head out on a tray across the kingdom in a display similar to that of these eight soldiers of yours for everyone to see. People will never challenge the authority of Devagupta. Your sons Rajyavardhan and Harshavardhan reclaimed your territory from us. When these eight poor bastards strayed into the area under our control, I thought, *What better wedding gift for my dear Rajashri than their heads nailed to a piece of wood?* I wish the courage to face my wrath for all of you. This is just the start; there is much more coming your way. Wait and watch.

—The Future Ruler of Bharatvarsh."

Yashomati was in tears. Rajashri looked horrified. King Prabhakar and Rajyavardhan held their composure, but Harsha and Bhandi were furious. This was the last thing they expected when the wedding rituals were about to commence.

Prabhakar said to the messenger, "You three understand the consequences of coming here like this at this moment and creating such a disruption, right?"

The messenger looked at the two Malava soldiers and said, "We came here knowing fully well the consequences of our actions."

Prabhakar signalled to the guards to take the Malavas away.

Rajyavardhan stepped forward and, with a smile on his face, spoke loudly to everyone assembled for the wedding, "Why should we let a mad man, an addict, his reckless antics and his wild fantasies ruin such a great day? It's just a matter of time before Devagupta's own people end his misery. Let's just forget about it. Please join me in wishing the best to this lovely couple who have taken the decision to be with each other for life."

Only Rajyavardhan, with his smile and infectious positivity, could have turned the situation around so that almost everyone brushed aside what had happened and joined in the wedding ceremony.

Vakul and Vamsi watched the proceedings, hidden among a sea of people. Once the ceremony was over, they decided to go back.

"I have that sick feeling in my stomach!" remarked Vakul.

Vamsi asked, "What is the reason for it?"

"That giant guard crossed the line with us. We have unfinished business," said Vakul.

Vamsi said, "I agree!"

The next morning, children playing outside the palace complex found something next to a sewage line near the grain storage warehouse. It was the dead body of a well-built palace guard who had left for his home after his shift much after midnight. He had been gagged with a strip of cloth whose marks were visible across his cheeks. One eye was wide open, almost popping out, while the other had stab marks from a sharp object. The veins on his head stood out over his pale skin. The bones of his palms and his toes were bloodied and crushed as if someone had battered them repeatedly with a heavy object. His left ear was severed, and his bloodied jaw detached from his face and thrown carelessly a little ahead.

seven

Collapse

"As usual, Narana does not believe in starting anything on time," remarked Prabhakar.

In the discussion hall of Thanesara palace, the royal delegation was waiting for the Hunas. King Prabhakar sat on the throne while Chief Minister Janardhan and Army Chief Chakravarti sat on both sides of him. The trio of Rajyavardhan, Harsha and Bhandi sat a little further on the right. In front of the podium with the throne were three cushioned wooden chairs. All eyes were on the entrance where the curtains fluttered.

"Let's disperse since he is taking his time," said Prabhakar, who hated people who turned up late for meetings.

A moment later, Narana appeared with a copper cup of wine, which he handed over to an attendant at the door out of respect for King Prabhakar. Trailing him were two of his deputies with long hair and a beard like him. It was impossible to guess from their expression what they were feeling at any point of time. Bhandi and Harsha used to call them 'stone-faced'.

Narana and his deputies sat in front of the throne. "Greetings, King Prabhakar!" he said. "Apologies for the delay."

"You made it just in time. I hope you all enjoyed the wedding and festivities," said Prabhakar.

Narana replied, "It was all going great until Devagupta's men created a scene."

"It is time everyone joined forces to contain that insane addict. It's just a matter of time. However, I called you here to ask about all the arrests across the Huna territory of Buddhist, Jain and tribal religious leaders. What's going on, Narana?"

"It was absolutely necessary. There were concerns about the way these people were spreading their religions through monasteries targeting vulnerable poor people with free food and gifts. It's religious propaganda spreading like an epidemic. It needs to be kept in check."

"Narana! The Hunas came along the Sanatana Dharma way and adopted Hinduism some generations back," said Prabhakar. Clearing his throat, he continued, "How come you are behaving like fanatics? Our way of life believes in multiple paths to the divine. We don't create barriers for people to follow their faith."

"We were nomadic vagabonds for generations. Good fortune came our way after we took refuge at the feet of Lord Shiva. We were shown the path by our legendary leader Mihirakula. I am only following the tradition. Our religion is our pride and strength. It provides us support to run a robust administration," said Narana, scratching his beard. "It's a sign of weakness to sit and do nothing while people of other religions increase in number."

"So what if they increase in number?" Prabhakar was curious.

Narana chuckled, "Isn't that obvious? They will come after us! What will happen to our authority?"

"These are peaceful communities. Why be threatened by them?"

Narana leaned forward and said, "They are all peaceful when they are in small numbers. When they become big mobs, things will not remain peaceful any more."

"Religion cannot be the source of one's power; it's his moral standing that gets a leader long-term support. What is this *us* versus *them*? So much lack of trust? These are your own people. There are rational people everywhere who will not allow anyone to unreasonably dominate the other," said Prabhakar.

"It is not an ideal world out there. Our view of the world is different. I need to run a kingdom here and with the required amount of force," commented Narana.

Prabhakar interrupted, "All I am saying is that when the governing authority shows this kind of bias, it empowers the fringe elements and some miscreant groups in the society to escalate the situation. For them, the governing body has endorsed their hate and they take advantage of this. It will lead to full-fledged anarchy."

"I have ruled my kingdom for years and I know when to stop," remarked Narana.

"Hate does not know where to stop. Anyway, my bigger worry is that since we are all viewed together now, it affects our image in Sthaneshwar."

"Yes! I am your vassal, and you use every opportunity to imply that."

Prabhakar was losing patience. "All I want to tell you is, do not promote anarchy in a stable situation, blinded by love for your religion. The only reason why Hinduism has survived for the longest time is because it is open to other religions and faiths. Don't be divisive."

"You are asking us to sit quietly and do nothing while all this continues to happen around us!" exclaimed Narana.

Harsha interrupted, “Maybe you can use the time more productively to focus on the issues of human slavery that plague your kingdom.” The young prince could not resist the temptation of speaking on something that he was passionate about. King Prabhakar was not pleased with Harsha’s emotional bluster. “You people do whatever you may deem fit,” he said. “The only thing we don’t want is our name to be associated with any kind of injustice or anarchy. We don’t support it.”

Before leaving, Narana assured the Vardhans that he would do whatever was best in the given situation.

“I don’t expect him to do much. He is blinded by his faith,” Prabhakar remarked to the others present. He also told Harsha to keep his emotions in check during such discussions.

The royal family proceeded to the dining section, an enclosure with a stone-cut lotus pond on both sides of a large teak table with chairs. The attendants served the evening meal for their king, the princes and Bhandi. The women of the royal household had their last meal before sunset. Today, on the cushioned bench next to the dining table, only Yashomati sat instructing the attendants. The king was on a liquid diet since he found it difficult to swallow food.

“I hope these turmeric-based medicines you are having make the swelling in your neck subside soon. You are looking very weak, my king,” said Yashomati.

Harsha added, “If this goes on for a few more days, then I really fear for your health.”

During the past few days, a strange silence had settled among the family members during meal times. Every eye darted around to finally rest at the place next to Yashomati, which was now vacant. Rajashri used to make the evening meal time fun with the constant banter between her and her brothers. She seemed to have taken that happiness away with her.

"It's remarkable how much patience you exercised with Narana," said Rajyavardhan to divert everyone's attention.

Prabhakar replied, "He always seems to bring out the worst in me. We need to plan how to keep him under control."

In the silence that followed, Yashomati shed tears thinking about her daughter.

"Yashomati! Please control yourself. I could not have kept Rajashri inside our palace forever. It is the way of the world that a woman gets married and moves on in life," said Prabhakar.

Rajyavardhan added, "We must all be happy for her."

"She promised me that she would visit us regularly," added Harsha.

Bhandi looked very affected by the conversation, but as always, he found it difficult to articulate his feelings.

"I have lost my appetite. I will have milk with mashed bananas and ground dry fruits before going to sleep," saying so, Prabhakar got up to leave. He felt giddy and abruptly slumped back into his chair.

eight

Fraternity of Evil

"Every time he calls us in the middle of a mission, I lose sleep at night," said Vakul.

They rode together along a mud road with wetlands on both sides. The twins were anxious since their master had summoned them rather abruptly.

"Do you think he is disappointed with us for not completing our mission?" asked Vakul, pulling the reins of his horse with his good hand.

Vamsi replied, "I don't know. The task he gave us was to stalk the Vardhan family and launch a lethal attack if any opportunity arose. They are the most protected family in the whole of Bharatvarsh. We honestly tried, but no opportunity came our way."

"I hope he remains patient with us and does not get into a fit of rage," remarked Vakul.

"You sound so scared!"

"Aren't you worried, Vamsi?"

"Actually, I am not worried but tired of all this," growled Vamsi as he ran his fingers through his hair. "Everyone who knows us believes that you have the sharper mind in the team, and I have the might. I don't know why the *smarter* you can't see the obvious, which I can."

"What is that?"

"Vakul, our master is just using us, from one dangerous and dirty job to another. We are just expendable men for him. He doesn't care."

"I think he does have plans for us," commented Vakul.

"That plan is to push us into dangerous situations and finally get us killed. In a way, no better than cocks with strapped metal claws made to fight before the village games for everyone's amusement. We are creatures that will die for nothing." Until recently, the brothers were aligned in all their thoughts; one mind and two bodies, one synergetic team. Now, there were more differences of opinion between them, which particularly bothered Vakul.

"The way I see it, Vamsi, we were dead people when we were out there on the streets. The other gangs were after our life, and it is his protection that has kept us alive."

"Alive! This is not the life I wanted for sure. Sometimes I want to quit," declared Vamsi.

Vakul sighed, "With what we know and what we have done for him, from assassinating ministers to killing army officials and spies, if we were to quit or abscond, I can see him tracking us down to wherever we escape to, and then the inevitable will happen."

The key skill of the twins, tactfully used by their master, was to execute assassinations that seemed like death by natural causes. The chain of assassinations executed by the twins spanned years; they had lost count.

The mud road now turned around a lake; the twins galloped fast. It was evening. A swarm of locusts crossed their path. There were numerous mahua trees all around.

"Vakul, I think it's just blind faith you have."

Vakul smiled, "After what he did to my hand, I should actually hate him. On the other hand, I understand him better. He is our only means to a good life."

From a distance, they could see four tents erected in the middle of the jungle, a bonfire between them. To the twins, it appeared like the end of a successful hunting day for their master. A spotted deer layered with seasoning was roasting on top of the fire. Another one hung on a wooden pole face-down, skinned by the assistants. At the sight of their master, the twins bowed down and clasped their hands.

"Come! Come! It took you longer than I thought."

"I apologise, master," said Vakul. "We were inside Thanesara town looking at our best options to get near the royal family."

"There has been a change of plan. Das! Get some water for them."

Vamsi murmured, "Change of plan?"

Their master signalled for them to sit. The twins squatted on the ground, their master on a wooden bench.

"I had wanted you both to create a vulnerable situation for the Vardhan family. Fortunately for us, I hear that King Prabhakar is unwell. The kingdom is going through a tenuous phase. So, I want you both to help me with something else."

"Please command, and we will do what is needed," Vakul responded.

"I have never been so excited. I cannot sleep at night thinking about the possibilities. This is our time finally." The twins had never seen their master so animated.

"I hope it's not a high-risk mission like the last one," said Vamsi.

"Has high risk started to bother you?"

The master got up and went to the skinned deer, which was over the bonfire. He took out his knife and cut a piece of meat from below its ribs. He then threw the piece on the ground in front of Vamsi.

"Eat!" Their master stared unblinking, his gaze pinning down Vamsi to his place. There was a moment of uneasy silence.

Vamsi looked at his brother, took a deep breath, then picked up the soiled piece of meat from the ground and reluctantly ate it.

"Is it cooked and spiced properly?"

"Yes, master!"

"Good! Come here! Let us discuss my plan for you over a meal."

"Looks like you had a good day hunting spotted deer." Vakul's voice was soft.

"It wasn't a good day, actually. The deer and antelopes in these parts are too quick for our horses. These are actually two young ones which fell to my arrows by the end of the day since we didn't want to return empty-handed."

As their master walked forward, the twins followed obediently.

nine

End of Bliss

Harsha and Rajyavardhan were at their father's bedside. Over the last few days, he had turned from being the epitome of royal grace to becoming a *nar-kankaal*, a human skeleton, just skin stretched over his bones. In all probability, he was bleeding inside. Whatever had been growing inside and below his neck had by now spread through his upper torso. His face was ghastly pale, his beard grey, hair shabby and eyes blank as he stared at the ceiling. He was unable to swallow and could barely open his mouth for the liquid food he was having. Tears rolled down his cheeks every now and then, the haggard face of a once-powerful king. He was too weak and too feeble even to speak. The few words that occasionally escaped his mouth were indecipherable. Two days earlier, he had called Rajyavardhan, Harsha and Bhandi to his side and, in a barely audible voice, said to them, "Always be there for each other. Above everything, dedicate yourself to our people and motherland." Queen Yashomati hadn't left her husband's side throughout his illness; she had become pale, was perpetually in tears, and her eyes were ringed by dark circles due to the lack of sleep. She had also stopped eating food.

"Ma! This is not a solution to anything. You need to take care of yourself," urged Harsha as he held his mother's hand.

"Don't worry about me," his mother said softly. "Please tell me that the physicians have a way around this ailment he is suffering from. I have no life without him; please save him!"

Rajyavardhan placed his hands on his mother's shoulders. "They are putting in their best efforts. His condition is deteriorating, but hopefully some miracle will happen. Our father has done so much for the welfare of his people during his reign that their blessings will save him. My heart says so."

The brothers decided to walk to the royal hall where the physicians had assembled. In spite of being generously lit with fire-torches, the hall was so huge that it was still dark in the corners. Tonight, there were 48 physicians from in and around Thanesara, who rose to their feet as the princes entered.

"Has anything changed since last night? Please tell me that there is hope." Rajyavardhan's voice quivered even as he fought back the tears.

The chief physician, an old man with a bushy grey beard, said, "This is your moment to show courage. I am afraid we need to face the truth. King Prabhakar is battling death and we are losing him with every passing moment."

Harsha's tears flowed uncontrollably, "Now that we have exhausted all normal alternatives, we have nothing to lose. Is there anything different from the normal that can be tried?"

The chief physician put his hand on the shoulder of a young physician standing to his left, "This is my nephew Anandam, a brilliant physician. He has read some ancient texts on *Shailyachikitsa*. There is a very risky alternative of making a small incision so as to reach directly into the ailing person's stomach."

"Reach with what?" asked Rajyavardhan.

"The mouth of a very thin wooden funnel. Then we can inject something nutritious like milk to give his body some energy to fight the weakness," elaborated Anandam.

"I am sorry to sound sceptical, but is this practical? Sounds to me like a reckless method," remarked Rajyavardhan.

The old physician thought for a moment and said, "To be honest, we have never tried something like this and we don't know if it would work. Given King Prabhakar's health condition, it is actually not recommended."

The physician's nephew added, "There is another method. We could try inserting a thin flexible bamboo pipe which may help to clear his throat. If we are successful, we can keep him alive for a day or two."

"A day or two? Will the pain and inconvenience be worth it?" asked Harsha.

The chief physician kept quiet.

Rajyavardhan queried, "Do you think it is worth giving more pain and suffering to a person who is already fighting life and death?"

"That is a tough one, but we leave the final decision to you both," said the old physician.

Harsha said, "It's unfortunate that our only two choices are to either let our father die or give him more pain to keep him alive for a day or two."

"We will be back here shortly. Come, Harsha!" said Rajyavardhan as he tried fighting back his tears. Putting an arm around his grieving younger brother's shoulder, he led him outside towards the royal court.

On their way through the external corridor, they could see the glow of fire on a hillock near the palace. It was called the 'Hillock of Gods'. There were 60 stone-cut stairs that led to the top where there was a ritual podium. Today, throughout the day, 108 priests from temples big and small around Thanesara had performed a *mahayagna*, rituals and Vedic chanting around a huge holy bonfire, offering prayers for the survival and good health of their beloved King Prabhakarvardhan. The ritual was slated to be performed for seven days to appease the gods. In one corner of the podium was a humongous, neatly arranged pile of firewood for the bonfires, large containers of flowers and pots of milk for the coming day. All the priests had just left, but the fire continued to burn.

"What do you think we should do? Should we go ahead with the reckless measures suggested by the physicians?" asked Rajyavardhan.

Harsha replied, "My worry is that, in his current state, are we prolonging his life by a few days or prolonging his pain and suffering? If given a choice and if he could speak, what would he have opted for? How can we decide for him? Is the life of a few days with extreme pain and suffering better than a life shorter by a few days? I cannot live with the burden of having taken a wrong decision." As Harsha broke down, Rajyavardhan embraced him tightly, fighting hard to conceal his own tears, feeling as though his head would burst with the number of thoughts crashing into each other.

"This is our moment to show courage and calm. Come with me, brother! We need to go to the court to hear the news from Kannauj," said Rajyavardhan as he led his brother through a turn in the corridor. Once again they glanced at the fire slowly going out on the hillock. Their family was exactly at this stage, light struggling relentlessly against darkness from all around. As they entered the court, Army Chief Chakravarti, Chief Minister Janardhan and Bhandi rushed towards them. Everyone looked at Bhandi since he now had a difficult task to perform.

"We have disturbing news from Kannauj. Grihavarman and Rajashri had been on a long pleasure trip to the lower

Himalayas." Bhandi sighed for a moment before he continued. "There was sudden flooding in the region followed by major landslides. Village after village was destroyed and hundreds of people have lost their lives."

Chakravarti added, "We are unable to trace the whereabouts of Rajashri and Grihavarman since all the mud roads and forest routes leading to those places were destroyed by the landslides. Since horsemen and chariots are not an option, administrators of Kannauj palace have sent their foot soldiers to rescue their king from the disaster-hit region."

"I just hope they are both safe. Father is fighting for his life; Rajashri needs to be here," said Rajyavardhan.

Janardhan interrupted, "Given the perilous situation and bad weather in the flood-affected lower reaches of the Himalayas, anything could have happened to the newly-weds and we should be prepared for the worst, realistically speaking."

They were suddenly distracted by the sound of anklets rushing away from the entrance of the court. "Do you think someone was overhearing us?" Harsha queried as he walked towards the entrance.

"I think I just saw a glimpse of mother Yashomati near the entrance," said Rajyavardhan, the concern clear on his face.

"You think she heard what was being said?" asked Harsha.

Rajyavardhan looked at Janardhan with resentment. "I think we should stick to facts during briefings without wandering away to what we feel and assume."

Harsha called out to his brother, "Come, *jyeshta-sri*! If she had heard us, then we must locate mother at once and comfort her." The brothers were about to leave the court when they heard the sharp cry of a woman from the king's bedchamber. They rushed into the room and found their father motionless, his eyes wide open, a drop of blood at the corner of his slightly open mouth.

"He is dead!" cried Rajyavardhan as he held his father's cold hands. Prabhakarvardhan, the glorious, powerful king who had protected his land and people against barbaric invaders, lay motionless, transformed from an intimidating, mighty king to folklore from the past, all in a matter of days. Harsha could barely control his tears as he clasped his father's pale feet, the cold of the lifeless limbs sending a chill down his spine, making his hair stand on end. "Where is mother?" he asked.

One of the female attendants near the bedside said, "Prince Harsha, she had gone to the royal court looking for both of you. Then she came back and our king stopped breathing. Queen Yashomati looked as if she had been struck by a bolt of lightning. She screamed that our king was not breathing and rushed out of here."

The brothers ran out in opposite directions, mobilising the guards along with them. Harsha looked around the palace garden and pond, trying hard to suppress the myriad feelings inside him. "Ma!" he called out loudly as he moved from one part of the palace to another, tears rolling down his face. Near the garden, Rajyavardhan appeared in front of him along with the guards from the outer gate of the palace.

"They saw mother walk out of the main gate, crying uncontrollably," said Rajyavardhan.

"Where was she going to? Which direction?" Harsha asked agitatedly.

"We should search all around Thanesara town at once," Rajyavardhan instructed the guards.

The brothers were thinking about their next course of action when their faces were lit up in the dark night with a burst of light from far away. "What is that?" asked Rajyavardhan as they both looked towards the Hillock of Gods. A huge bonfire engulfed the tall stacked-up structure of the wood for the rituals to be performed in the coming days. Without wasting another moment, Rajyavardhan and Harsha rushed towards the gate, followed by the guards. As they panted and sprinted towards the hillock, little did they realise the enormity of the towering inferno at the top. As they came near, they could see the faint outline of a woman standing in front of the flames. Harsha knew at once that it was their mother. After setting the whole structure ablaze, she had thrown a fire torch away. Rajyavardhan and Harsha called out loudly, pleading with her to come down, asking her to stop. As they stumbled up the hillock, she looked behind and paused for a moment. This woman had lived her life for her family. They had been her purpose, accomplishment and driving force. She had chosen her family to define herself; there was nothing else in her life other than her husband and children. Today, she had received the biggest jolt of her life—she had lost her husband and her daughter was either dead or in grave danger. Rajyavardhan kept pleading at the top of his voice as he climbed the steps, "Ma! Just stop. Come back!" Harsha shouted to her, "Please don't, Ma!"

Yashomati turned around, as if she had not heard anything, and walked straight into the inferno in what appeared to be a spur-of-the-moment decision. What followed was a loud, sharp cry which reverberated all around the vicinity. It was difficult to fathom whether it was due to the pain or the letting go of the grief inside. For the brothers, who had been rushing to the top of the hillock, the cry pierced their ears and numbed their mind and body. They stood mortified, in utter despair and disbelief.

ten

Disaster-Struck

Water had dripped from the ceiling and seeped into the wooden storage, making inroads into the sacks of millets and barley. Rajashri looked at the head cook in dismay. The soldiers, squatting in the hall of the stone castle, were coughing almost in turns and Rajashri could hear them inside.

"We need to cook and eat these today. By tomorrow, these wet grains will be inedible," commented the head cook.

Rajashri said, "Please boil it with the pink rock salt and the spices we have. You have dry firewood?"

"Yes, Ragyi! Thankfully, we do."

"Send two bowls of that downstairs for me and the king," said Rajashri.

"No, my dear queen! We have rice and pulses for you and our king," said the head cook. The more expensive grains for the royal couple were intact in their metal storage bins.

Rajashri replied, "We are trapped here with the devastation of nature all around us. It's time to share whatever precious little we have and move ahead one day at a time. We'll share the rice and pulses in the next few days until they last."

"How can royals have something as frugal as a millet cake or barley porridge?"

Rajashri smiled, "I am sure we will relish it. Hunger adds flavour to the taste of food."

She came out into the hall and saw the squatting soldiers. They got up, but she signalled to them to be at ease.

"Is anybody missing?"

One of the soldiers replied, "Some of them have gone outside to take positions in the guard cabins."

"Please call them inside. Both the guard cabins are made of wood. They will fall sick. I hear most of you coughing and sneezing anyway," said Rajashri.

"We need to guard the complex!"

Rajashri interrupted, "I don't see any safety concerns other than the fury of nature. We are surrounded by debris, fallen trees, dead animals and destroyed villages. Everybody stays here inside the main complex throughout the night without exception, please."

"Yes, Ragyi!"

Rajashri asked, "How many more days do we need to pull on as per your estimate?"

"God willing, if it does not rain overnight, we can leave for our capital in the afternoon," replied the main guard.

"Let's all pray for that!" said Rajashri as she looked out of the window.

The sky was not cloudy. The stone castle was at the edge of a flat hilltop surrounded by mountains. All around them was devastation as far as the eye could see. At intervals, the breeze wafted the stench into the castle. Rajashri turned and clasped her hands to greet some goat herders who were seated behind the soldiers in one corner of the hall. They were in the vicinity when calamity struck and had managed to take refuge in the castle. Some were still shedding tears at the loss of a loved one or of their home. Everyone was petrified by what they had seen and were worrying about what they might yet have to see. There was a limited stock of fresh water. All of them were dirty, their clothes soiled.

"Here, Ragyi! The hot medicinal potion for the king," said the head cook as he handed over a copper cup of brown liquid to Rajashri.

As she walked down the stone stairs to the basement, Rajashri wondered how things had taken such a surprising turn. After their wedding, the couple had decided to spend some days in the pristine natural heaven at the foothills of the Himalayas. As their convoy of chariots passed each village, people cheered on both sides of the mud road, ecstatic to see the royal couple. They left their chariots and horses in the last leg of their journey. After crossing the bridge over a stream, they climbed up a slope to reach their final destination. The rains started just as they were about to reach the hillside castle. From this vantage point, they could see snow-clad mountains on one side. A stream right below them rushed into a valley on the other side, dotted with villages. It rained relentlessly for two days. Grihavarman and Rajashri were too lost in each other to notice anything. On the third day, ear-shattering thunder erupted from the direction of the mountains. Then it came, a sudden deluge from the heights, uprooting trees, washing away animals and crops. From the castle, they saw the placid stream transform into what looked like the tall waves of a violent sea flooding the villages in the valley within moments. The waters receded as fast as they had come. The royal couple decided to leave even though the rains hadn't stopped. Then one side of the hill in front of them came crashing down, an avalanche of sliding mud, rocks and debris. Within moments, everything that was left downhill was buried.

All the mud roads leading out of the castle, including the bridge, were covered with layers of rubble from the landslide and wreckage from the sudden flood. It was dangerous to venture out. They had all been holed up inside the castle for four days now.

The basement of the castle was spacious, carpeted and complete with exquisite décor. Grihavarman was relaxing on a royal bed made of teak with ivory inlay. Even with all the misery and tragedy around, the sight of Grihavarman lit up Rajashri's worried face.

"Here is the hot medicinal potion for your sore throat, my handsome king," said Rajashri as she handed the copper cup to her husband.

"It has a very strong smell," he took a sip and raised his eyebrows. "Does not taste bad. So, what were we talking about before you went upstairs?"

Rajashri replied, "We were talking about my cousin Bhandi."

"What happened after that tragic night when he lost his parents?" Grihavarman took another sip from the cup.

"Bhandi was brought to our palace as a little boy with burns and blisters on his body. Later he developed rashes, which eventually healed but left some permanent scars," said Rajashri.

"Having lost his parents and then going through so much physical pain must have been traumatic for a child," remarked Grihavarman.

"All that misery is probably the reason he has such a rough exterior. Inside, he is a gem. He loves all of us beyond words," said Rajashri.

"I am told he is very skilled in horse riding and with a sword," said Grihavarman.

"Father says that if he trains hard, one day he will replace Army Chief Chakravarti who wants to retire in three to four years."

"What is your father's plan for Rajyavardhan?"

"In a couple of months, father wants my elder brother to shadow him in each meeting or event he presides over. By next year, my father plans to bring the whole administration under my elder brother's control," said Rajashri.

"I believe Rajyavardhan is ready for that."

"My mother thinks that under the warrior facade, my elder brother is a saint. After his recent personal tragedy, he has become even more spiritual. She believes he is too innocent for dirty politics."

"Mothers have a soft image of their children, that's the way it is. What is planned for Harsha?"

"We all think that he has the sharpest mind and an extraordinary ability to learn quickly. My father thinks he will take some time. Maybe it's because of his age, but he gets carried away by his emotions."

"I think in a year or two he will be ready to take up important roles," said Grihavarman.

"To be honest, Harsha is just preparing himself to be as useful as possible when our elder brother becomes king. He is happy playing the assistant role. Poor thing! Left to himself, he might just sit in a secluded peaceful corner and write love stories without troubling anybody," said Rajashri.

"I hear he is very good at that."

Rajashri asked, "Tell me something, how were you prepared to lead a kingdom?"

"Ha! In my case it was abrupt. My father died when I was 13 years old. My coronation was held immediately while my mother took the role of regent queen. I pretty much learned everything first-hand."

"Must have been a difficult journey for the young king!"

Grihavarman held Rajashri's hands and pulled her towards him, "Yes, it was! It's important to fail and learn from it. From now onwards, will you assist me in matters of the state, my queen?"

"Depending on what it is and how much I know about it!"

Grihavarman smiled, "I have thought of something. Anyway, for tonight I want you to assist me in feeling loved."

"Feeling loved? You can phrase it better than that, my king!"

Grihavarman said, "I am a king, not a royal court poet! Come closer."

Rajashri laughed out loud, "What about dinner?"

"Let's skip that. We need to preserve foodgrains in this time of adversity, you see."

Rajashri smiled, "Really! Saving foodgrains is not the real intention."

"You might be right, my queen."

That night, there was no rain. The next morning too, the weather was fine. By afternoon, the royal couple decided to return to their palace at Kanyakubja.

eleven

Silent Palace

A sea of people from across Sthaneshwar, along with dignitaries, vassals and neighbouring kings flocked to pay their last respects to the departed king. King Bhaskaravarman of Kamarupa could not stop himself from shedding tears for his old friend throughout the ceremony. King Shashank of Gauda constantly consoled the princes. King Prabhakarvardhan was cremated in the afternoon on the next day. In the evening, surrounded by priests, the princes went to the Hillock of Gods with their cousin Bhandi, Chief Minister Janardhan and Army Chief Chakravarti to perform the ritual of collecting the remains of the departed to be sealed in a holy urn. It was a painful ritual, but for centuries it had been performed as instructed in the holy text despite the agony it caused the mourning survivors. Rajyavardhan and Harsha extended their hands forward, opening up their palms. Attendants went to the spot where Queen Yashomati had immolated herself, picked up the remains of charred bones, and placed them one by one on Harsha's open palms. Tears blurring his vision, Harsha avoided looking at the bones that were once his loving mother. The attendants moved on to the spot where Prabhakarvardhan had been cremated. As they placed the charred remains of his bones on Rajyavardhan's open palms, Harsha could see that his brother's hands were trembling and his face was ghastly pale. There was so much discomfort in their minds that each moment of the rituals seemed like eternity. Bhandi too was uncomfortable. His grief was choking him, but he was not used to expressing himself. He left before the ritual ended. The priest poured holy water from the River Ganga over the charred bones, followed by neem water, turmeric water and a scented liquid. He then asked the brothers to place the bone fragments into the respective holy urns. Reciting Vedic hymns, he then covered the urns with flowers and sealed them. The two urns with the mortal remains of Yashomati and Prabhakarvardhan were to be taken to the sacred town of Haridwar to be immersed in the holy Ganga. For now they were placed in a tent in the garden.

Rajyavardhan and Harsha returned to the palace and went to the family's chambers. After a ritual dip in the pool, they changed their clothes. Food was served by the attendants, but after what the princes had held a while ago, they could not eat with their hands, not today; not even for the next couple of days. King Shashank and King Bhaskaravarman bid a tearful adieu to the brothers as they left for their kingdoms.

Rajyavardhan looked out of the window into the horizon, lost deep in thought. Every once in a while, Harsha kept looking at his palm, remembering the creepy feel of the charred bones. Not a word was spoken, not a tear shed. Their minds were numb after the shocking turn of events. Harsha looked at Rajyavardhan and he could see the strain that this series of misfortunes had caused him. Just a year back, he was in the lap of luxury in a grand palace with caring parents, a loving wife, and a child on the way. Today he was a man with nothing but grief surrounding him. Rajyavardhan looked at his younger brother. At the age of

17, young Harsha had received his first big jolt from life. In a normal situation, they would have hugged and cried to pacify each other, but this was grief beyond pacifying words, beyond comforting acts and beyond consolation of any kind. They remained motionless like statues.

Army Chief Chakravarti and Chief Minister Janardhan entered. "Prince Rajyavardhan! I suggest that we should conduct your coronation ceremony tomorrow itself," the army chief announced as he stepped into the room with Janardhan.

Rajyavardhan replied, "Chief, please excuse me for now. I am in no frame of mind for anything right away. Give me a couple of days please, I want to be left alone."

Chakravarti's expression changed to one of concern, "We cannot have a kingdom without a head of state. I understand how much agony you both are going through, but we may need to keep that aside for the larger good of the people of this kingdom."

"I am sorry! No matter what you say now, my mind is just too numb for all this," said Rajyavardhan.

Janardhan intervened, "This state of mourning and inactivity cannot be our permanent state. I suggest we keep personal grief aside and think practically, without losing time."

Just then a familiar odour wafted in from the entrance. Harsha turned to see the Hunas approach, led by their king Narana. Whether it was the herbal oil they used or the hides to wrap around their body or the excessive use of leather accessories, their approach could be smelled from afar. The hard soles of their leather footwear made a creaking noise as they walked in.

"I apologise for not being able to make it here in time. The distance and the rugged terrain make it really difficult to reach here at short notice," said Narana, looking tired but sharp.

Rajyavardhan stepped forward to greet them. Harsha gazed at Army Chief Chakravarti and Chief Minister Janardhan as they keenly observed every move of this interaction.

"My deepest condolences, Prince Rajyavardhan! You lost a loving father. We lost a dear friend and a long-time ally," said Narana as he advanced to hug Rajyavardhan.

Then he hugged Harsha. "Prince Harsha! I am so sorry for your loss. Your father was a great man. History will remember King Prabhakarvardhan as one of the greatest kings to have ruled these lands. Your mother was nobility personified."

From the corner of his eye, Harsha could see the discomfort on Chakravarti's face. Was Narana really sad at the loss? Had it not been for King Prabhakarvardhan, the Hunas would have been in control of this palace and most of Bharatvarsh long ago.

The guests settled down in the row of chairs around the chamber while the princes sat on the royal chairs.

"So, when is your coronation, Prince Rajyavardhan?" asked Narana.

Startled by the abruptly timed question, Rajyavardhan replied, "I was just telling them that we are not in a hurry. As of now it is not our priority."

Narana's eyes narrowed as he exclaimed, "You never know how a delay will be perceived by the general public. A kingdom without a proclaimed head of state! What if someone tries to take advantage of this vulnerable situation?"

"We will see when that happens!" intervened Harsha, seeing how hassled Rajyavardhan got under intimidation. Even in grief, he still mustered the presence of mind to be of support to his brother. Uncomfortable silence filled the chamber.

"I hope I was not too assertive. I was just saying that for the benefit of your kingdom since you are not doing the obvious thing," said Narana. The Huna king leaned forward as if intimidating the princes.

Rajyavardhan said, "Let's not be worried about Sthaneshwar and instead talk about your kingdom. In the last month or so, we heard about violent acts in the territories under your control. Religious shrines were ambushed and monks injured." Harsha knew that in tight situations, Rajyavardhan's way of defending himself was to turn the offensive on the other side.

"There are these groups within our kingdom which became uncontrollably violent. They believe that we should not promote shrines of other religions within our territories," stated Narana, scratching his stubble, as if it was the most obvious thing to say.

Harsha intervened, "We had cautioned you before that fringe elements go out of control if the administration shows a slight inclination towards their ideology."

"We are not showing any inclination. You boys are young; there is so much about the world, politics and governance that you don't know. That is the reason you have such idealistic beliefs. Once you reach my age, you will better understand why such power games are necessary for good governance," said Narana, his tone that of an experienced elder.

Harsha remarked, "Even with our limited experience we know that playing such games with your own people to create situations that benefit the ones in power is undesirable."

"Don't get me wrong, but I was just saying that there are reasons for our style of governance, considering the groups and sects of people we have to deal with inside our kingdom," said Narana. Janardhan and Chakravarti looked at each other, wondering where the argument was heading.

Rajyavardhan spoke out, "My view is that this should stop! We are allies, and it can tarnish our image if we are associated with regimes that allow injustice upon their own people, prosecute them or subject them to atrocities by fringe elements."

Narana fixed Rajyavardhan with a piercing stare. "Has this got to do with your newfound interest in Buddhism and your being influenced by some of these monks who visit your palace?"

For once even Rajyavardhan was furious, "My personal choices have nothing to do with my official stance on policies and governance."

"I fail to understand why it is so difficult for you people to stop the discrimination and harassment of people hailing from different backgrounds," added Harsha, knowing that his brother was about to have an outburst that would deteriorate the situation.

"Noted," said Narana as he asked to be excused with his team, so as to take rest after a long journey. After Narana left, so did Janardhan and Chakravarti. Once the brothers were by themselves, there was silence in the chamber again. Finally, Rajyavardhan said, "I just seem to have a bad feeling about everything around me now."

Harsha went up to his brother and placed his hands on his shoulders, "Suddenly we are thrust into a hostile world."

"These are really testing times and we both need to be careful..." remarked Rajyavardhan, cut off mid-sentence by Bhandi, who suddenly rushed into the chamber. Rajyavardhan and Harsha stood up immediately, sensing something from the look on Bhandi's face.

"There is some really bad news. After being stuck in the flood and landslides in the lower Himalayas, Rajashri and King Grihavarman managed to escape from the calamity-stricken region. However, even before they could reach the capital, Devagupta of Malava took advantage of the vulnerable situation and attacked their kingdom, capturing the king and our sister."

"What are you saying? Kannauj has been captured by Devagupta?" queried Harsha in disbelief. "Where are Rajashri and Grihavarman now?" Bhandi had no clue.

Rajyavardhan muttered, "That scheming snake Devagupta could see that both Kannauj and our kingdom are going through a vulnerable phase. He just used the opportunity."

"I am worried for the newly-married couple," remarked Bhandi.

Rajyavardhan instructed, "Call in the army chief! The army needs to be ready by tomorrow morning to march towards the border of Kannauj. A war between Sthaneshwar and Malava is inevitable now. I will lead the army."

"I am coming with you," said Harsha.

"No! In my absence, you will be thc leader in charge of the palace and administrative affairs. Army Chief Chakravarti, Chief Minister Janardhan and Bhandi will stay back here to assist you," ordered Rajyavardhan.

"No, but..." interrupted Harsha.

"It's an order! Our sister is in grave distress and I am going to get her back to Thanesara," said Rajyavardhan assertively.

Next morning, as he marched out of the main gate, Rajyavardhan turned and looked at his palace. It was unbelievable how within a matter of days the family's fortunes had taken a sharp dip. Rajyavardhan knew that he needed to take control before it became any worse.

twelve

Human Sacrifice

For the first time in her life, Rajashri felt what it was like to have her hands and legs bound by a restraining chain and padlock for days. She experienced the burning pain of the cold hard metal bruising and rupturing the skin of her wrists and legs. The princess of Sthaneshwar, who had spent her life in the lap of luxury, had just woken up after sleeping on the cold stony surface of her dark prison cell. When they were trapped in the hills, the enemies of Kannauj had been keeping track of the proceedings and made an opportunistic strike. Devagupta attacked and captured the capital town of Kanyakubja. The newly-weds had assumed that the worst was over for them when they escaped unhurt from the disaster-struck region, but when their convoy was attacked outside the capital, their soldiers, already starving and fatigued, could not save the royal couple. Grihavarman and Rajashri were captured and sent to separate prisons.

The light in the cell was dim, the air heavy and the smell similar to that of a horse stable. Her cell was in the middle of a corridor on the first floor of a complex that had many unoccupied cells.

This prison was specifically for political prisoners. Rajashri was lost in thought as she looked across the prison bars to the small window in the adjacent cell where the setting sun was visible. A large grey lizard crawled on the wall next to her. Terrified, she moved backwards and as she did so, the chains clanked. A moment later, in front of her appeared the tall and well-built King of Malava. She had seen him at a royal wedding at Vallabhi two years back and he had not changed much in appearance. Devagupta had a dusky complexion, long curly hair, bushy moustache and a scar across his face from one of the numerous battles he had fought. Due to his addiction to mandrake root with belladonna infusions, which his men sourced all the way from Mishrarajya, his eyes were always bloodshot. He examined the queen of Kannauj keenly. Devagupta had two trays in his hands, one covered and the other with a royal meal. Three attendants quickly placed a wooden table and chair for their king in front of Rajashri's cell. He placed the trays on the table and went to the black stone sink near the adjacent cell, drawing water from a metal pot kept below the sink to wash his hands. His smile remained intact throughout.

"I know that you have grown up surrounded by luxury, pampered by everyone. This must be a harrowing experience. Do the chains and padlock hurt?" he asked.

"They do. Where is my husband? Why are you doing this, Devagupta?" said Rajashri, fighting back her tears.

Devagupta smirked, "I saw you at that grand wedding of the princess of Vallabhi and I was smitten by your beauty. I wanted to make you mine. My guru agreed that you indeed are my lucky charm, but your father had other plans."

"Which father in the world would agree to get his daughter married to a delusional man following his family guru verbatim?

Ready to get into a marriage just to bring good luck, satisfy his lust and then sacrifice his bride on the altar on Durgashtami? My father did what anybody in his place would do."

Devagupta sighed, "My guru has always been right and it has worked for me in the past. You wait and watch, one day I will be the most powerful king in the whole of Bharatvarsh. Your father and the likes of him have looked down upon us and our Gupta clan since the beginning. I will prove everyone wrong." In his drugged state, he slurred his words with long pauses in between.

"My father and other kingdoms of Bharatvarsh have a problem with you and the Guptas of Malava because of the land-grabbing and plundering you do for expansion. After all this you claim to be the direct descendants of the illustrious Guptas of Magadha, the bloodline of Samudragupta and Chandragupta Vikramaditya. My father thinks it is unfair," said Rajashri.

"What your father thinks about our clan does not matter any more."

At this moment, Devagupta's brother Visnugupta walked in. He had a dusky complexion like his brother, but straighter hair and a beard. He was tall and muscular, and his eyes darted all over the place, as if he were contemplating something all the time. Visnugupta came dragging a leather bag behind him, but he froze when his glance moved to Rajashri.

"O Rajashri! Meet my brother Visnugupta. Not only is he a fierce warrior in the battlefield, he has other skills also. Visnu dear! Look at this delicate flower, the queen of Kannauj," said Devagupta as he gestured towards Rajashri, who was now reduced to nothing but a caged animal who could not avoid the prying, ridiculing gaze of her captors.

Visnugupta looked at the prisoner carefully from head to toe and declared, "She is a delicate flower which anyone would want to trample under their feet, brother! You will have the time of your life when you consummate your marriage." As the brothers giggled, Rajashri wondered how bad her fate was to get trapped between such insane people. Visnugupta opened his leather bag next to the water pot. One by one he took out bloodstained knives, choppers, a cleaver, pointed rods, a saw and scrapers. He took water in a clay cup out of the pot and cleaned them.

Devagupta commented, "Ah! I forgot to tell you that Visnu here is a torture specialist also and he loves doing it." His smile widened. "You will be surprised to know how he can literally reduce a full-grown person to just a heap of flesh, ligaments, cartilage and bits of bone. It's sometimes impossible to imagine that those blood-drenched heaps were once a walking talking person."

Rajashri looked at the blood running with the water into the drainage pipe. She gulped in fear and said, "So you are going to torture me? For what? To get even with my father?"

Devagupta sighed, "I can only imagine how horrified the old man would be if he came to know that I captured you and your groom alive. Seated on his throne, imagining the agony I am putting you through. My bad luck. The old man escaped the horror by dying before that."

"Not just him, but his wife also walked into a fire," added Visnugupta.

Rajashri could not comprehend what Devagupta was saying. She looked dazed and her eyes filled with tears.

"I don't think she believes me. Visnu! Look at her. She thinks I am speaking gibberish because I am intoxicated. Let me show you something." He held up an invitation from Thanesara palace, which had been sent to the various vassals and warlords of Sthaneshwar. A document which Devagupta's spies were able to get their hands on.

"Look at this! An invitation from your palace to people asking them to attend the 13th day ceremony after the death of the king and queen. Look at the stationery and the royal seal. Read this!"

He thrust the document at her. Rajashri burst out crying. The brothers giggled.

Devagupta brought his face close to the wailing princess. "Only a little more than a lunar month separates us. After that, your body is mine. For the one night I have it, I will make the most of it. The next day you will be gone forever, sacrificed for my good luck. Here, eat something and keep yourself alive till then." He pushed the tray from below the cell door towards the princess. She stepped away. The clanking of the chain around her hands and the padlock on her legs drowned the sound of her sobbing.

Visnugupta stopped cleaning the knives and stepped forward. "My dear *jyeshta-sri*! How can she eat when her hands are chained? I think she needs a helping hand." Saying so, he removed the cover from the other tray and flung something towards the princess through the bars. It landed on the royal meal plate in front of Rajashri, splashing everything. She started to scream loudly in horror. It was a severed hand that was still bleeding. She recognised the rings on its fingers. It was the forearm of her husband Grihavarman. Rajashri's shrill cries reverberated around the corridor. Petrified, she crawled backwards on the floor.

Devagupta said, "Visnu just reduced your husband to shreds of flesh. You also have a few days left. Enjoy the real world while it lasts, my delicate flower."

thirteen

Battle with Malava

Rajyavardhan had the benevolence to send a messenger of truce one last time to his enemy's camp. His heart still believed that they should be given one final chance. The terms were simple: Devagupta should surrender Rajashri at once and unconditionally. In return, Sthaneshwar's army would allow the Malava army to set up camp on the recently annexed disputed lands around the Dharini.

The response was prompt. The messenger returned and conveyed to Rajyavardhan how Devagupta and his sadistic brother Visnugupta had made fun of this proposal. In their words, they were overjoyed to see the future king of Sthaneshwar down on his knees begging for a truce. They emphatically stated that the strained relationship between the kingdoms was beyond repair. Devagupta had dismissed the messenger with the parting words that the slaying of each and every member of the Sthaneshwar royal family was his first step towards the total domination of Bharatvarsh.

Rajyavardhan stepped out of his tent with his soldiers behind him and looked at the rising sun. On the southern horizon he could see the Malava soldiers getting ready for battle. Still mourning the death of his parents, the young prince clad in his metallic battle armour was not in a state of mind to command an army into a battlefield, but he had no choice. Rajyavardhan had come to know that his sister's husband had been mercilessly butchered, shredded to pieces by Visnugupta after being tortured by his elder brother Devagupta. In less than two lunar months, on the day of Durgashtami, they would do the same to his sister at the sacrificial altar. Holding a heavy sword, Rajyavardhan walked to the peak of the mound where they had set up their camp, his leather footwear with alloy buckles throwing up dust as he surveyed the barren battlefield covered with bushes. Following him closely was his inner circle of 50 young Yuva-Sena men who had been selected after a rigorous elimination process and had trained under the supervision of his cousin Bhandi. Rajyavardhan's eyes narrowed as he inspected the Malava soldiers carefully.

"They are about 10,000 in number. Look at their defensive formation. Split into three parts with a left, centre and right wing. Foot soldiers in the front of each wing and cavalry behind. Surprisingly, no war elephants," commented Rajyavardhan.

A young Yuva-Sena soldier said, "We are just short of their number. At around 8,000 in strength and with our level of skill, we can definitely defeat them."

"My worry is not what you see, but what you cannot see," said Rajyavardhan.

He pointed southwards, "You see how the farthest line of cavalry at the very back of this formation looks out of place? They are so closely placed. Looks like they are cordoning off something behind them. Why would their army generals do that?"

"That is a good observation. It is looking odd for sure!"

"Well! You see those ravines behind them near the horizon? I strongly believe that their master Devagupta or his brother Visnugupta are hiding there with reinforcements." As Rajyavardhan elaborated his hypothesis, he could see that his men were intrigued.

"You mean to say that there are more soldiers than we can see. That means they will pounce on us at an opportune moment," said a rugged-looking soldier.

"Yes! When we are tired, worn-out and would have wrongly assumed that we have won the battle, they will make a surprise ambush and finish us," added Rajyavardhan. There was momentary silence as they pondered over the situation.

"Master, should we then direct our offensive in that direction?"

Rajyavardhan thought for a moment before saying, "That will come later. The only way we can turn this situation to our advantage is by first creating a commotion so that the Malava generals are not able to instruct or control the direction of their soldiers. Then later, we will penetrate deep inside their formation."

Rajyavardhan and his men retired to the tent where they quickly devised their strategy for the day. He instructed the 1,000 well-trained soldiers under Bhandi to split into two equal groups and take the treacherous routes through the ravines on either side of the battlefield to await instructions. These teams were told to cover as much ground as possible in a clandestine manner on both sides while the armies engaged in the battlefield. Another 1,000 soldiers were earmarked as reinforcements. Rajyavardhan explained the battle formation to his residual 6,000 soldiers.

Having briefed them, Rajyavardhan stood in front of the polished metal mirror in his tent, looking at his reflection as he tightened his alloy-plated armour. As he donned his helmet, he remembered something from a few years ago. He was newly married and was about to accompany his father for a battle campaign. His wife had entered their palace chamber just as he was getting ready like this. They were both little more than adolescent, a stage of life in which love has no limits of intensity and is totally devoid of logic. He remembered how beautiful young Swaranya looked in her long flowing dress, beautiful jewellery made of multi-coloured precious stones, with small fragrant flowers in threads encircling her dark hair. Initially she was full of playfulness as they teased each other. “You look so good in this armour, my prince, but it seems as if your body has outgrown your tiny face,” she had said. “Tiny face? Just look at yourself and your tiny body which is like that of an adolescent. I am worried that our children will look like fragile stick-men if they turn out to be like you. See, I can lift you with one hand!” He had grabbed her in his arms, picked her off the floor and turned around in circles. Swaranya screamed out of fear of falling down even as Rajyavardhan had continued to laugh. The laughter from the past reverberated in Rajyavardhan’s ears, flashes of scenes from that lost time made his present more unbearable than it was. He remembered that just when he had been about to leave, the teary-eyed Swaranya had asked him to be careful and stay out of danger. She would wait for him by the palace window, she’d said. In that one year of togetherness, Rajyavardhan had experienced the ultimate bliss of loving someone and being loved beyond any boundaries. It defined a lifetime which so many others are deprived of, a piece of heaven on earth. Those who preach that love and attachment should be kept separate to make life less complicated don’t understand the essence of love. The true depth of love can be reached by making yourself totally vulnerable and embracing the fear that comes with attachment. So even if Rajyavardhan missed Swaranya every day and shed tears while remembering her in private, not for once did he regret exposing his totally vulnerable self to her. Rajyavardhan tried to shrug off the memories of his past and joined his hands in front of the idol of Lord Shiva in his tent, murmuring a prayer, "*Aum mani padme hum*," in praise of Buddha. Buddhism had been his solace after his wife's death. Rajyavardhan followed every religion and yet did not follow any one in particular. He believed that if everyone did so, the world would be a more peaceful place. Today, peace was the last thing on his mind.

On the battlefield, the Sthaneshwar army made the *Deva-vyuha* battle formation. It was a reverse pointed arrow-shaped hollow formation like the open mouth of a stork. The foot soldiers were concentrated on either side while the cavalry was in the centre, far behind the other foot soldiers. Rajyavardhan was right in the centre of the formation on a large white stallion. Once in a while, his eyes wandered to the horizon where 500 soldiers were secretly crossing over to the other side, away from plain sight.

The tension was palpable as the armies prepared to clash. Rajyavardhan took a deep breath and closed his eyes. Horrifying images crowded his mind—his father reduced to a sack of cold bones, his mother walking into a tower of flames, his sister's face glowing at the sight of her groom Grihavarman on the day of their wedding.

"Har Har Mahadev!" He let out the war cry.

The Sthaneshwar army roared like thunder, then charged at the rival formation. Their open mouth formation induced absolute commotion. Rajyavardhan watched as the left and right wings of the enemy came under severe attack. Soldiers mauled each other with their weapons, war cries of invincibility and of pain rent the air. The centre of the enemy formation right ahead of Rajyavardhan was largely intact. The scorching sun and the dust generated by the fierce fighting continued while Rajyavardhan and his cavalry waited with bated breath. On either side, the Sthaneshwar foot soldiers tore into the enemy. The Malava commander of the central formation directed some of his foot soldiers and horsemen to move in as reinforcements. Seeing the centre of the enemy's formation spread thin, Rajyavardhan cried out to his men, "*Akraman*!" The prince and his contingent charged forward in an instant. Two Malava riders charged towards Rajyavardhan, swords drawn, but he ducked swiftly. He slashed the neck of one of the soldiers, drawing blood and dislodging him from his horse. Rajyavardhan nimbly turned his stallion sideways to avoid the other soldier's attack, then swung his sword into the hapless man's shoulder, throwing him off balance. Rajyavardhan charged forward, cutting into the line of cavalry which was at the rear of the rival formation. As he and his men tore into it, the fighting slowly concentrated more towards the middle of the battlefield. More reinforcements came from behind to support the charging Sthaneshwar army.

"Oh lord!" gasped Rajyavardhan as the soldier riding next to him flew off his horse after being hit by a spear. This was followed by more spears being hurled in his direction. He quickly picked up the shield hanging near the hind side of his horse to protect himself.

"The enemy seems to be very upset that we are moving in this direction," he thought as more of his soldiers fell victim to the flying projectiles. From the corner of his eye, Rajyavardhan watched as Bhandi's trained soldiers, who had swiftly moved in on either side, used this opportunity to enter the arena and quickly head for the ravines right behind the battlefield. Rajyavardhan held his mace in his left hand, sword in his right hand and his horse's reins between his teeth. His stallion dashed forward as he continued to knock down rival horsemen. They joined the other teams as they rode into the ravines. The galloping horses threw up a storm of dust as they dashed through the zigzag paths surrounded by the dry foliage and thorny shrubs of the arid terrain. The scorching sun was overhead now. They went for some distance without spotting anything.

Then, suddenly, as the dusty path led them around a barren dune, they saw the Malava camp with around 1,500 soldiers.

"Looks like they were not expecting guests for lunch," remarked Rajyavardhan to the soldier next to him. As they moved ahead, he spotted Devagupta and Visnugupta on horseback riding away. The brothers quickly surrounded Rajyavardhan and launched a combined attack on him with their swords. Visnugupta swung at Rajyavardhan's neck, but he moved sideways, taking the blow on his helmet. In retaliation, Rajyavardhan swung his mace at Visnugupta and simultaneously slashed at Devagupta's shoulder. They blocked Rajyavardhan's strikes with their shields and attacked him again. He ducked just in time to save himself and at once swung on both sides. Devagupta shielded himself well while the mace missed Visnugupta but hit his horse on the back of its head. The animal neighed in pain and reared. Sensing that Visnugupta was temporarily imbalanced, Rajyavardhan kicked him down from his horse. Visnugupta was now on the ground and moments away from Rajyavardhan's sword beheading him. Sensing that his brother required help, Devagupta wheeled his horse towards him. Rajyavardhan pointed his sword at the head of Visnugupta who had just got up from the ground with giddy steps. Both warriors galloped in from either side towards Visnugupta. Something occurred to Rajyavardhan. Visnugupta was not his main target for now. He held the mace in his other hand close to his chest. "Here!" cried Rajyavardhan as he swung his sword at Visnugupta. Devagupta, who was rushing in to save his brother, blocked Rajyavardhan's sword but unexpectedly got the backhand strike of Rajyavardhan's mace right on his face. The mace cracked his skull around his nose, the only area unprotected by the metallic helmet, leaving his face a bloody mess. Devagupta fell off his horse, dead. Visnugupta's face turned red with fear, sorrow and anger. With their king dead, the Malava soldiers started to flee. Rajyavardhan looked around. Within moments, most of the enemy, including Visnugupta, had disappeared.

Victory!

Rajyavardhan sighed in relief.

fourteen

Word of Caution

For the young prince, writing was like floating in a placid lake, a state of being calm and peaceful. Harsha wrote poetry occasionally, but writing plays was his way of escaping the noise of the world around. His current creation was tentatively titled *Ratnavali*. It was about a shy and docile princess from Lanka named Ratnavali. As part of a marriage treaty, her father agrees to send her overseas to be the queen of the king of Kaushambi. Unfortunately, a major storm breaks out in the middle of the ocean and their ship is wrecked. Washed ashore, Ratnavali finds herself stranded on an unknown coastal beach with nobody around to help. Vulnerable and lonely, she traverses the mysterious lands.

Every time Harsha picked up his stylus dipped in lamp black and wrote something, he was appreciated for it. When he read out his creation to his father in front of the royal court, many agreed that his talent for writing was extraordinary. Some, who did not understand literature, felt that the praise was only because he was a prince. Harsha wrote not for praise but for the joy of writing. The noises inside his head travelled down his neck and shoulders to his arms, from the stylus to the writing leaf. Then these dark energies moved out of his body. Writing was an act of being at peace with the world. Like the princess he was writing about, he too had weathered an unprecedented storm to be thrust into unfamiliar territories. Like the helpless Ratnavali who had to summon all her internal strength to face unimaginable situations, even Harsha was going through a similar phase. He could actually feel her standing on a windy beach at twilight, feet in wet sand with no one around and nowhere to go. His thoughts were going into the writing leaf as her thoughts, his agony blending into the agony of his character; the character becoming the writer's partner in pain, standing united in grief, his constant companion, someone who voiced his angst and feelings without judgement. They laughed together and cried together. Explored thoughts and feelings together. Took their flights of hope together. Healed together.

Harsha decided to stop writing for a while. He was not feeling well. A slight pain in his abdomen had been bothering him since morning.

An attendant came in just as he was keeping his writing materials away. There was a message from Princess Sharada of Gauda. Harsha's eyes lit up at the mention of her name and he asked that the messenger be ushered in immediately. It is not that we are drifting apart; she does care for me, thought Harsha. A colourfully dressed messenger with a red turban presented himself and handed a scroll to Harsha.

The peculiar slant in the writing was typical of Sharada, so she had written the scroll herself, rather than dictating it to a scribe.

My betrothed Prince Harsha of Sthaneshwar,

I am so deeply saddened by the loss of King Prabhakar and Queen Yashomati. It was shocking, sudden and tragic. They were both gentle by nature, full of wisdom and very caring. Whenever they saw me, they would say that they could not wait for our marriage to take place and for me to shift forever to Thanesara palace. My father attended the final rites with you on our behalf since we women are not allowed to do so, as per tradition. This whole episode is very sad and I don't have words to console you, but that is not the reason why I am writing to you today.

There is something I need to talk to you about, urgently and face to face. I cannot mention what it is about in this letter out of the fear that it might fall into the wrong hands. Believe me, nobody around you can be trusted at this point of time and you need to be wary of that. We need to meet at the 'hunting mansion' in the bordering area of our kingdoms towards the Gauda side. The map to the location, with landmarks, is behind this scroll. It will take less than a day for you to reach there. Remember, there is danger lurking around us and you must not mention to anybody where you are going and why. Not even to cousin Bhandi.

Your partner for life and princess of Gauda,
Sharada

Harsha pondered over the scroll, turned it around and looked at the map with landmarks. "Please tell Princess Sharada that I will be there," he told the messenger.

Harsha walked across the corridor to the royal court. The place was empty except for Army Chief Chakravarti who was discussing palace security with two of his deputies. Harsha signalled to the two deputies to leave.

"I need to be excused for a couple of days since something urgent has come up and I need to be out of town," he told the chief.

The old warrior was surprised, "Prince Harsha, can it be avoided since it is important for you to be here?"

"It's a matter of two days. This is unavoidable, otherwise I would have not insisted. I will be back by the time my brother returns to the capital," replied Harsha.

Just then, Janardhan and Bhandi walked into the court in apparent excitement. The Chief Minister said, "There is news from our border that the armies of Sthaneshwar and Malava are engaged in fierce battle as we speak."

"It will not be easy, but I am sure Rajyavardhan will emerge victorious!" remarked Bhandi.

Harsha said, "I wish I was there to assist him, but he wouldn't listen. He will be triumphant for sure."

"We should never underestimate Devagupta and his penchant for surprise treachery in such situations," added Janardhan, scratching his bald head.

Harsha said, "We will see what happens. I will be out of town for two days. I am leaving now."

Bhandi walked along with Harsha to the entrance and asked, "Where are you going?"

"Nearby. I will tell you when I am back, but for now you must stay here and be watchful. Just keep me informed about the urgent matters through messengers," said Harsha.

"Looks like you have already made up your mind," commented Bhandi.

Harsha replied, "I think it will be better for me to spend a couple of days away from here."

"I understand," said Bhandi.

A little later, accompanied by a convoy of a hundred soldiers, Harsha left the gates of Thanesara palace on horseback towards the border of Gauda. Just behind him rode a thin soldier who was well-versed with those parts. He introduced Harsha to the changing landscape and flora as if he were a toddler. Harsha wondered why people kept treating him like an imbecile prince. He had overheard the staff using a nickname for him—'*aprabhu*', a dig at the young prince for being naïve. Could this gawky image and word of mouth be the reason why Sharada did not seem interested in him anymore? Harsha wondered and wanted to ask her face to face tonight.

As they journeyed on, Harsha sensed that the mansion was situated right in the middle of a dense forest. There was no fluorescent green long grass but trees with trunks wider than the foot of a fully grown elephant. Even though it was noon, the rays of the sun were mostly blocked by the wide green leaves of these trees before they reached the ground. However, this was not a calm, serene forest. The sounds made by insects and birds made it lively. The convoy passed through uneven hilly terrain, crossed the border of Sthaneshwar into Gauda, and arrived at a placid lake surrounded by three hills.

Harsha asked the thin soldier, "How far is it from here?"

"Not very, Prince Harsha. It's right in the middle of those two hills."

"This is the most beautiful water body surrounded by forests I have seen in a long time," commented Harsha.

The soldier smiled, "Looks like all this natural beauty has deceived you, my dear prince. At first glance this water body looks so placid that you would want to take off your clothes for a refreshing dip. The reality is that this lake is popularly known in these parts as *Naraka Sarovara*."

Harsha wondered why something this beautiful was called Hell's Lake. "People don't even go near the vegetation around it. There! Look carefully." Harsha looked at where he was pointing. Three sets of trailing large ripples crossing each other. He could see some snouts and waving spiky dark brown tails. Within moments, they disappeared. The trails continued before other ripple trails could be seen a little ahead.

"Those are humongous *magars*. I have never seen them grow this big!" exclaimed Harsha.

One of the soldiers at the rear commented, "We heard in the palace that one of our new recruits went to wash his face in this lake. A *maha-magar* bit into his leg. He screamed for help as the reptile rolled him numerous times in the water. By then some of our soldiers reached the lake and they stabbed the crocodile with spears till it died. They dragged the soldier and the reptile ashore, but the jaws were clamped so tightly that it took three men with iron rods to open them and release whatever remained of the soldier's blood-drenched foot."

Another soldier added, "The local saying is that if anything goes into this lake, it does not come back in one piece."

They continued their journey. Harsha touched his abdomen, wondering why the pain had not subsided.

Suddenly, they heard cries for help coming from somewhere ahead. Harsha dashed in the direction of the sound, towards the edge of a small cliff. Below he could see rows of trees. An adolescent tribal boy was on the top branches of one of them, screaming for help. The moment he spotted the royal convoy, he started to cry out in broken Sanskrit. A ferocious leopard was about to climb the tree, his growls echoing between the hillocks. One hind leg of the animal was bleeding because a crude tribal spear had injured it. In one leap, the wild cat made it to a low branch, clinging on to it with remarkable agility. Looking at the beast's bloodthirstiness, the soldiers around Harsha were intimidated.

The thin soldier mumbled, "This tribal boy must have done something to irritate the leopard."

Harsha knew that in a couple of leaps the leopard would reach the stranded boy, knock him down and maul him. He pulled out an arrow, mounted it on his bow and focusing on his target, drew the string to the maximum. His target was below, which was an advantage, but he had to keep the wind direction in mind and also estimate where the leopard would reach in its next leap. The boy was terrified and continued screaming. The wild cat's grip loosened and it slid down a little. Grabbing the opportunity, Harsha fired the arrow at its back, but it luckily dug into one of the leopard's paws, bringing it crashing to the ground. Rising up, the beast looked at the hillock. In apparent rage, it started to rush in the direction of Harsha. It was a tedious effort, but the leopard sprinted up the slightly vertical climb. The soldiers gathered around Harsha, on guard, while the prince took out his sword. The beast paused, intimidated by the numbers. It pondered for a while before withdrawing slowly and reluctantly, eventually disappearing into the trees.

The adolescent tribal who was trembling and pale until now looked visibly relieved. He clasped his hands and bowed his head as a sign of gratitude to the prince. Harsha smiled at him and raised his hand in acknowledgement. The convoy turned around and started their ascent up a slope leading to the hunting mansion. Around 20 Gauda soldiers welcomed the 100 Sthaneshwar soldiers escorting Harsha. The chief of the army unit in the region, Ashwath, along with his team of cooks and attendants, greeted Harsha, "Welcome, Prince of Sthaneshwar!

It's an honour to have your presence here in our kingdom of Gauda at this royal hunting mansion."

Harsha remarked, "I appreciate all the effort you have put into this. Please don't get worried by our numbers. I can see this place is small. My soldiers will set up tents outside the mansion and arrange for their own food and requirements."

Ashwath said, "They can camp in the front porch of the mansion. Rest assured, everything to make your stay comfortable is taken care of. Your food, which will include multiple courses of delicious dishes, and any other requirements will be fully taken care of by the cooks and attendants."

"Sounds great after a long day of travel."

"Our pleasure! We are known in these parts to give a memorable welcome to our guests. Local jugglers and acrobats will also be performing for your entertainment tonight," said Ashwath.

"That was not required, but we appreciate the gesture. I have a slightly upset stomach so I will skip the dinner, but you can serve everyone else. By the way, when is Princess Sharada likely to join us here?" asked Harsha.

"A messenger had arrived this afternoon. He informed us that their convoy is running a little late and will be here only by midnight," replied Ashwath.

"All right! Then I guess we need to wait."

Towards evening, Harsha took a warm bath in a black stone tub with sandalwood paste and turmeric. His stomach continued to ache a little as he went around the mansion with his soldiers, admiring the natural beauty. By the time he returned to his bedchamber, it was getting dark. A multi-course dinner was kept on a side table, but Harsha did not feel like eating anything because of the pain in his abdomen. He sat on his bed, wondering when Sharada would reach and what she wanted to reveal to him. Soon, the tiredness of the journey got the better of him and he sank into a deep sleep.

From the time Harsha entered the mansion, two prying eyes had kept a watch on the prince's every move. Now it was time to move from the wilderness into the mansion.

fifteen

Message of Truce

It had been a hectic but victorious day on the battlefield. As he rested on his bed in the army tent, Rajyavardhan wondered whether his soldiers would be able to capture Devagupta's brother Visnugupta soon. Considering the large expanse of these ravines, it was a difficult task to trace Visnugupta and his men. All Rajyavardhan wanted was the release of his sister. Visnugupta was free to take the throne of Malava and rule it, as long as he maintained peace with Sthaneshwar. From what the spies had said, Visnugupta had tortured and killed Rajashri's husband. He had to pay for it with the slaying of his elder brother Devagupta. For the sake of long-term peace, both sides had to forget the past and move on.

"The royal messenger from Gauda is here, my master!" announced the chamberlain from outside the tent. Rajyavardhan wondered why his father-in-law King Shashank was trying to reach out to him. When the stout messenger read out the scroll to him, he was perplexed.

> To my beloved Rajyavardhan,
>
> I am told that you are out in battle with Malava with the objective of defeating Devagupta and rescuing your

sister Rajashri. I am surprised you did not reach out to me for help in this time of crisis. Maybe you acted on impulse, driven by emotions. The standing army of Gauda is always ready to help our extended family in Sthaneshwar in this hour of distress. I am leaving Karnasuvarna with an army of 12,000 soldiers. We will join your army tonight and together we will finish the Malava army in the battlefield tomorrow. Also, I wanted to talk to you about something very important regarding you and my daughter Gautami. So, looking forward to meeting you tonight.

May Lord Shiva's blessing be with you!
King Shashank of Gauda

While Rajyavardhan understood every other portion of the message, he was not clear what his father-in-law wanted to discuss regarding him and his deceased wife's youngest sister. Was the old man going to propose marriage with his daughter? Gautami was too young. If King Shashank did propose marriage, he decided not to agree to it. In his mind he knew that he would never be able to love anyone after Swaranya. He did not want to be unfair to anybody. Engrossed in his thoughts, he did not see the large rat that had scurried into the tent, knocking things down. Almost immediately, one of his commanders entered the tent with a distraught and dishevelled soldier from Malava.

"Sorry to disturb you, Master Rajyavardhan! This Malava soldier just rode in with a message from his master Visnugupta," said the commander.

"Go on, tell me what Visnugupta wants to convey."

The Malava soldier said, "Master Visnugupta has offered unconditional stoppage to this conflict and truce from his side.

He has requested you not to send out soldiers into the ravines for a manhunt."

Rajyavardhan pondered over the message for a while, then asked, "What about Rajashri?"

"My master has offered unconditional return of your sister to you in four days."

"Right now, you are trapped and in a vulnerable state. How can we be assured that your master Visnugupta will not try to consolidate all your soldiers from across Malava once he reaches your capital Vidisha to declare war on us to avenge his brother's death?"

The soldier was taken aback by the query, "My master Visnugupta realises that his elder brother was rather reckless all along. Now that he is head of the kingdom, master Visnugupta will make amends."

"Tell him that this gesture of friendship between the two kingdoms is always welcome. However, I want Rajashri to be sent to Thanesara palace not in four but in two days."

"I will convey the same to him, Sri Rajyavardhan."

After everyone left, Rajyavardhan sat on his bed wondering whether he should indeed trust Visnugupta. The rat was still running around his tent. Rajyavardhan asked his soldiers to do something about it. After the battle, they were fatigued. Four of them who were assigned to this task went about it half-heartedly. Rajyavardhan was having fun watching them chase a rodent with their spears. It felt good to have a carefree laugh after a day of toil spent in close proximity to death and suffering.

"That poor thing has strayed into the tent in search of food. I don't want you to stab it, just get a thick piece of cloth, catch it and leave it outside. For now, just get me my evening meal and you can try to get the rodent out of the tent when I am out on my night stroll," said Rajyavardhan.

The soldiers left.

A little later, the evening meal was served for Rajyavardhan. He closed his eyes to whisper a prayer, "I use this food not for fun, not for pleasure, not for fattening, not for beautification, but only for the maintenance of this body, for keeping it healthy, for helping with my spiritual life; believing so, I will dispel hunger without overeating, so that I may continue to live." Prayer completed, he put the first morsel of food into his mouth.

Midway through his meal, he sensed a rumbling sound of infantry and cavalry approaching his tent. Rajyavardhan paused. He then heard the chamberlain announce outside his tent that the Gauda army was here and King Shashank was coming in. Soon after, his wife's father entered the tent. "Rajya, my dear! I must admit that today you proved beyond a shadow of doubt that you, the future king of Sthaneshwar are the future of the whole of Bharatvarsh. I had estimated a long drawn battle between you and Malava. I came in with my army just for that. However, I hear that you have finished the job already."

"We planned it well and luck was with us. You came in at the right time. Join me! This sweet milk porridge is hot and tastes like heaven," said Rajyavardhan.

"All that later. Tell me what happened."

"Be seated, please! It was an exciting and unpredictable day. They made a very deceptive army formation. I figured that out and managed to track down Devagupta. He was killed while trying to protect his brother. Visnugupta is absconding but ready for a truce. We destroyed the Malava army but lost 3,000 men in the process, which is very sad."

"And Rajashri?"

"She will be released in two days. That is the message we have sent out to Visnugupta. Anyway, this conflict with Malava is behind us now. I read your message; what did you want to discuss with me?"

"It was regarding you and Gautami. Not tonight, you are too tired. Take rest for now," said Shashank.

Suddenly there came sounds of fierce fighting and cries of pain outside the tent. Rajyavardhan got up from his meal and as he dashed towards the tent entrance, he felt a sudden sharp pain in his spine. He turned back in shock to find that Shashank had stabbed him in the back with Asi, the family sword. It was symbolic, the sword of the Pushyabhutis plunged into the body of their own scion. Blood spurted on the ground as Rajyavardhan fell down.

"You? I thought of you not as my wife's father but as my own," he said chokingly.

"I was also fond of you once upon a time. Not any more." Shashank had a stoic expression as he looked at the fallen prince bleeding profusely on the tent floor. He wiped the blade of the sword with his shoulder cloth.

"But why? Why your own family?"

Shashank smirked, "You know the reason for this. Don't pretend you don't! You should have taken the right stand."

Rajyavardhan sighed, "That cannot be the reason. You are a man without morals."

"I am a man who knows that I don't have unlimited time at my disposal, but I will make the most of it from now on," said Shashank with a smile.

A little later, Visnugupta appeared inside the tent with a sword and leather bag trailed by Gauda soldiers. Going straight to Shashank, he said, "My dear cousin! You turned the story around for us."

"Don't patronise me with that cousin talk. I am in this for a reason. The same as yours. Rajyavardhan is all yours; you are free to avenge your brother's death," said Shashank as he prepared to leave. Visnugupta's eyes bulged like a maniac's as he examined the moaning pale body of Rajyavardhan on the ground. He laughed out loud, running his fingers through his hair again and again, "Oh poor thing! Let me think. I just have the deep inner urge to skin him alive."

Rajyavardhan's head was swirling as Visnugupta examined him closely. A big rodent appeared from the corner of the tent, moving forward cautiously towards the fallen warrior. It darted ahead and took a bite out of Rajyavardhan's ruptured skin.

"This little bastard is loving it. Even I will relish this," muttered Visnugupta as he took out his cleaver and chopper from his leather bag.

As death took over, Rajyavardhan had a smile on his face. He was going to another world. Perhaps Swaranya was waiting for him there.

sixteen

In the Jungle

The forest became unusually silent at midnight except for the roars of the tigers. In the mansion, Harsha was in deep sleep. The eyes that had been keeping watch on him were distracted. From the other side of the mansion came sounds of commotion and muffled cries of pain. Just a glimpse of what was happening there was petrifying. It was time for some quick action.

Harsha was jolted out of his sleep. In the dim light, he could make out the face of the same tribal adolescent whose life he had saved from the leopard. The boy clamped his hand on Harsha's mouth, signalling silence and pulled Harsha towards him, leading him to the balcony. Harsha grabbed his sword on the way out. *What was the boy trying to show him?* The boy leaped up on to the strong branch of a *khair* tree which was leaning against the balcony, nimbly turned around and motioned to Harsha to follow him. Harsha wondered why but nonetheless, he climbed up the branch and they moved carefully towards the thick trunk of the tree where the boy picked up a sack. They shifted to a lower branch so that the trunk did not hinder their view of the mansion.

No sooner had they settled down than they saw hordes of fire torches barging into the room where Harsha had been sleeping. They heard instructions being yelled and grunts of exasperation.

"What is going on? Check there!"

"Here! Below the bed."

The soldiers looked around desperately. Right in front of them, in the darkness between the trees, was Harsha, looking at them, barely breathing, droplets of perspiration rolling down his neck. He could see their faces, their swords, fire torches; waiting for a glimpse of him to shred him to pieces.

"He has escaped, you worthless bastards! Something must have alerted him. He must have jumped down the balcony," yelled Ashwath. Some of the soldiers took out their battleaxes and, giving in to their frustration, chopped down the branch leaning into the balcony.

To gain better balance, Harsha leaned against the tree trunk and shifted his sword to his other hand. The moisture on his hands caused his grip to loosen and the sword fell to the ground.

"What is that sound?"

"Run! Follow me," the tribal boy said and they were down the tree in a flash. Harsha picked up his sword and they sprinted to the other side of the boundary wall. In the moonlight, Harsha glimpsed the dead bodies laid out in the courtyard of the hunting mansion. Each and every Sthaneshwar soldier accompanying Harsha had been slain. Their food or water had been drugged and they had been stabbed in their sleep. With the rumbling of soldiers trying to nab them approaching, the thought racing through Harsha's mind was of remorse. *So many loyal soldiers killed while protecting my life*, he thought. Seeing Harsha slow down, the boy whispered urgently, "They are catching up, we need to run fast and noiselessly." The flicker of many fire torches behind were closing in on them like a swarm of vengeful bees.

They fled among the dense trees through whatever space the thick vegetation provided, unperturbed by branches and thorns that caused bloody scratches all over their bodies.

"What is your name?" asked Harsha.

"Soma, from the Koruwa tribe. I was keeping an eye on you from the trees so as to evade security and give you this sack of wild fruits and rare herbs. A small gesture of thankfulness for having saved my life. That is when I happened to see the carnage of your soldiers outside the mansion and felt that there was a threat to your life." He spoke with a thick accent.

"You just saved my life! I am Prince Harsha of Sthaneshwar. How big is your tribe?" Harsha remembered the name of this tribe at the Yuva-Sena training ground where the tribal boy Radheya had mentioned that three tribes including the Koruwas were adept at selecting forest herbs and natural ingredients to create the fumes to keep rampaging tuskers at bay.

"We are a small tribe of 46 people including children. Our settlement is on that hill."

Harsha was clear that he did not want to be spotted with this adolescent. Whoever wanted Harsha's life would not hesitate to butcher this boy and his whole tribe of innocent people for having provided him assistance. Harsha did not want these poor nature-loving locals to get involved in this conflict. Other thoughts were racing through Harsha's mind. *Why were Gauda soldiers engaged in such a conspiracy and carnage?* The only logical reason Harsha could fathom was that a faction of the Gauda army had rebelled against King Shashank. They were targeting the royal family, the extended family and well-wishers. Abruptly, Harsha paused. Princess Sharada of Gauda was slated to arrive at the mansion around midnight.

Soma sensed something was wrong and turned back, panting and sweating, "What happened, Prince Harsha? This is not the moment to stop, we need to keep running."

"No! I need to go back. The girl I am going to marry will reach the hunting mansion soon, unaware of the fact that her life is in danger."

"It's dangerous to go back."

"I know, but there is no way I am letting her walk into an assassination trap at the mansion. I think it's equally dangerous for you to be seen with me. Hear me carefully, tomorrow at noon, meet me at that rock on that hillock," said Harsha, pointing at a hillock towards the east. "Bring some food, a sack, strong ropes, a stick, a blanket, a fire torch and something to cover my head. If I don't come, then assume that I have managed to rescue my princess or I am dead."

"Please think it over..."

"I need to do this. Now, take all this because these make it easier for people to identify me." He took off all his gold ornaments except for his tiger-claw necklace and the ring gifted by Sharada and handed them over to Soma. With his sword held firmly in his hands, Harsha returned to the mansion.

The advantage Harsha had over the soldiers split into groups of three or four on the manhunt was that they carried fire torches and he did not. Whenever he saw the glimmer of a fire torch approaching, he would hide behind a thick tree trunk or climb one. He had to be careful to make no sound. The walk back to the mansion did not turn out to be as troublesome as he had imagined, because the last thing his enemy would think of was that he would dare to return.

Once he was near the compound, Harsha spotted more Gauda soldiers guarding two royal chariots. *She is already inside*! Harsha was petrified by the thought. *How do I get in?* The angry soldiers had chopped down the branch of the tree leaning against the balcony of his room. It would be foolish to try and enter the same way as he had absconded. He decided to scale the boundary wall at the rear of the mansion. He fastened the sword to his waistband, tore off his tunic sleeves and wrapped them tightly around his palms. The tough soles of his leather footwear would protect his feet, but he had to use his hands to get across the wall topped with sharp nails. The sound of footsteps came from the other side of the wall. Harsha almost stopped breathing and concentrated on the sound. Soldiers were guarding the wall on the other side. Two—Harsha knew from their steps. He listened carefully, positioning himself at exactly the place opposite to where the guards intersected each other's path. Just as one of them paused to speak to the other, Harsha leaped and grabbed the top of the wall, pulling himself up. His palms started to bleed from the nails that dug into them. Sharp pain streaked along his hands to his spine. The soldiers stopped. They had spotted a dark figure standing on top of the wall, but before they could shout for help, it jumped towards them, sword swinging in mid-air, catching one of the soldiers on his neck and the other on his mouth. The first collapsed but the other one stumbled up, gargling blood even as he dashed for help. As soon as he landed, Harsha drew the dagger out of the fallen soldier's waistband and threw it at the man fleeing, dropping him dead. Harsha loosened the cloth on his palms and clenched his fists to release the pain. It caused more bleeding but made his pain bearable.

He could hear a loud conversation from the mansion. Now, he had to quickly figure out how to observe the happenings inside.

If Sharada's life is in danger, I might have to barge in, he thought. No window was open, but one had a gap caused by termites. A pair of twins were questioning Ashwath, almost bullying him.

"Ashwath! So how come the poison did not work?" asked the crippled twin, almost unable to control his fury.

Ashwath replied, "Vakul, I had mixed poison in his food and placed it in his room. Looks like he did not eat it."

"And he just vanished from his bedchamber after that?" asked the muscular one.

Ashwath replied, "Listen, Vamsi. From what I understand, something alerted him of the impending danger before we could nab him."

In the darkness, Harsha could not believe that such an elaborate plan had been hatched to eliminate him in this wilderness.

"It's a slip, but I am in control and will nab Harsha in no time. This is a hostile forest where he has no clue what dangers await him at each corner. Will Princess Sharada be joining us in some time?" asked Ashwath.

The twins looked at each other and smiled sarcastically. "You incompetent fools don't get it! Princess Sharada is not coming and she never intended to come. She set up a trap for us to nab Harsha," replied Vakul.

Harsha was stunned. He could not believe his ears. The one who was his betrothed and was soon to be his partner for life had set up a trap for him. *Why?*

Vamsi gripped Ashwath's tunic in rage, "Now tell me before I smash everyone's skull. What are we supposed to tell King Shashank when we are back at his palace? He coaxed his own daughter into helping us, but Harsha has escaped."

Ashwath looked nervous but spoke with confidence. "Harsha was saved by luck today. There is nothing we could have done better."

Vamsi said, "Both the brothers should meet the same fate! You understand, that is the order from King Shashank."

What did he mean? Both the brothers? Harsha wondered what was going on.

"Listen, everyone! Let me make you the deal of your lifetime," said Vakul. "Harsha is out there in the jungle. Find and behead him by afternoon or all of you will lose your heads in a public execution in the town square at Karnasuvarna. Is the message clear?"

Ashwath was irritated. "Enough! This area is under my jurisdiction and if there is any slip-up, I will take care of it. You cannot threaten my people like this, so watch your words."

At this, the twins started to laugh and looked at each other. Vakul said, "You know what? Let me tell you about something that happened a year back."

"I don't want to listen."

"You must! It's the most important story of your life. So, inside my brother's shoe, the left toe is only half there. Do you want to know the story behind it?"

"No! I told you that I don't have time for your stories. You may leave since I have a task at hand to nab Harsha," Ashwath replied defiantly.

Vamsi clamped down on Ashwath's shoulders, not allowing him to move.

"Hold on, it's not irrelevant!" cried Vakul. "You need to listen because this is important. Tell him about your toe, Vamsi!"

At Vakul's urging, Vamsi spoke up, "King Shashank ordered me to trace and execute the leader of a tribal rebel group in the forests of the Ganga delta. On the second day, I was ambushed and wounded in the toe. It was the rainy season and my toe started to rot. So, I chopped my own toe off with an axe and put a burning torch on the stump to stop the bleeding."

"Very interesting! Now that you are done with your story, please leave," remarked Ashwath.

"Wait! There's more to it," Vakul intervened. "Do you think he returned to the capital to recuperate after that? No! Not at all! Vamsi ventured to the forest and came back with the heads of the tribal leaders. You know why?"

"No! And I don't want to know," replied Ashwath as his eyes darted between the two men.

"I am sure you want to know."

Vamsi picked up Ashwath by his throat and started to bang his head against the wall in a vicious rhythm, "You must know why. The reason for that, my dear friend... is that... we never... ever... disappoint our king."

"Aagh! Aagh!" Ashwath cried out in pain.

Vakul exclaimed, "We don't disappoint our king! Not yesterday, not today and not any day. Never… Ever..."

"Don't disappoint King Shashank!" added Vamsi.

Looking at Vamsi smash Ashwath's head against the wall, the legs of the other soldiers started to tremble. The spot on the wall where his head was being banged became a bloody mess as Ashwath continued to scream. From his hiding place, Harsha could hear Ashwath's skull crack. Vamsi flung Ashwath's body aside.

Harsha's mind was numb with the revelations. There were more questions than answers, but he had no time to think. He heard the footsteps of a guard coming from the left of the mansion. Harsha decided that it was time to leave. He had to let it all sink in and then decide what to do next. He leaped up and grabbed the top of the wall, the cold nails digging into his palms again, making them bleed. This time the pain was less, his palms were almost numb. Once he was on the other side, he ventured into the forest, walking towards the direction of the rock on the hillock where he planned to meet Soma.

Vakul and Vamsi waited patiently throughout the next day, pacing all around the mansion like beasts in rage. The whole day passed and the soldiers were unable to catch Harsha. In the evening, they decided to return to their capital town and inform their master, King Shashank, about it.

They mounted a chariot with the best breed of horses and sped towards their destination, lost in thought as to how they would pacify their master after such a colossal failure. Vakul looked at his crippled hand, the reminder of the last time he had failed their master. It was late in the evening when their chariot took a sharp turn around a hill. The horses were galloping at the speed of wind, when suddenly, the twins were flung into the air and the chariot crashed into the side of the mud road. The loud noise echoed through the forest as they fell. Vamsi blacked out as his head banged into a thick tree trunk. Vakul slammed face first into the ground and rolled away. Dizzy, he looked around and saw Prince Harsha standing next to a rock which he had placed on the other side of the sharp turn. He had tied a rope between two trees on either side of the road just ahead of the rock. *Clever bastard!* Vakul lost consciousness. With Soma's help, Harsha had caught the twins by surprise.

The forest was silent again but not for long.

seventeen

Wild Animals

When the twins regained consciousness, they found themselves in a dingy cave in the middle of the forest. The air was heavy and it smelled of bird droppings. There were definitely bats inside, who started to get more active as the darkness grew. A fire torch fixed firmly in a crack on the rock face illuminated the entrance to this dark enclosure. The twins realised that their hands and legs were tightly tied with rope. "I can't see a thing!" Vamsi cried, the dried blood on his face had a layer of soil stuck to it so he could barely see. As Vakul rolled over and looked around, he spotted someone—Prince Harsha was seated on a rock near the cave entrance, his body covered with dust, full of scratches, palms bleeding. He wore no gold ornaments, only the tiger-claw necklace and a ring. The red birthmark on his left cheek made him recognisable as the prince of Sthaneshwar.

Vakul smiled sarcastically and declared, "That thing you did with the rope and rock to topple the chariot. That was commendable indeed!"

"I had the whole day to plan. In my kind of situation, it took all my resourcefulness to get my hands on both of you," said Harsha.

"You got us. Well done! Now what?" asked Vamsi.

"I need answers for some of my questions. Needless to say that if you keep quiet, I will put you through misery you have never experienced in your life," said Harsha.

To Harsha's surprise, the twins started to laugh aloud, revealing their bloodied teeth. It was irritating to hear like the sound made by a pack of hyenas. Harsha would never be able to put these two through misery that they had never experienced. Decades ago, the twins, eight years old at the time, were beaten, along with their mother, by their drunkard father every single night when he returned home. Finally, their mother lost her patience one day and poisoned their father's supper. They watched him vomit chunks of barley and blood till he eventually collapsed. Already horrified, they watched as their mother hanged herself with a rope inside the house. Those were the three years of continuous drought. The orphaned twins were homeless wanderers, spending days in the wilderness in extreme heat without food and water for days together. By adolescence they were small-time criminals in Karnasuvarna before King Shashank took them under his wing after noticing them during a royal court session where they were being prosecuted. "You are not the regular small-time criminals we deal with every day. Something about you sets you apart. Looks like you are trying to get even with the world. With my years of experience, I can spot the difference between a wild animal and a tame one. I need people like you. I will suspend your sentence but you should work for me," Shashank had said. He had kept his word. The two turned into Shashank's trusted henchmen.

Harsha stepped forward and punched both the twins on their face, "Try laughing now!"

"You bastard!" swore Vakul.

"Now that we got rid of the laugh, it's time to answer me. Did Sharada call me to the mansion knowing what was going to happen there?" His voice quivered through the last few words.

The twins looked at each other and as usual, Vakul took over the proceedings, "From what I hear, she played along with her father to set up this trap for you."

Harsha was taken aback, "Why would they do that? Tell me the truth or I will drive this sword right through you."

"Do you think so many Gauda soldiers would do something on such a large scale all by themselves, without being ordered by their king?" said Vakul after a pause.

"Why would King Shashank want to get rid of me? We are family. I am slated to marry his daughter Sharada."

Vakul smirked, "You ask him the reasons. How do we know?"

Vamsi stretched out, trying to break the rope restraining his hands and legs. Harsha stepped forward and kicked him in his stomach, "There is no way you can free yourself from that."

Vamsi looked at Harsha with bloodshot eyes and muttered, "I swear, one day you will be in my grasp. That day I will crush your skull, splattering your brain on the ground while blood gushes out of your nose, ears and mouth."

"My brother saying that makes me really worried for you. He has an elephant's memory, neither forgets nor forgives," said Vakul, glaring at Harsha. They giggled again, as if enjoying the situation. It was unnerving, similar to being alone on the street surrounded by aggressive barking stray dogs at night.

Harsha turned to Vamsi and said, "What did you mean when you said inside the mansion that the brothers will meet a similar fate? What are you people planning for Rajyavardhan? Is he in some kind of danger?"

"I think you are looking at it the wrong way. It's you following him and not the other way round," said Vakul with a grin. "You see this scroll in my waistband? This is a message we received last evening at the mansion and were asked to personally deliver on our way back to your father's closest friend, King Bhaskaravarman of Kamarupa. Read it and you will understand."

In Vakul's eyes was a sense of achievement that King Shashank was slowly showing faith in the twins by upgrading their status. They were no more men in the background doing his dirty jobs, but actually representing him as envoys.

As Harsha pulled the scroll out of Vakul's waistband, they heard a horse neighing outside the cave followed immediately by a crashing sound. Harsha looked concerned.

"You took our horses?" asked Vamsi.

Harsha replied, "One of them was injured after the chariot toppled. The other one is fine and tethered outside to a tree. Now, you both watch me escape unharmed from here."

"So, you think you will escape out of here alive on a horse! You are 17 years old and talk your age," they started to laugh like mad men, white teeth gleaming through blood and mud-smeared faces. Harsha went outside to check on the horse, carrying the scroll but unknowingly leaving his sword behind. His worst fear had come true. The horse had broken loose.

Harsha ran into the wilderness hoping to find it, but to no avail. *That horse was my only chance to escape!* He glanced at the scroll, opened it and tried to read it, but it was well past sunset and very dim. To his horror, when he turned around, he could not see the light of the fire torch at the cave entrance. In a moment of indiscretion, he had been humane enough to tie the rope a little loosely around Vakul's crippled hand, though he had tied up his muscular twin tightly. Harsha realised that he had left his sword too inside the cave. It was possible that the twins had set themselves free and were waiting for him. He decided not to go back. Instead, he dashed towards the hillock where he had met Soma at noon. *The twins will intensify the manhunt for me*, he thought.

The forest was denser here and had a damp leafy smell. He reached a familiar broad banyan tree on the hillock. At the base of the trunk were all the articles that Soma had handed over to him in the afternoon, except for the rope—baked grain cakes, fruits, flintstones, blanket, turban, bow and arrow. He surveyed the hills around; there were dots of light moving all over them. The Gauda soldiers were looking for him. Harsha collected some dry leaves into a heap and rubbed the flintstones together. He could keep the fire going only for a short period of time. The light and smoke could catch the soldiers' attention and draw them here. As soon as the heap caught fire, Harsha started reading the scroll which was on official Gauda stationery with the royal seal.

King Bhaskaravarman of Kamarupa,

I hope you are in good health. I hear that you have been unwell and bedridden since your return from Thanesara. The purpose of my writing this letter to you is to keep you abreast of the recent events and to serve as a cautionary note. In the battle between Sthaneshwar and Malava, Rajyavardhan defeated the Malava army, eventually slaying their king, Devagupta. Tonight, I and Devagupta's younger brother, Visnugupta, managed to trap Rajyavardhan in a vulnerable position and assassinated him…

Harsha froze, it was as if everything had come to a sudden standstill, even the forest breeze.

> ...By the time this message reaches you, his brother Harsha would have also suffered a similar fate in the middle of the forest. As you are aware, Rajashri is counting her days imprisoned by the Malava royals. With the whole of the Sthaneshwar royal family eliminated, it is inevitable that between me and Visnugupta, we will bring a new order in the plains of the great rivers. I know that King Prabhakar was your closest friend for decades and you are like family. Don't let your emotions provoke the worst in you and make you take up any form of confrontation with us. In the coming months, Visnugupta and I will use aggression and diplomacy to establish total dominance over all the small kingdoms in the plains. If we face any hostility from you, we will not hesitate for a moment before focusing our attention on your kingdom. So do the right thing, keep your emotions under check, think practically and stay out of our way.
>
> With your best interests in mind,
> King Shashank of Gauda

His brother was dead! Three months shy of his 21st birthday, when most people start their life, Rajyavardhan's life was taken away. Maybe someone as noble as him was not meant for this world. Two years back, Rajyavardhan had stood on the podium with his newly-wedded wife, their faces aglow with wide smiles. A child on the way made everyone in the royal household beam with happiness. Then, a year ago, this match made in heaven could not survive the ways of the world as Rajyavardhan lost his wife in a tragic manner. He'd lost his parents early too, and finally his own life was snatched away from him. Harsha felt his legs give way as he broke down and wept.

On either side he could see the dots of fire torches held by Gauda soldiers. They were fast approaching this hillock from all sides. It started to rain heavily. Harsha walked towards the dreaded lake between the hills. Midway through the denser part of the forest, he slipped, ruptured the skin on his left thigh against a sharp stone and fell into the slush between the trees. All over his body, he felt a strange itching. When he touched his arms and chest, he realised that numerous leeches were clinging to him, sucking his blood. If he tried to pull them out forcefully, their fangs would remain under his skin, leading to a purulent discharge across his body.

At the lake, four crocodiles rested on the shore, three enormous and one small. Harsha climbed on to the branch of a tree near the lake and waited for the rain to subside. The soldiers looking out for him also seemed to be waiting, since their fire torches had been extinguished in the rain. As he sat there with scratches all over his body, his palms bleeding and leeches sucking his blood, he knew that he was at his lowest point in life. He could not control his tears for his brother; his short life, his tragic love story and everything that had not worked out for him. Nobody would remember Rajyavardhan, not even history. A young man who was never given an opportunity to reach his full potential because his life was cut short by deception. Deception reminded Harsha of Sharada. The girl that Harsha loved had sent him towards death. Tonight, he was alone and fighting for his life. He had no father, no mother, no brother and no lover.

The leeches bloated to three times their size. Once satiated, they started to fall off Harsha's face, chest, stomach and limbs into the leaves below, leaving behind perforations that continued to bleed. Once the rain subsided, the flickering dots reappeared on the hills around him. This time he heard noises. He listened carefully. Wild dogs, definitely not domestic ones. Not one, not ten, but many more.

Harsha had no choice now. He could not take the land route because the twins and their soldiers would easily nab and butcher him. He walked a little distance away from the resting crocodiles and dipped his feet into the cold waters of the lake people called Naraka Sarovara. Harsha remembered what they had told him—the reptiles' sharp rows of teeth, their tight snapping and rolling of their prey, and the iron rods that were needed to force open the locked jaws. Waist-deep in the lake with the water slowly washing off all the blood on his body, he was so heartbroken that he wished the crocodiles would just rip him apart and end his misery forever. The only thing that kept him going was the thought of his sister locked far away in some dingy prison among savages, counting her days to the inevitable. She would be hoping that a loved one would reach out and save her. Or maybe like Harsha, a part of her also wanted to die.

eighteen

Dreaded Lake

The moon shone bright on the surface of the lake. Quietly, Harsha moved further into the lake, trying his best to avoid drawing attention of either the bloodthirsty men behind him or the dangerous reptiles around him. He took deep breaths. The task was uphill and would test his strength to the limit. When they were children, Harsha, Bhandi and Rajyavardhan used to go for a swim in the large water tank of Thanesara palace. Harsha would continue the practice even a month into the winter season, much to the amazement of his brother and cousin. *What are you, a Naga sadhu from Mount Kailash? Don't you feel cold?* Bhandi would ask. The lake was very cold at this time, even by Harsha's standards. From what he had observed earlier, the crocodiles were actually as big as the saltwater alligators or the gharials that Harsha had once seen in the kingdom of Gauda near the delta. The blood oozing out of his wounded palms and punctures created by the leeches added to his troubles. He had heard tribal representatives in the royal court say that these reptiles could sense traces of blood in water and then they searched desperately for the source. He was about to find out whether this was true or village gossip. Harsha started to swim very slowly. He gradually got used to the extreme cold of the water. At his speed it would take forever to reach the other side but he had no choice. Once he swam a little towards the middle of the lake, he turned face upwards and started to float, gently flapping his feet, his movements slow and soundless. The middle was the real danger zone where disturbances in the water could attract the bloodthirsty beasts from all sides. If that were to happen, Harsha would be torn to shreds within moments. This floating and gentle thrust was slow, painstaking and draining Harsha of energy, but there was no choice.

Harsha continued to inch forward. Suddenly, he heard a splash to his left. Harsha felt as if his heart would leap out of his chest. He halted, barely moving except for his feet, stopping his breath and hoping for the crocodile to pass. It turned out to be a big fish. Harsha continued drifting across the lake and now he could see the shore which was part of his kingdom. The gamble had worked. Harsha remembered a lesson in his gurukul regarding reptiles. The guru had said that too much heat or too much cold makes these reptiles stay burrowed inside the soil in an inactive state. For once it looked like the extreme chill in the atmosphere had caused most of the crocodiles to stay away from the lake. Maybe fear is all in the mind. Once you face it, it may not be all that bad. Harsha smiled. If he had been shredded to pieces by the crocodiles in the middle of the lake, then these words of wisdom were of no use. Half in their sleep in the dead of night, the Gauda soldiers on a manhunt for him could not fathom that he would do something as risky as swimming across the dreaded lake.

Exhausted beyond words, he sought refuge below a tree. Finally, he had reached Sthaneshwar. No Gauda soldiers would chase him here.

Weakness and fatigue muddled his head. He fell into a deep sleep and woke up with a heavy head. The sun was shining on his face. He looked at his palms and legs. Huge patches of sticky dry blood were around his wounds. *I need to eat something*, he thought as he looked around. He had eaten some bananas Soma had given him last afternoon. Limping, he went around looking at the trees, frantically hoping that he might find something. These dense parts of the forest did not have anything to offer. He noticed something in the distance and rushed towards it. On the ground were two half-eaten fruits monkeys had tried and dropped. The strange-looking fruit had a green spiky covering and white insides. Harsha washed the fist-sized fruits in the water of the lake and eagerly took a bite. Within moments he vomited it out; it was not edible.

After he regained some strength, Harsha wandered inside the not-so-dense forest looking for something to eat. There were some wild berry trees but they could have been poisonous. Well past noon he spotted a camachile tree with ripe fruits and devoured the pulp of some that had fallen on the ground. For the time being, he was satiated.

nineteen

Lost Wanderer

Far below the hill where they stood, the camps could be seen. One group of settlements near the lake and the other near the horizon, next to the river. The air was misty around them. It was getting dark. Rajyavardhan looked tired and worn out but a smile still lit up his face.

"Mother has asked you to come back to the palace. She is really worried about you."

"No, Harsha! There is a lot to be done here and we have had some success in containing the outbreak after segregating the sick ones from the healthy ones."

"It's an epidemic, my dear brother. It spares nobody. What if you get the disease?"

"I believe that it does not spread as long as we keep our food and water clean. Harsha, nothing will happen to me."

Harsha was getting anxious. "Nothing will happen to you? You are the future king. You cannot take such risks with your life."

"I cannot leave these people here without assistance at this crucial juncture. Just because I was lucky to be born inside the royal palace and they were born in huts in these remote villages does not make me special. We all are equal before nature."

Harsha woke up with a jolt inside the rock crevice where he'd fallen asleep. It was well past afternoon. Tears had filled the corners of his eyes while he was asleep. He wiped them and wondered which direction to take. But first, he wanted something to eat. He walked around, looking for fruits and berries. He could hear faint sounds of trumpets and kettledrums. Was he imagining them? He walked quickly towards the music, crossing numerous trees on the way. Reaching there, he saw a procession of around 20 tribal men. In the front were men playing trumpets and drums, followed closely by people carrying three open palanquins with an idol in each as well as various offerings. From the knives, tools, flowers, fruits and clothes scattered around each idol, it was evident to Harsha that these were tribal gods being taken around for their annual procession.

The men halted on spotting the stranger, wounded and covered in dirt. Harsha was worried about their next move. He clasped his hands and bowed before each palanquin. The main god was the divine feminine, another was a small child, Bal-Nath and the third was the sun god. The men understood that this young man meant no harm.

"I am the prince of Sthaneshwar. Which direction do I go for Thanesara palace?"

The tribals looked at each other. When they spoke, Harsha did not understand a single word. They pointed backwards and Harsha started to move back, tripped and almost knocked down one of the palanquins. He smiled while two of the men helped him get back on his feet again, bowing to them all. Looking at his sorry state, the men felt pity; one of them tied up some bananas and berries in a cloth pouch and gave it to Harsha who grabbed it eagerly. The prince of Sthaneshwar had fallen way below his status today, not any better than a wayside destitute. The men left, chanting something; the only words Harsha could make out were something about the sun god, Aditya Bhagawan shining upon Devi, the divine feminine. Harsha had pretended to trip and fall, in the process pulling out a small dagger from the offerings on the palanquin. He wanted something to protect himself against wild animals. When he looked at it now, it seemed to have been a futile effort—the knife was blunt—but he did not throw it away; everything is useful in a forest.

Harsha sat on a low branch devouring the fruits, hoping that either a caravan of traders or some villagers would pass by and help him out of this wilderness. In the worst case, he decided to spend the night on this branch. Evening was fast approaching. At a distance Harsha spotted five soldiers patrolling the forest road.

Excited, he scrambled down the tree and dashed towards the soldiers. From the blue and yellow uniforms, Harsha could see that they were indeed soldiers of Sthaneshwar. Just as he was about to call out, he spotted something. The flag they were holding was not the orange one with Mount Kailash and the sun in the background. Instead, it was a blue one with a flying eagle. Harsha paused, wondering why Sthaneshwar soldiers were holding a different flag. Having encountered a lot of unexpected problems recently, Harsha decided to approach cautiously. He trailed the group behind the trees, trying to overhear what they were saying.

The leader of the group was a hefty man with greying hair, followed by younger soldiers. All of them were holding their evening meals wrapped in *patravali* leaves. Harsha trailed them at a distance, but was unable to hear anything. He knew that they would have their food before sunset since the insects in the forest would be out after dark. As anticipated, they settled down on a rocky platform below a leafy tree for their meal. Harsha tiptoed from one tree trunk to another, finally reaching close to the soldiers. To his dismay, they were speaking in Apabhramasa, a very local variant of it. He could barely understand what they were saying; something about their supervisor's insatiable appetite.

Harsha peeped from behind the tree trunk as they unpacked their *patravali* leaf packets. One of them, a lean man, told the others that he was going to urinate. The others made fun of him and told him to go as far away as possible.

The soldier was urinating and enjoying the breeze below a Mahua tree when Harsha clamped his hand on the soldier's mouth from behind. Placing the blunt knife at his neck, he dragged him further away from his group.

"Why this new flag?" asked Harsha when they were at a safe distance.

The soldier looked at the knife pointed at him and said something which Harsha did not understand except for the words 'King Janardhan'.

"When did Janardhan become king?"

The soldier remained silent.

"Where is Army Chief Chakravarti?"

To this the soldier said something in which the words *nidra* and *mrityu* were understandable. Harsha tried to make sense of it. Was Chakravarti assassinated in his bedchamber? Janardhan had made the most of the opportunity created by Rajyavardhan's death and Harsha's absence from the capital to seize power.

"Anvesh! Anvesh!" Harsha was distracted from his thoughts. The other soldiers had come looking for their mate. Taking advantage of the diversion, the soldier thrust hard on Harsha's wrist. The blunt knife flew out of Harsha's hands. Harsha tried to grab him, but the soldier escaped. Hiding behind another tree, he called out to his fellow soldiers, "Here! Come and help me."

Harsha's mind was racing. If Janardhan was king, then he, Harsha, would be the most wanted man in the kingdom.

"Here! This side! The attacker is trying to flee."

Harsha ran as fast as he could and tripped across a ditch that he hadn't noticed. He started rolling down a slope and tried to grab something but to no avail. He kept falling till his head hit a rock protruding out of the slope.

twenty

Thrust into Darkness

In the faint light, Bhandi could barely see his commander Keshav who was in the prison cell opposite his. They had been beaten and harassed in the morning. Keshav was in a crouched position on the ground, still moaning. Chained and confined, Bhandi wondered how he could have evaded all this, but he had been caught unawares.

They could not face him man to man, so they had drugged his food and captured him. It was easy to kill him, but he knew the possible reasons as to why he had been spared. To be more specific, his life had been spared only for the time being. His enemies believed that he had an important piece of information which he honestly did not have, but for now it was useful to pretend that he did.

Bhandi could constantly hear the faint sound of a waterfall nearby. He knew that by some ways or means he had to get out of there. Get out and do what? His only objective now was to destroy everyone who had conspired against the royal family. Like the others in the Vardhan family, Bhandi knew about the three secret tunnels leading to Thanesara palace. He would use this knowledge to his advantage to surprise his enemies. That was for later; for now he had to figure out how to escape.

The prison attendant placed metal plates with millet cakes inside each cell.

"What should I instruct my brother and his team?" whispered the attendant. His brother was in the Yuva-Sena and had offered his help to Bhandi.

Bhandi said softly, "Day after tomorrow." It was the day of the Vinayaka temple festival and he knew the advantage of trying to escape on that day. He pointed to a small hole near the ceiling of his cell.

"I will drop something from there at night. That is the signal for your men to engage the soldiers below. Tell them not to come upstairs," whispered Bhandi just as the guards came in, scolding the attendant for not doing his job more promptly.

"What is taking all this time? Go to the next one!" said one guard.

Though he knew who was responsible for what had befallen the Vardhan family, deep inside Bhandi thought that it was somehow related to him. He felt that he had been a bad omen all along. A moving, breathing personification of bad luck. First, his own family had had to face it and now, his adopted family had borne the consequences. Like rotting wounds attracted flies, he attracted negative energies.

Keshav got up and looked at Bhandi. He gestured to ask whether it would be that day. Bhandi gestured in the negative, it would be the day after. They withdrew to the wall in the corner and murmured to the captives held in the adjacent cell—two full days to prepare.

twenty-one

God Particle

The Buddhist monastery bustled with activity well before sunrise. The monks did not belong to the Hinayana or Mahayana sects, but followed a more purist Sarvayana variant of Buddhism, which was a merger of Buddhist principles and alignment to the forces of nature. The monastery was a mud brick extension built around natural caves. The gust of fresh air swirling through the structure constantly reminded one of the sandalwood trees surrounding the place. The monks rose early each morning, bathed in the monastery's lotus pond, and followed it up with meditation and chanting.

After three days of complete rest, healing and eating nutritious food, Harsha had joined them today. Two monks, out to collect alms from the villagers, had found him in the woods in a half-conscious state. He was barely able to murmur that he was the prince of Sthaneshwar and needed to be saved from the enemies of the state. They had carried him to the monastery where they treated him with local medicines under the supervision of expert resident monks hailing from the north of the Himalayas. Harsha spent his time between his resting room and the prayer hall, careful not to be spotted by people from the nearby villages or visitors to the monastery. He was a wanted man in his own kingdom. A green medicinal paste was applied on his wounds during the day and a dark yellow one at night. A slow-heated broth of turmeric and other medicinal herbs mixed with warm goat's milk was given to him four times a day. Harsha's wounds were healing well. However, his mind was in turbulence. He had requested for a private conversation with the head monk of the monastery after the morning prayers.

Bhadrapala had the face of a child, albeit with grey stubble and a balding head. He was seated on the podium in the main hall which had numerous prayer mats laid out in neat rows. Harsha sat in front of him. The hall was dimly lit by fire torches; inscriptions, murals and carvings on the walls gave the place a vivid and lively feel.

Clad in the light red robe of the monastery, almost teary-eyed, Harsha asked Bhadrapala, "The question that keeps haunting me is what wrong did I do to deserve all this? Why was everything that was dear to me so mercilessly snatched away from me?"

Bhadrapala looked at the young prince with compassion in his eyes, "Not just you but everybody goes through these thoughts at some point of time in their life. In nature, it's a privilege to be born as a human being. This privilege comes at a price of suffering in various forms, which is the human condition."

"A series of misfortunes was unleashed upon me, all of a sudden. While everyone else seems to go ahead with their regular life, why am I the only one thrust into this darkness?"

"Harsha, for some, the pain and sufferings start with big mishaps. For others, it is spaced out in multiple smaller episodes of suffering, not any lesser than one big sudden jolt. A person cannot evade this during their lifetime. We cannot see other people's misery and assume we are the only ones in the dark place. No man's suffering is less than another's. The important thing is to move on."

"I have no faith left. I believe that god is against me all the time."

"God is not an entity or an object. If god were a thing, then he himself could not have come from the void and would require a creator. The balancing force in nature is what we believe is god. Actually, the balancing force in the whole universe is god. It works around us quietly all the time. It balances emptiness with matter, inactivity with energy, rise with fall and happiness with suffering." Bhadrapala raised both his hands to demonstrate how all-encompassing this force is. "Good karma and doing your dharma tones down the volatility of this force. A prayer is our means of submitting ourselves to the force to align ourselves to it. Most importantly, this force cannot be directly communicated to, persuaded, manipulated. It is disproportional and impersonal. So, it will do what it is meant to do, but have trust that in the end, balance will be maintained."

Harsha felt that this was a very different way of looking at the creation and workings of the universe. Man complains about god only because he imagines god to be like a person, a human manifestation with unimaginable powers. As per these monks, god seemed to be a force beyond being a saviour to every person. A force which does not exist to cater to individual needs but to balance the universe.

Just then a group of young monks walked through the adjacent corridor with a clay pot of fuming incense. The hall was suddenly filled with fragrant smoke. Other monks quickly followed them, sweeping and dusting the corridors. Bhadrapala and Harsha glanced at them knowing that the younger monks were finishing up their chores to have their morning meal. Bhadrapala had the most carefree childlike smile.

Harsha asked, "So, you mean that it is our fate to go through all these ups and downs?"

Bhadrapala spoke in his calm demeanour, "That's how nature functions. One should move forward all the time being fully aware that these forces are at play. Don't blame yourself for your miseries or take credit for your success, since bigger forces cause that."

Bhadrapala sensed the brimming anxiety on Harsha's face. The young man was taking too much stress upon himself, he thought. He got up and gave him a bowl of water from a wooden shelf nailed to the wall. "Drink this and take a deep breath," he said as he comfortingly placed his hand on Harsha's shoulder.

"I know some of these things are difficult to articulate, but what exactly is bothering you so much?" he asked.

Harsha drank the water and sighed before speaking, "The past haunts me and I feel totally inadequate to handle the present or face the future. I am drifting towards becoming what the palace staff calls me, an *aprabhu*. The incompetent one."

"Harsha, the past is our imagination of what has happened coloured by our emotions. The future is imagined uncertainty. Be in the present and do what is required. Don't bother about people around."

"My constant worry is that I don't think I will ever be happy or light in my mind again."

"Harsha, you feel like this right now, but like everything else, this too will pass."

"I understand all this, but I still can't overcome my emotions."

"Channelise those emotions. Be in the moment, not in the grief of the past or the stress of the future. Just focus on what needs to be done, one day at a time," said Bhadrapala with a smile.

"I understand. Pray for me," said Harsha.

Harsha bid adieu to Bhadrapala and the other monks in the monastery with all the gratitude in his heart for having given him a fresh lease of life. He thought about the conversation he had had at the monastery—about god, the human condition, cycles of life and happiness. Maybe happiness is indeed highly addictive. Prolonged exposure to it cuts one off from real life. Harsha's privileged upbringing had made it even more difficult to tolerate the harsh realities of the human condition. He now had to learn to persevere in hostile environments. The challenges that lay ahead of him looked impossible to subdue and he did not know where to start. Now that he was inside Sthaneshwar, there was only one place he could think of which was safe. It was hidden away in the wilderness, not known to anyone except the royal family.

twenty-two

Days without Sunshine

Janardhan sat on the throne with a bejewelled crown on his head. He still sat a little towards the corner of the throne, as if a little unsure of being seated on it. For more than two decades he had sat in the right front row of this very throne, head bowed and hands folded, a humble, loyal servant of the king. Today, the turn of events and the right moves at the right time had thrust him into this long-aspired-for position of power. He looked at the two messengers in his court and their insulting demeanour. They had brought with them two huge salivating dogs that had leather straps along their body held by a chain. Those present in the court had not seen such animals; they looked more like overgrown wolves. Their roars despite the metal jaw-restraints and their aggression made everyone around feel uncomfortable. The messengers represented King Shashank of Gauda. They had introduced themselves as Vakul and Vamsi, twins, one with a crippled hand, the other muscular.

The crippled one, Vakul, was reading out a scroll from his master.

> "...the toppling of the previous regime has resulted in a situation of unrest and rebellion across your kingdom. Numerous soldiers who were loyal to the Vardhan family

have left the army and a similar crisis is brewing in the administration councils also. We have no objection to your continuing as king and we will support you to gain full control of your people and army. The only thing we ask in return is that you acknowledge us as the supreme power, and pledge complete loyalty and allegiance to the throne of Gauda. Think over it well before you decide, since what is decided now will decide the course for the future.

Your well-wisher,
King Shashank of Gauda."

Janardhan took a deep breath and said, "I was looking forward to a partnership of equals and you people want my servitude. You want me to be your vassal?"

"Our master believes that with control over less than half of the erstwhile army of Sthaneshwar, you don't have any choice but to seek our help to tide over the commotion inside your kingdom," remarked Vakul.

The twins were now comfortably settled in the more public role that King Shashank had recently laid out for them. No more were they faceless men doing dirty jobs in the background, but envoys who were capable of intimidating even kings. They had shifted the blame of their failure to kill Harsha in the hunting mansion on to the commanding officer of the unit, Ashwath. To impress their king, they also made up a story about getting into a scuffle in the forest with Sthaneshwar soldiers loyal to Harsha, so as to explain the injuries they had sustained.

Janardhan shrugged, "If Shashank, your master, thinks that he will subdue me because he believes that I have less bargaining power at this moment, he is wrong. Go and tell him that I reject his offer. If armed conflict between us is inevitable, so be it. I don't trust Shashank. The world has seen how he deceived his family by treacherously killing his own daughter's husband."

"With due respect, we should not be talking about deception. As we have seen, even the closest friends resort to treachery in their pursuit for power," said Vamsi. It was a thinly veiled dig at Janardhan who had assassinated his closest friend for decades, Army Chief Chakravarti to claim the throne.

Suddenly everyone in the court including Janardhan stood up and drew their swords, "You are messengers and I don't want to set a wrong precedent by slaying you right now. First you insult us by bringing in your rabid dogs and next you have the audacity to make snide remarks directed at me. One more word and we will cut you all into so many pieces that it will be difficult to figure out which are human and which are the dogs. Go and tell Shashank that I have made arrangements. If he invades, he will regret it."

Once the twins left, Janardhan, who until then had pretended to be calm and composed, left his palace along with a convoy in panic. His heart was beating rapidly throughout. *It took a lifetime to reach here; will I lose it all?* he thought. Fear was corroding him from inside. The royal treasury was not in good shape after Rajashri's marriage and because taxation had been waived off in the border areas plagued by floods. As the convoy crossed the Thanesara town checkpost, and the tributary of the Nirjhara River before the waterfall, Janardhan's mind was racing. *How reckless had the older administration been with expenditure?* He needed gold coins, lots of them, to save the situation. Finally, he reached his destination, the Udayawar Prison complex. This was where all the rebels—soldiers, administrators, powerful civilians—had been imprisoned. The ones who were more serious threats to his regime had been assassinated; the ones held here did not pose any serious threat, except for one young man—Bhandi.

Bhandi had been interned on the first floor of this well-guarded prison complex. Tortured, beaten and bruised, he had been subjected to the wrath of Janardhan's soldiers in the last few days. A restraining chain secured his hands and legs. Janardhan looked at him from across the metal bars of the cell. The warden, a thin rough man, and his assistant, a muscular short man, stood behind him.

"No matter what we do and how much we torture him, he does not reach breaking point," said the warden to Janardhan. Bhandi could not hear him over the sound of the waterfall near the prison complex, especially in this section.

He looked weak. His eyes were half open. "I heard the guards talking about Gauda and Malava launching an imminent attack on us. I am not surprised to see you here again."

"I have had enough of patience with you, Bhandi! Your time is running out. By tomorrow morning, I need my two demands to be met unconditionally. First, you will reach out to all your Yuva-Sena leaders and convince them to pledge their support to me. Second, and more importantly, you will tell me the exact location of the Vardhan family treasure," said Janardhan.

"With most of the Sthaneshwar army deserting your regime, you sound desperate for skilled soldiers. What do you require the treasure for? To lure greedy chieftains and warlords to join forces with you?" Bhandi cleared his throat. He was thirsty.

"I know how to use money properly and have done that all my life. You should save your kingdom in this hour of need and

I will spare you with an exile. If you don't, I will behead you. I mean it! Think it over," commented Janardhan.

"Save my kingdom! More like save you. You are a traitor to my family and our kingdom. Why should I help you?"

Janardhan smirked, "To save your life. Also, don't get unnecessarily emotional since those people were not your family but relatives. They were not your parents, brothers or sister."

"It's natural to expect such remarks from you. What do you know about human relationships, you stray dog? You killed your closest friend for the throne, low-life bastard! After years of pretending to be loyal, you treacherously seized power."

"I have my reasons. King Prabhakar was becoming too lenient with spending and was disinterested in strict law enforcement in the last few years. I was frustrated. Once the king was dead, it was evident to me that the two young princes were incompetent to manage this kingdom," said Janardhan, not looking at Bhandi. "I love my motherland and have had enough of this family mismanaging it."

"Everybody lies to themselves in various degrees. You are committing sins and creating a story around it. These are not truths, but it is what you want to believe. The truth is that you are a sinner and everyone hates you," said Bhandi.

"Ha! People's opinions about anybody are as wavering as the farmer's relationship with the rains. At the beginning of the season, farmers look forward to the rains; later their emotion begins to border on irritation, and if the rains are heavy enough to damage the crops, the feeling turns to hatred. You see, it's all based on self-interest. If I take care of every group's interest, sooner or later they will be with me. They will see that I did all this for the larger good." Janardhan's voice was brimming with confidence.

"I don't see that happening."

"Enough of this! I don't care what you feel about me. I came here with an offer. Don't make me change my mind. You are the last surviving male member of the family. It would be easy to just kill you, but I am offering you a chance to save yourself."

Bhandi smiled, "I loathe kindness from a venomous snake like you. What makes you think I am the last one surviving?"

"Harsha is presumed dead. Badly wounded, he must have been eaten by wild animals in the jungle."

"That is what you think. I know that boy since childhood. Don't underestimate his perseverance and resourcefulness."

Janardhan said, "He is dead for sure and if you don't fall in line by tomorrow morning, you will be dead too. This could be the last night of your life."

When they left, Bhandi looked at the bald army commander Keshav locked in the cell in front of him. The row of cells held key army commanders whom Janardhan perceived as a threat to his position. Towards his right was the strong metal door that allowed entry to this corridor. Towards his left were four similar cells on either side. When they were being dragged into the cells, Bhandi had seen that the other end of the corridor led to some stairs and another metallic door. *Where did it lead to?* He had yet to figure it out. The sound of the waterfall meant there was a water body nearby.

Bhandi's right wrist was very flexible. In the afternoon, he had managed to twist and half squeeze it out of the restraining chain's bangle-shaped part around his wrist. Now he applied saliva to the metal loop and tried hard again, but with no luck. He couldn't afford to attract the guards' attention. He banged the metal on the stone floor at well-spaced-out intervals, trying to bend it. He repeated the process—bang the metal, apply saliva to his wrist—till at last, he was finally able to free his hand. Bhandi wrapped the chain around his wrist to conceal his now free hand and waved at Keshav. The guards were on the right of Bhandi's cell; they had to depend on gestures to discuss and finalise their plan.

The change of guards took place late in the evening. Bhandi and Keshav moved quietly to the wall at the side of their cells; from there, they could murmur instructions to the prisoners in the adjacent cells. These were repeated all the way to the last cell in the corridor. They were trained and highly skilled army commanders; if all of them did their best, they had a chance.

The evening meal of millet and barley balls along with yam was served to all the prisoners. There were no toilets inside each cell; every morning, noon and evening, the inmates were taken out into the open. However, on the ground floor, there were close to a hundred soldiers, making escape even more impossible.

When the warden and his assistant came along a little later, accompanied by four soldiers, Bhandi tossed his metal plate across the wall through the small hole near the ceiling of his cell. It crashed below, the cue for the Yuva-Sena men hiding outside the premises to spring into action.

The guards freed Bhandi and Keshav from their respective cells. The warden and his assistant stood in front of them while the four soldiers opened the doors of the other cells. They were asked to form a straight line so as to be escorted downstairs. Whatever they had to do had to be done before they reached the metal door at the end of the corridor leading to the staircase going downstairs. If the soldiers stationed below heard them, they would swarm the first floor like wild bees to subdue the prisoners. Bhandi heard a commotion below, which, in all probability, was the handful of Yuva-Sena soldiers ambushing the guards. There were fewer soldiers that night since most of them were assigned to the Vinayaka temple festival to manage the crowds; precisely why Bhandi had selected that night to try and escape.

"Now!" yelled Bhandi. The warden's assistant said, "What now?" when Keshav put his chained hand around his neck and flung him into the open cell, shut the door with his leg and began to strangle him. At exactly that moment, Bhandi used his free hand to pull out the dagger from the warden's waistband, pushed him into his cell and shut the door. The other prisoners overpowered the four soldiers.

"Now hear me clearly and nobody makes any noise! I have a dagger on your warden's neck and will not hesitate for a moment before plunging it inside," said Bhandi.

Keshav added, "And I have his assistant who is fighting for his breath, as you can see." They knew they had very little time before the soldiers downstairs who were fighting the intruders would decide to head upstairs.

"Tell your men to release those prisoners," said Bhandi. The warden repeated his words. The soldiers used their metallic levers to free the others, who in turn freed Bhandi and Keshav from what remained of their shackles. They took away the soldiers' weapons and except for the warden, locked everybody else in Keshav's cell. They dragged the warden, a dagger to his throat, to the other end of the corridor where a door led to a flight of stairs towards the terrace.

"How many soldiers up there?" asked Bhandi.

"Two."

"All right! Now do as I say," instructed Bhandi. They pulled the warden near the metal door and told him to call the guards.

"Guards! Open the door," shouted the warden as Bhandi dug the dagger into the skin of his neck.

"What happened?"

"I need to have a word with you," said the warden.

As the handle slowly started to turn, Bhandi glanced across the corridor. A soldier had come up to check on the reason for the delay. He saw the warden held hostage by prisoners and rushed down, yelling for help. Within moments, Bhandi felt the rumbling of army leather footwear rushing up the stairs towards the first floor. The latch on the other side of the door was slowly, creakily being opened. The moment the terrace guards opened the door, they were knocked senseless by the escaping men. It was twilight. Bhandi surveyed the terrace in the little light available.

"Look there!" shouted Keshav.

A strong, wild tree leaned against the terrace. Bhandi instructed everybody to leap on to its strong branches and stay there, not climb down since the soldiers were on the alert. One branch of the tree was bending towards the fast-gushing stream.

"If you people move, I will put this dagger into his neck," threatened Bhandi as the soldiers rushed into the terrace. In a sudden motion, he pushed the petrified warden to the side and leaped to grab the bent branch of the tree. He pulled himself up, tiptoed on the branch and called out to the others, "Just jump! Don't think. Jump!"

One by one they climbed on to the branch, ran along it and jumped into the water. The speed of the stream swept them away. Trained soldiers all, they grabbed on to the rocks in between to avoid being swept down the waterfall. It was not as big as

Bhandi had estimated, but it was wide. At that moment, Bhandi saw Keshav being swept past him, yelling for help.

"Hold on!" Bhandi left the support of his rock, swam forward, grabbed Keshav and clung on to another rock, saving his life.

Keshav laughed nervously as he saw the torrent gushing down the waterfall a little ahead, "My grip slipped on the rock! Thank you for saving me." Water flowed past them on both sides. Once they were all ashore, they walked across the forest. Night had fallen.

By the next afternoon, they had traversed the forest to a place that was special for Bhandi. Once the eight fugitive army commanders reached there, they saw two adjacent mansions in the middle of the forest, one destroyed and covered in soot, dirt and dry moss, the other liveable.

"What is this place?" asked Keshav.

"This place is tightly entangled with my past," Bhandi replied. "It's a story that goes back to when I was eight years old."

Keshav was eating berries and offered them to Bhandi who took one and ate it. "So, what is it with you and this place?"

"Back then my mother was unwell, could barely walk and for her better health, my father brought us all here to this natural paradise in the middle of the jungle."

"To this mansion?" Keshav indicated the better-looking mansion.

"No! The burned-down dilapidated one. We spent some memorable days here until one night everything changed. Probably a loose fitted fire torch on the wall. The whole structure caught fire in the middle of the night. My father managed to carry me to safety by knocking down a flaming door. In spite of his bodyguards' repeated cautioning, he went back to save my mother. Within moments, the place had turned into a towering inferno. Neither came out of it. They burnt to ashes in front of my eyes."

"It must have been very difficult for you."

Bhandi smiled, "I remember the pitying looks people gave me. I thought it was because of my loss, but they were also worried about my future. Now, it is happening all over again and it is every bit as painful as before. I think I need to get used to losing the people around me."

Keshav put his hands on Bhandi's shoulders. In all these years, he had never seen Bhandi speak about his feelings, but today, in this moment of vulnerability, he had confided in him about his past and his feelings. Bhandi had built the new structure next to the old one, to come here once in a while. Here, in this wilderness, he felt as if his parents were around him.

The fugitives rested through the day and night after their tiring jungle trek.

Early the next morning, they heard an unexpected sound in the hedges. Bhandi, Keshav and the others assumed that it was a patrolling soldier.

"Harsha!" exclaimed Bhandi, as he saw him coming out of the woods.

Harsha said, "I knew in my heart that if you were on the run, I would find you here."

"I was so worried for you. What happened after you left the palace?!" exclaimed Bhandi as he hugged Harsha in one of those rare moments when he showed his emotions.

"I can't even start to talk about what I went through. It's a long story and does not matter as long as both of us are here."

twenty-three

Devil's Sibling

The footsteps of someone approaching her cell woke Rajashri up from her slumber. Her beautiful face was soiled with layers of dried tears and dust, her clothes were dirty, her hair limp and dishevelled. The grandeur of the queen of Kannauj was gone; she was like an ordinary, less fortunate woman on the streets.

When she saw Visnugupta in front of her, the royal crown on his head, dressed in a fresh tunic with a sleeveless leather coat and lower garment, she started crying. "Please go away! I beg you. I am terrified of you both."

"You will not hear from my brother Devagupta any more. He is dead. As for me, I just don't have anybody to talk to. I am both miserable and happy. You know that feeling, don't you?"

Rajashri looked at him, puzzled. The way he spoke about his brother's death, so matter-of-factly, she was taken aback. His eyes darted all over the place, his expressions were incomprehensible, his voice husky. His demeanour was more intimidating than before.

"When we were children, my brother and I used to play with servant boys and attendants inside Vidisha palace. Once, one of the boys accidentally pushed me down the stairs. I broke two front teeth. My brother punched and kicked that boy. I joined in too. By the time we had vented out our frustration, the boy was barely alive and damaged for life." Visnugupta sighed every now and then as he spoke. "Our father was furious. He made us work along with workers on the irrigation canal work outside the capital in the scorching sun for two months. My brother and I took the digging and toil in our stride. We were partners in everything. I cannot imagine that he is not around any more. Your brother Rajyavardhan killed him."

Rajashri pleaded, "I am still requesting you to end this blood feud. Let me go and we can end this bitter rivalry."

Visnugupta stared at her for some time and spat out, "Huh! Even if I were to let you go, things will not change. You will never be able to forget how Devagupta and I killed your husband and threw his severed hand into your plate. Can you?"

Rajashri started to cry bitterly.

"And I cannot forget how you people killed my elder brother. So, on the day he was slain, I vowed to complete his wish for him. On the day of Saptami, less than a lunar month from now, I will marry you, violate you and the next morning, on Durgashtami, behead you at the sacrificial altar, just like he had planned."

"Please go. Please go away."

Visnugupta came close to the bars. "I am not doing it for some prophecy by our guru, so that this ritual makes me the most powerful man in Bharatvarsh. I will do it to give peace to the soul of my departed brother, as a tribute to him."

"May Lord Shiva save you from the wrath of my brothers!"

"Brothers! It's not brothers any more. This leather coat that I am wearing, do you think it's so cold that I need one in this season? Come here and touch this. Come here! Tanned in a liquid of salt, exotic leaves and a rare tree bark, this is what remains of your brother Rajyavardhan."

Rajashri stood wide-eyed, terrified.

Visnugupta turned around and showed her the puncture marks on the back of his coat. "See this hole? This is where Shashank of Gauda stabbed him. And your elder brother, the scion of the Pushyabhutis, bled to death knowing that this world is a dark place full of betrayal."

Rajashri froze.

"I never wanted to be the king. I was content enjoying my space while my brother did all the hard work. Now that I am the ruler, I must tell you that this feeling of power is the best thing I have ever felt. Good times are here!" exclaimed Visnugupta.

"Please, I beg of you. Go away!"

"You have less than a lunar month, my queen. Enjoy your time here!"

twenty-four

Temple Siege

Harsha's immediate objective was very clear to him. Sthaneshwar, his own kingdom, had to be under his control before he could even think of waging war with Gauda and Malava to save his sister. Only a few army commanders in Sthaneshwar supported Janardhan, that too because they were worried for their families. A full-scale battle or a civil war was not required to seize power. If Janardhan could be assassinated, his commanders would not create any trouble. Other commanders, who had absconded with their men, left or turned hostile, would return.

Harsha and Bhandi had to figure out where the assassination could be attempted. With the high security around Janardhan, it was next to impossible; but, like his elaborate evening dive from the top of the palace wall into the palace pool, Janardhan had a few more eccentricities. On full moon nights, he fasted the whole day and visited the Neelkantheshwar Mahadev temple in the middle of the town. Once a year, he would also head south to Dandakaranya to spend a month in the forest. After setting up a makeshift tent, he would stay inside clad only in his loincloth, for his inner peace, he said. No religious text prescribed such rituals, but Janardhan believed it brought him good luck.

In their safe house near the royal granary in the middle of the town, Harsha and Bhandi were getting ready. The house belonged to Keshav's relative, who lived in Indraprastha but stayed here during his trips to the capital for business. It was getting dark outside. There were eight other highly trained Yuva-Sena soldiers in the room including Keshav, all getting ready for action. Two of them wore black clothes with a black cloth face mask. The others stuffed the bottom of their leather footwear with as many pieces of soft cloth as possible. The fall, in all probability, would be impactful and they did not want to break their toes. After tightly tying on their footwear, they padded their elbows and knees, donned metal helmets, strapped their swords to their waistbands, and picked up ropes on their way up to the terrace of the safe house.

It was a moonlit night and the gentle breeze brought in the fragrance of marigold and night lily from the flower market adjacent to the royal granary. As far as the eye could see, there were small, illuminated dots made by lamps in the numerous mud brick houses around Thanesara town that gave it the appearance of being carpeted by bright yellow dots. But in each house, there was a cloud of unease ever since the stable regime of the Vardhans had become a thing of the past. Their new ruler had the reputation of being too occupied with his own greed. Within days of coming to power, he had increased taxes for farmers and artisans and cancelled the free mid-day meals for the poor. There were rumours that Janardhan was considering a reduction in remuneration for administration and palace officials. People across the kingdom stared at an uncertain future.

Janardhan always visited the temple when it was about to close and the streets were deserted.

Harsha, Bhandi and their team waited with bated breath on the terrace. A little later, they heard the faint sound from below of horseshoes along the cobblestones.

"Crouch!" Harsha whispered.

The preliminary scouts sent by the palace to secure the lane before Janardhan arrived, rode all the way to the temple and back, their fire torches brightening up the street as they did so.

"We have a few moments before the royal convoy comes in," said Bhandi. "So let's do this quickly."

All structures on this lane leading to the Mahadev temple were two floors high with gaps between them. The assassination team had performed a trial run the previous night and went about their task with ease. Harsha and Keshav remained on the terrace with two soldiers while the others went down the stairs to the street. The two men clothed in black remained on either side of the lane while Bhandi and three others took the external stairs to the terrace of the opposite building.

Nobody was around, and the three teams moved like a synchronised battle formation. Harsha's team moved forward on the terraces in tune with the two men in black on the street below; Bhandi and his men moved on the terraces on the opposite side, a little slower, keeping an eye on the street behind.

Every now and then, the teams had to leap from one terrace to another till they reached the end of the lane. It was the only entrance to the temple; the other sides were covered by a boundary wall. The last two buildings in the lane had a huge arch concealing a connector between them. This grand arched entrance to the temple was used during festivals to hang long floral curtains and had a suspended fire cauldron right in the middle of the arch. During celebrations, people stationed on top showered flower petals and rose water at visiting dignitaries. The

Vardhan family used to visit the temple twice a month, especially during the Shivaratri festival. Harsha had very fond memories of this place; it was difficult for him to even imagine back then that one day he would be attempting an assassination on the reigning king outside the same premises, and as a commoner.

The lane and the arch were in darkness, except for intermittent fire torches at a distance. The two men in black removed the sewer slabs covering the now dry sewage line on either side of the lane and hid inside. The previous night, they had placed two iron rods and boulders beneath the slabs, which were to be used tonight. On the top of the arch, Harsha and Bhandi's men had positioned themselves on either side of the cauldron. They tied one end of their ropes on the stone-cut railing of the arch. The ropes had to be tied tight and be just the right length. Not too long and not too short. They had equidistant knots to avoid skidding and the men wore leather gloves. Crouched on the arch, hands holding their ropes, a prayer on their lips, they waited with their hearts pounding inside their chests.

A group of four horsemen were heard in the lane below. "Janardhan's royal scouts," whispered Bhandi to Harsha from across the cauldron. It took a while for the scouts to thoroughly inspect the temple premises before they left.

"I think they have cleared it and have gone to call the convoy," murmured Harsha.

Janardhan and his men would come in at any time. The plan had been well-thought-through. The foot soldiers would enter first, then four armed riders in a two-by-two formation. They would be followed by Janardhan's long, open, four-horse drawn chariot. Four bodyguards would surround him as he sat on a throne in the chariot, and they would be followed by four riders and some foot soldiers. The lane was very narrow, which meant that when the chariot passed through, it blocked the space, preventing the riders or the foot soldiers from moving ahead. Bhandi had selected this spot because of the constricted space and limited mobility. When the chariot was right below the arch, the two men in black would pop out of the sewer, thrust the boulders in front of the wheels and push metal rods across the wheel spokes on either side. This would halt the chariot. At that precise moment, Harsha's and Bhandi's soldiers would slide down their ropes on to the open chariot. Within moments, they had to get rid of the bodyguards and kill Janardhan. The soldiers ahead and behind would have no time or space to prevent the assassination or retaliate.

Harsha and Bhandi waited, their faces red with anxiety. Finally, rows of fire torches approached and the convoy appeared. The assassination teams were waiting for the exact moment to strike when Harsha spotted something. His eyes widened and his lips pressed together.

"We need to abort this and leave."

Bhandi asked, "Why?"

"Look! Janardhan is not on a chariot but on horseback tonight."

Bhandi swore under his breath. "Luck favours the devil!" On Bhandi's instructions, one of their men cawed like a wild crow, signalling to the others to abandon the plan.

"Let's leave! We have to come up with another plan," said Harsha.

twenty-five

The Art of Hunting

The balcony on the topmost floor of Kanyakubja palace had a long platform which stretched a little ahead. Below, on three sides of this platform, was a semi-circular enclosure with a black stone wall. There were numerous thorny shrubs half the size of a fully grown man with paths crisscrossing around them. Only one metal gate stood on the east side of the enclosure wall. Kettle drummers were stationed at multiple places around the perimeter.

King Shashank pulled out an arrow from his quiver and loaded his bow. He glanced at the metal cage that had been wheeled to the gate.

"Release!" he commanded.

The cage opened, and a large black boar emerged. Terrified by the beating of the drums, the animal began to run among the shrubs. Shashank stretched his bow and shot the arrow. He missed. Every time the boar reached the wall, a drummer started to beat his drum. The boar would retreat in panic again towards the centre of the enclosure. Running among the thorny shrubs caused excruciating pain to the animal, aggravating its terror. Shashank shot a second time and a third time but missed.

"Very sharp for a wild pig!"

Shashank's eyes narrowed; he held his breath and took his time before releasing the arrow. It dug into the boar's rear, and it fell, grunting in pain.

Wearing a red flowing dress, fresh flowers in her hair, Sharada appeared on the balcony. She tiptoed to the extended platform towards her father.

"Release!" called Shashank. Another wild boar entered the enclosure. This one was smaller and more grey than black. Shashank smiled at Sharada and took aim at the boar, which was running in fright.

"Father! I came to know that you sent the twins to the hunting mansion when Harsha was supposed to be there."

"I did."

Sharada said, "When we had spoken about destroying the Vardhans, I thought we meant bringing them to a humiliating downfall. Possibly sending them into exile. To kill them was not part of the plan, right?"

"It still isn't," said Shashank, stretching the arrow loaded on his bow. He missed. The small wild boar was nimble and fast.

"I know what kind of people the twins are and what kind of jobs they do for you. Why send them after Harsha?" asked Sharada.

Shashank said, "I have upgraded the status of the twins. They are not my assassination team any more. Their mission at the hunting mansion was to capture Harsha."

"Father! I would like to believe you." Sharada hesitated for a moment before saying, "I don't know how to say this, but are the rumours true that you killed Rajyavardhan? They are false, right?"

Shashank continued to aim at the hapless boar below, but his voice had risen in pitch. "Blatant lies! These are baseless rumours. Malava is the only ally we have against the Vardhans. I was there to ensure that Rajyavardhan did not annihilate them totally. Visnugupta had killed him before I reached the spot."

"I am not sure whom to trust."

"Just trust my words!" Shashank said. "You are too young to understand this kind of politics, my girl. I played the game intelligently and ruthlessly. Hence, I am winning. You see that boar below? Do you know the trick to kill it?"

"No!"

"The trick is to initially fire some arrows just to see where it moves. You need to understand its movement, speed and directional preference. Subject it to the pain of thorns to baffle it. Then you aim the arrow not at the animal, but where it is likely to move," said Shashank. Sharada looked at her father and wondered if it was someone else who was talking.

"I observed and planned against the Vardhans for months. I anticipated some of their actions correctly. I improvised as per the situations. Most importantly, without emotions. That worked," said Shashank as he moved his bow around. "Hunting or politics, you need to always be ahead of your opponent whatever may be the means. Morality is secondary. Don't break your head thinking about all these complications. Leave it to me!"

The little wild boar was moving around the enclosure very fast. Shashank's arm was moving equally fast.

"You have changed!" said Sharada as she left.

Shashank smiled to himself. Yes, he had changed. It had taken a life-threatening illness and a near-death experience to bring about the change. As he lay on his bed for months, fighting death, shedding tears thinking about the final moments of his daughter, he reached a stage of clarity that had eluded him till then. He realised that the dream he had once seen as a young king, of dominating the whole of Bharatvarsh had mellowed with age. That the difficult forgiveness he had granted to the Vardhan family was superficial. That his rage against them knew no bounds. He would be pacified only after each and every one in that family was destroyed. On his supposed deathbed, he felt that he was carrying this immense burden of unfulfilled wants that would have died with him. Sharada would never understand him. One needs to reach a particular age to understand the dead weight of unachieved ambitions and wishes. It's like a robe of thorns one wears throughout the day and takes to bed at night. He survived miraculously after an expert physician from Kamarupa was called in to intervene. When he recovered, he realised that god had given him a second chance to make his dreams come true. To make those who made him feel miserable suffer. Shashank had promised himself that he would make the best of this god-given chance.

twenty-six

Dark Tunnel

Three secret tunnels had been constructed two generations back. They had been made by a small group of loyal workers to assist in the escape of the royal family in case of a war, revolt or assassination attempt. Two of these were known to the royals and their close associates. There was a third long tunnel that ran all the way from the palace basement, around the Durga Devi temple and water tank to a thick patch of forest a little away from the palace. Once, at midnight, four years ago, Rajyavardhan, Harsha, Rajashri and Bhandi had been woken up from their sleep by their parents. They were secretly escorted to one of the numerous basement rooms to be shown the entrance to this tunnel. Harsha was pretty sure that nobody, including Janardhan, knew about this tunnel.

In the morning, the soldiers who would carry out the coup entered the capital town in small groups, disguised as farmers, monks and traders, their weapons concealed. By evening, Harsha, Bhandi and 600 of their most trusted and skilled Yuva-Sena warriors assembled at the forest patch near the tunnel exit. Their intention was to enter from here, cover the distance to the basement and storm the palace at night, catching unawares the 2,000 soldiers stationed inside the palace complex.

There was a cluster of small natural caves among the thick vegetation, one of which was covered by a massive boulder. It took five men to push the rock aside. Inside, there was enough space for around three people to enter at a time. When it was dark enough, Harsha and Bhandi, followed by their men, entered the tunnel with fire torches and swords. They were greeted with a damp stench and cobwebs as they slid down a steep slope to land on the rocky floor of the tunnel. A few steps ahead, the tunnel widened considerably. Harsha, Bhandi and their soldiers were hurrying in anticipation of reaching the palace basement, but the tunnel was longer than they had anticipated. Portions of it had collapsed to form piles of clay bricks and debris at various places. The one thing the team was wary of were poisonous snakes; one wrong step and it could prove to be lethal. Harsha and Bhandi hurried past a section where water trickled down the side, making the floor muddy. Within minutes, the whole group of warriors were inside the tunnel, but all of a sudden they heard the sound of shouting and a ruckus from behind. Harsha and Bhandi looked at each other. One by one, their fire torches got extinguished. Thrust into pitch darkness, Bhandi shouted, "What's going on?"

A soldier from far behind shouted, "Somebody said the entrance has been sealed."

"What?!" exclaimed Bhandi.

"Janardhan must have come to know about this tunnel through some means," said Harsha. Maybe years and years of association had led Prabhakar to reveal the details of this tunnel to Janardhan for the safety of his family.

"And we walked right into it. Now what?" Bhandi asked.

"We cannot go back to the cave exit and try to remove the boulder. There is a steep rocky slope before the exit and even if there are ten enemy soldiers on the other side, we will be unable to open it with brute force," said Harsha.

"We cannot go to the palace side where soldiers will be waiting for us. So, we wait here in this suffocating darkness while they mobilise their soldiers and send them in from both sides. Our luck!" Bhandi growled in frustration.

"Now that they know we are trapped, it's just a matter of time," said Harsha.

In pitch darkness, 600 young men waited helplessly for their eventual doom.

"Prince Harsha! Come here for a moment," a soldier called out.

"Here!" said the soldier, as Harsha and Bhandi looked at the roof. Water trickled down the side. At once Harsha realised that this was the part of the tunnel that ran along the perimeter of the palace water tank. After decades of no maintenance, water had started to seep through the wall of the tank into the adjoining section of the tunnel.

"Let's try to bring this down. We don't have any other choice," said Harsha.

Bhandi and the others struck at the wet portion of the wall with their spears. Cracks slowly began to appear. "Har Har Mahadev!" With all their might, they hit the wall in tandem.

Outside, Janardhan's commanders mobilised their men on the cave and palace basement sides of the tunnel. It was easy, all they had to do was barge in and butcher the trapped rebels. Within moments, they stormed in from both sides. As soon as they entered, Janardhan's soldiers heard loud sounds and felt tremors coming from a distance. The tunnel wall was shuddering and chants of "Har Har Mahadev" reached them. As they waited to close in on the rebels, wave after wave of water came gushing towards them, washing away some of the soldiers. The others moved ahead through the waterlogged tunnel, but when they finally reached the spot where the rebels were supposed to be, they saw a crater in the wall of the tunnel.

At a distance, in the fruit orchard adjacent to the palace, Harsha called out to Bhandi, "Our enemy thinks we have absconded."

"We are absconding!" Bhandi answered.

"What is the last thing he would expect from us?"

"What?"

"Janardhan will not be expecting us to dare come back again immediately after our failed coup," said Harsha.

Bhandi understood the merit in his statement. They had the advantage of surprise. As all other men escaped to safety, Harsha, Bhandi and two trusted deputies moved in the opposite direction.

"This is our home and we know it better than anybody else," said Bhandi.

Taking advantage of the darkness behind the bushes of the gardens, they tiptoed towards the inner palace wall near the Durga Devi temple. Once in a while, they saw soldiers carrying fire torches rushing in the water tank's direction while others came in from outside. As time went by, the commotion subsided.

"I think it has dawned upon them that the rebels have managed to get away this time! How do you plan to get in?" Bhandi asked in a hushed tone.

"Listen carefully," said Harsha, pointing in the direction of the Durga Devi temple where *saayan aarti,* the evening prayers and lighting of oil lamps had started. They reached the old entry to the temple, now locked and abandoned. The door was thick and small with the image of Nandi carved into it.

"Pick up big stones and go for the hinges when I tell you," instructed Harsha.

"If you knock down the door by force, the noise might alert the guards on the other side," Bhandi warned.

"Along with the bell! We have exactly 12 attempts in hand," said Harsha. They waited patiently as the din on the other side caused by chants, drums and trumpets increased. The noise reached fever pitch as the chanting intensified and the huge temple bell was rung.

"Bong!" A little later came the second bong and the group of four delivered their first blow in tandem. A layer of dust dropped from the door into their faces and eyes. The bell was rung at equal intervals of time; the group synchronised their blows on the door hinges with each peal of the bell. By the fifth bong, the door started to shake.

"We have another seven before we lose the chance!" muttered Harsha.

Three more blows and the door fell.

"Where to now?" asked Bhandi.

"Easy to guess. What does Janardhan do around late evening?" Harsha's eyes twinkled in the muted light. Bhandi smiled. They reached the rear of the temple and hid among the trimmed hedges. Just as they had settled down, they were spotted by two guards, but Bhandi and one of the soldiers pounced on them and slit their throats before they could alert the others.

Harsha and the other soldier proceeded to the fence near the pool and waited with bated breath, vigilant. After what seemed like an eternity, a dark figure appeared on top of the palace balcony leading to the wall-walk.

Janardhan was ready, as usual, for his dive into the pool. From this distance, Harsha could not read the expression on his face, but the way he walked showed dejection. Maybe it was because of the lost chance in the tunnel. The one opportunity when he could have easily finished Harsha.

"Quick! Give me the bow and arrow," Harsha commanded the soldier.

As Janardhan stood on the wall taking a deep breath before finally plunging into the pool way down below, Harsha strung the bow and stretched it to its maximum. This could perhaps be his last chance to get the job done.

Janardhan was ready to leap.

Harsha shot the arrow exactly at the moment Janardhan leaped. A sudden gust of air and Harsha knew it was no good. The arrow swung a little and brushed Janardhan on his shoulder. He plummeted into the pool.

"Bastards! Look at this! Someone tried to kill me. Go get them!" He started screaming the moment he emerged out of the water and continued yelling as he swam to the embankment.

"You good for nothing worms! I need the decapitated heads of those people who dared to try to kill me!" The complex swarmed with soldiers, but they could not find anybody.

Dejected for the second time, Janardhan went into the changing room to dry himself and change into fresh clothes. As he entered and swung aside the curtain, he saw Harsha.

"It was my hunch that at some point of time you would be here, in the changing room." Harsha stabbed Janardhan in the stomach and waited till the traitor collapsed, before stepping out with his sword. The guards saw him immediately. Seeing some 30 soldiers rush towards him made Harsha worried. If they were hostile, he had no chance. He gripped his sword and prepared himself for any eventuality. The guards stopped just short of him and contemplated what to do. Nobody attacked the young prince. Behind Harsha appeared the two deputies, dragging the half-dead Janardhan out of the changing room.

"Janardhan has been slain!" one of the soldiers yelled, and everyone raised their swords to cheer.

"Sthaneshwar stands with the Vardhans!" cheered another soldier. Bhandi, who was covering Harsha, and the soldiers sprung out from the hedges.

In his final moments, the thought that crossed Janardhan's mind was that poor Harsha did not know about the trap he had set for him. The young prince would never be able to sit on the throne.

twenty-seven

Suffocation

The physician checking Rajashri inside her prison cell was aghast at seeing an erstwhile queen in such a bad state. She was pale, with dark circles around her eyes, her throat sore, wheezing with each breath she took. Her gaze was like that of a dead person, without any expression. As the physician checked her pulse, throat and eyes, his assistant whispered something into his ears. Visnugupta, who was standing at the entrance of the cell, observed the proceedings.

"Maharajadhiraj! I am afraid her health situation is not looking good," said the physician.

Visnugupta replied, "That is fine. She just needs to survive till the day of Durgashtami."

"The way things are, she might not make it till then, your highness."

Visnugupta sighed as his eyes moved in all directions, "Then give her some medicines and make her better."

"I will give some ayurvedic medicines that need to be boiled with milk and given thrice daily. I am afraid that alone won't help. Her throat is the problem," the physician responded.

"If I had my way, I would pour red hot molten copper down her throat, but I can't kill her for now."

The physician cleared his throat, "She is choking in this dusty, damp and unventilated cell. Her *shwasakosa* is in a bad state. She needs to be out in the fresh air."

"No way! She is my prized possession. I can't afford to have her roaming around freely," said a furious Visnugupta.

"Just twice a day should improve her chances of surviving this ailment, your highness."

Visnugupta thought for a while, "I will think about it. You give the medicinal powder and instructions to the guard. Then leave!"

Once the physician and his assistant left, Visnugupta walked towards Rajashri. She was petrified and moved backwards. He touched her chin to raise her face. She was trembling.

"My little princess, brought up in the lap of luxury. A baby. A little discomfort and she becomes ill," he said, thrusting his face at her. "Bad upbringing by your parents. When my brother and I were very young, we were very mischievous inside the palace. In the peak of winter our father used to make us spend the night clad in our loincloths in the open as punishment. Do you know why he did that?"

"Uh! You are hurting me," said Rajashri as he jerked her face backwards.

"He did that to prepare us for the world. Get used to pain and suffering, pampered woman. It helps you to face life. You see this mark on my palms? A considerate palace caretaker once tried to save us brothers from my father's punishment and gave us refuge in his chamber for the night. My father ordered his right thumb to be chopped off, a thousand lashes for him, and placed hot metal rods on our hands for flouting his orders. Everybody should be groomed to be tough and disciplined.

Protected children like you become weak individuals. What a shame!"

"And what did you become with all the grooming?"

Visnugupta laughed, "All-powerful, as you can see. The man who controls a kingdom and your destiny." From being a childhood victim, Visnugupta had changed to victimiser. When inflicting pain, he felt relevant, alive, in control. Now in a position of power, he felt even better.

"Yes, you control my destiny. I fold my hands and request you, just kill me!" Rajashri broke down.

Visnugupta turned to leave and said, "You need to live for now, so that you can die later."

twenty-eight

Left Behind

As children, Rajyavardhan, Harsha, Rajashri and Bhandi would visit the Shri Ram temple near the old market of Thanesara during the month of Ramayana reading. Every day, the priest would read a portion of the holy book and share the underlying wisdom with the children. All of them, especially Bhandi, looked forward to these visits because on the way back they would stop to buy dumplings made of jackfruit and jaggery along with tender coconut water from a famous vendor on the same street. One day, Rajyavardhan asked the priest what had happened to Lord Ram after he was crowned king. The priest was not very keen to respond, but Rajyavardhan insisted on knowing. The next day onwards, the priest started narrating the verses of the Uttarkanda to the children. After his wife Sita left the palace, Ram lived an uneventful life for years. While the common man outside enjoyed the benefits of Ramrajya, the lord himself was going through dark ages. With no family of his own, his parents long gone and brothers busy with their own families, Ram was lonely. The image Harsha drew from the narration was that of a lonely, heartbroken king wandering across the dark corridors of a large palace. His life had been a series of tragedies. First it was the 14 years of suffering in the forest and then almost the same number of years of solitude in the palace. The days of glory and heroics had passed. A lingering nostalgia must have crept inside him. Harsha could now understand what it was to be in a situation like that. Thanesara palace had been his home since birth. Now it felt like a different place altogether. Like a discarded carcass whose flesh had been eaten by the vultures of fate. A ruined paradise. All those lively people who were now reduced to portraits hanging on the corridor wall used to live here, move around these corridors, talking cheerfully. There were good times when this place was the venue of grand celebrations and there were bad times when everyone stuck together till they passed. Today there was nobody. This place that once echoed with laughter and conversation had fallen silent. The only sounds were of the curtains fluttering and the tinkling of the oil lamp chandeliers in the wind. Other than that, there was an eerie, ghastly silence, a silence so deafening that it made Harsha's head hurt. Sorrow, like a wayward artisan, constantly painted every nook and cranny with colours of darkness while hope, like a novice worker, struggled to remove it. Grief loomed in every object and every corner, spread evenly on everything like a layer of dust.

What happened to people after they died? Harsha did not believe in life after death. He believed that every time a loved one shed a tear remembering the departed, they came back to life in that moment. That teardrop, the love and the longing, is something the departed ones had earned during their lifetime. In private, Harsha cried thinking about his family and the tragedy that they had encountered.

The thoughts that pestered him were not only of the people who were gone but also of those who had deceived him. The person with whom he had fallen in love for the very first time.

First love is like a mud road in farmlands. Even after years, seasons change, vegetation sprouts over it, but if one looks carefully, the trail is still there. Sharada had shaken Harsha's faith in relationships. Their story could have been so many things; it had been reduced to nothing.

Today, he could not afford to let his mind wander. Harsha had assumed that taking control of the kingdom would ease out things for him but more complications followed. After Janardhan's death, Harsha had declared himself the supreme commander of his army. He and Bhandi had decided against coronation in this moment of crisis. Harsha never wanted the crown and wanted to stay away from it at this moment. For him this crown of thorns, the power struggle for Sthaneshwar, was the root cause of the suffering and grief he had experienced. Harsha went up the stairs to the royal gallery where Bhandi was waiting for him. In front of them were about 100 commoners selected from within the kingdom after a day of intense thought and deliberation.

Bhandi proclaimed, "Today we have with us distinguished civilians, representing groups that have a mastery in the field of combat, making weapons or specific skills useful in a battle. Our kingdom faces grave danger and we need everyone's support. I give to you our leader, scion of the Pushyabhuti clan, Harshavardhan!" The toll of the recent series of misfortunes was evident on Bhandi and Harsha's faces. Bhandi had an implicit calm acceptance of tragedy in life unlike the latent rage and gloom that had crept inside Harsha after having faced tragedy for the very first time.

Clear with the thoughts and clear with the words, Harsha murmured to himself as he took a deep breath. He spoke almost immediately and did not let the self-confidence in his tone waver. People spot weakness very easily and his image was a hurdle for him. "Janardhan was not only a traitor who cheated everyone to grab power but he also turned out to be extremely foolish. To face the threat from Gauda and Malava, he made the most unexpected choice of inviting the Hunas for help." There was a mild rumble of disbelief in the crowd.

"Those people should be kept at arm's length is something even a fool knows!" said a woman from the audience whose sharp features, curly hair and dusky complexion had made Harsha notice her when he had started speaking.

"Janardhan is dead now but he had pulled us all into this immediate crisis of the Hunas before he left. Two scrolls were sent to the Huna king Narana asking him to come along with his army to Thanesara immediately. Many of our soldiers left the army and went off to their native places after Janardhan took over. Some are in the forests organised as rebel groups. It will take many days for us to track them and consolidate them here. Meanwhile, the Hunas will be in our capital in three days."

"The general public needs to step in for the sake of our motherland. We have 600 trained young men of the Yuva-Sena. We have war elephants and 700 soldiers from the royal army. How many more can we organise in three days?" asked Bhandi.

"My name is Simhananda. I am the leader of a tribe which migrated to Sthaneshwar when our native village near Lumbini was plagued by drought and ransacked by barbaric clans from the Himalayas. We have made this kingdom our home for the past four years. Our tribe has 300 men who are fighting fit. We are with you!"

A frail young man spoke up, "I am Kuntala. We teach horse riding to youngsters who want to join the army. I can organise around 200 young men trained in weapons and horse riding."

"I am Daksh and we are a tribe of warriors from Gorakhanagari. We migrated to these parts a year back. I can arrange for 400 fighters," said a muscular man.

"My name is Avanti. I retired as a minister under your father Prabhakar because I was fed up of being dominated by our then Chief Minister Janardhan. I am old but know about battle strategy and tactics which can be of help," said an old man with a flowing white beard.

"I have seen you many times in the royal court when I was younger. Then you suddenly disappeared," remarked Harsha.

Avanti smiled, "I quit! Internal politics have destroyed more kingdoms than external factors."

Blacksmiths, wrestlers, elephant tamers, carpenters, masons and groups of young men—all pledged their contribution towards facing the imminent attack of the Hunas.

"My name is Durgavati," the young woman Harsha had noticed earlier spoke. "This is my father Parikshit. He was in the army, the best archer in the kingdom. We are teachers of archery and we have trained a lot of people in this skill over decades. Some of them have joined the Sthaneshwar army also. We can put the word out and organise some 400 civilians, men and women who are good at archery." Her self-confidence and grooming made it look as if she could command the whole army herself. Harsha and Bhandi were impressed.

A private discussion was arranged in the royal court. A large clay model of the Thanesara palace complex was placed in the middle, around which stood Harsha, Bhandi, Yuva-Sena leaders, army commanders, old Avanti, Kuntala, Daksh, Simhananda,

Durgavati, her father Parikshit, and representatives of other groups.

Old Avanti was the first to speak, "The Hunas are largely horseback fighters, who use only swords. This makes them fast and agile. Our strategy should be to see that we exploit this trait and turn it into their weakness."

"Then I think we should rely on long-range weapons like arrows and spears to create an advantage," remarked Durgavati.

The huge temporary structure with a dome created in the middle of the vast palace grounds for Rajashri's wedding ceremony caught Harsha's attention. The main gate to the compound led to this vast space surrounded by the palace walls.

"This structure is still there, right? We need our masons and labourers to work on it overnight, and make the dome hollow so that we can fill it with something I'll ask for. It could turn the tide for us," said Harsha. He was very careful with his words because he knew that each person in the hall was evaluating him as a leader, contemplating placing their trust in the hands of a commander whose age was a disadvantage.

Bhandi pointed out the wide passage connecting the grounds to the court, residential palace and temple, "If we create a deep trench here, fill it up with sharp stones and route water from the palace pond here, it will serve as a barrier for those invaders on horseback and block their access to the main structure."

Harsha's eyes narrowed as he evaluated all possibilities and an idea flashed in his mind, "I have a very unconventional thought on dealing with this invasion. It will need our masons, workers, blacksmiths, archers, cavalry, war elephants and foot soldiers to work continuously for the next two days. Frankly, considering the large numbers of the savages, we have no choice but to take big risks. The Hunas have fantasised about capturing Thanesara palace for more than half a century now. Let's just give it to them. Let them have it!"

Appalled, everyone looked at each other. Harsha smiled, then set out to explain his plan.

twenty-nine

Deserted Palace

Narana the Huna brushed aside the hair that fell over his eyes as his army of horsemen stormed into the outskirts of Thanesara town. In the dusty background, he could see the outline of the fortified palace far away. His gaze remained transfixed on it for some time as he ran his fingers over his beard. A smile lit up his face. The army had taken a full night of rest before starting their assault early in the morning. The Huna dream for decades, to subdue the kingdom of Sthaneshwar, was right before him. His spies believed it was as easy as it could get. All Narana had to do was eliminate a 17-year-old boy and his army of soldiers put together in a hurry. The scouts who had come before them at the break of dawn had informed him that most inhabitants seemed to have deserted the town. Some people who were nabbed confirmed that Harsha and his close associates had fled out of fear. From what he could see, it appeared to be true since even the main marketplace, which bustled with activity during his last visits to this town, was empty today. Carrying sharp straight swords in each hand, his soldiers were mounted on the best breed of Arabian horses. The distinctive head shape, high tail carriage, height, stamina and the brute strength of these stallions added to the Huna army's sense of intimidation.

A dust cloud trailed them as they reached the palace complex. Narana noted that the main gate, massive and embedded with spikes, was unguarded.

"Get this open!" the Huna king ordered his men.

Once the gate opened and the invading army entered, they saw no one in the huge open ground behind the gate. A breeze raised dust across the empty arid ground. The solitary structure right in the middle of this ground was the big dome-shaped temporary structure that had been constructed for Princess Rajashri's wedding. Narana noted a lot of new curtains fluttering around the structure and the dome seemed to be broken and hollow in some places. *With all the turmoil happening inside the palace following Rajashri's wedding, the royal family did not even have time to demolish the structure*, thought Narana.

The wide passage leading to the main complex had a deep trench across it, filled with water. Narana looked around suspiciously and found a lot of rubble in various corners, as if something had been demolished. What could it be?

Narana tied his long hair with a black string and put both his swords into the sheaths on either side of his horse's saddle. While his men roared in delight at having scared away their enemy, Narana scratched his beard and said, "Don't celebrate too early. We need to be careful. This could be some kind of deception. We need to be very alert, especially at night. March ahead with me!"

On his instruction, his army rode along the wide path to the water-filled trench. The large ground was covered with 5,000 Huna soldiers on horseback. Narana surveyed the trench. It was too deep for the horses to cross. *There is something inside the palace complex and they want to block us from reaching it*, he thought. The silence sounded unnatural to him. When he looked carefully, he noticed that the stone stairway leading to the walk on top of the palace wall was demolished on both sides. *That explains all the rubble, but why would someone do that?*

Then suddenly he heard a woman's voice loudly calling, "Soldiers, load your bows! Ready! Now!"

It was a young woman commander instructing her archers all around the palace wall-walk as they emerged from their hiding places. Many of them were women, their skill and focus a sight to behold as the arrows rained from all sides on the Hunas.

The field was filled with cries of pain from the Hunas and the neighing of their horses. Harsha, standing with the archers, watched Durgavati in awe as she directed and controlled her archers, covering the perimeter on top of the wall. Her father Parikshit was doing the same on the opposite side.

"Not so quickly. Cover more distance," she instructed, pacing like a trained general. "Aim and shoot!"

As she passed by, Harsha said, "I must say that you have risen to the occasion."

"Under duress, it happens! Time for you to proceed, chief. All clear from our side. The rival army is contained," said Durgavati.

Harsha went quickly to the corner of the wall with its concealed stairs and the secret passage used by messengers, moving towards the inner palace where his part of the mission awaited.

The Hunas could do nothing amid the rain of arrows. There were no stairs to reach the wall-walk to attack their rivals. They could not use ropes to scale the walls while the archers were above. As the main gate closed behind them, they realised that they were trapped. More than 1,000 Huna soldiers had perished to the arrows and most of their horses were badly injured. Narana's eyes blazed. "Take your swords," he commanded his men. "Get off your horses and move towards that structure. Don't worry, we are twice their number!"

While the endless arrows continued showering under Durgavati's instructions, the Hunas dashed towards the centre and took shelter under the temporary structure in the middle of the ground. Behind them, the massacre continued.

"I always believed that having no shield in our armoury was a weakness, and today we stand exposed. We step out of this structure and they will finish us one by one," said Narana. The arrows indeed did no harm to them, sheltered under the huge structure constructed for a thousand wedding guests at a time. For a moment, everyone felt relieved.

The main gate opened to let in war elephants that positioned themselves all around the palace wall. Narana saw Bhandi leading his soldiers outside the gates supported by Simhananda and Kuntala's warriors. On the palace side across the trench, Harsha led his men supported by Daksh's group. Narana knew that he was encircled, but he still had many more men than his enemy. "Nice surprise!" he smirked. "It won't amount to much in the end."

He looked up and saw that the structure under which they were sheltering had a false wooden ceiling, which seemed to have been modified. Pieces of cloth were dangling from between the strips of wood above. The stench of clarified butter wafted all around when the curtains fluttered in the breeze.

On Durgavati's instruction, archers from four sides shot fire-tipped arrows, some of them zooming into the cavities inside the dome. Suddenly, the dome, which was stuffed with dry hay and long rolls of cloth dipped in clarified butter, caught fire along with the false wooden ceiling. Within moments, it turned to ash the wooden platform which supported it from below.

"My lord!" screamed a soldier behind Narana as the long curtains caught fire and an inferno dropped on the numerous Hunas taking refuge below the dome. The soldiers suffered severe burns as they ran in panic. The war elephants charged towards the structure, trampling panic-stricken Huna soldiers. Some who survived fell prey to the archers; those who were trying to escape by moving towards the gates were chased and killed by Bhandi's riders; those trying to run towards the palace were killed by foot soldiers led by Harsha after they crossed the trench.

From between the smoke and dust appeared Narana, tired, dirty, burnt and injured. He charged towards the palace, swords in both hands and came face to face with Harsha on horseback with his soldiers. Behind Narana appeared Bhandi who dismounted from his horse and went after the Huna leader. Narana swung his sword, Bhandi ducked and made two quick strikes. One hit Narana's right shoulder and the other his left wrist. Both his swords fell to the ground. Unarmed and bleeding, Narana dropped to his knees. Bhandi held his sword to his neck, the bright sun shining over him.

"Stop!" said Harsha as he dismounted and walked towards the Huna king across the trench in waist-deep water.

"Well done, young man!" exclaimed Narana.

Harsha said, "You have two options now. One, we finish you right here. Two, we let you go if you give your word that you will not look in our direction ever again."

Narana, who was expecting to be beheaded, was taken aback. He looked around at the faces of the rival soldiers surrounding him. He could not believe that he had an escape route.

"It was Janardhan who provoked us. I was over-enthusiastic to increase my influence, and fell for it," said Narana.

"Whatever the reason, it ends here! What do you choose?" Harsha towered over him.

"I want to be spared and promise to never create trouble again. I take an oath on the name of my children," said Narana.

Harsha exclaimed, "Good! My physicians will take care of you for the next few days and my soldiers will respectfully escort you out of our kingdom after that."

Harsha had decided in consultation with his group that they would give Narana another chance if possible. The death of Narana, who was a feared warrior in his region, would cause his kingdom to disintegrate. The situation could become worse with the 22 barbaric tribes that existed to the west of his kingdom stepping in. These had been kept in check only because of the Huna kingdom. If the Hunas collapsed, these savage tribes would venture east and create regular problems for Sthaneshwar and other kingdoms. Conventional wisdom states that all enemies should be eliminated. Harsha believed that sometimes it was better not to enter every battle or eliminate every enemy. Some things had to be kept aside to take care of themselves. Even an enemy can be useful sometimes. Bhandi was happy that at a young age, Harsha had started to keep the bigger picture in mind while taking decisions.

thirty

The Element of Surprise

On the night of the victory against the Hunas, a feast was held inside Thanesara palace. It was less of a celebration and more a show of unity. Harsha expressed his gratitude for the contributions of Simhananda, Kuntala, Daksh, old Avanti, Durgavati and her father Parikshit for ensuring the victory against the Hunas. Drunk on *somras*, Bhandi, Simhananda, Kuntala and Daksh erupted into a warrior's song and huddle.

"How come you don't look happy even after such a comprehensive victory?" asked Durgavati as she took a sip from her copper cup of flavoured buttermilk and offered a cup to Harsha.

Harsha took the cup from her, "I don't know what is wrong with me. Nothing really excites me."

"What is the problem?" asked Durgavati.

"I am not sure myself!"

"Prince Harsha, try opening up, it helps!"

"Even if I forget the incidents of the recent past, when I think about what my sister is going through every day, it makes me numb with grief and rage," said Harsha.

"We are making progress, right! You have the kingdom of Sthaneshwar and all its resources under your control now. You can go after your main objective," remarked Durgavati.

Harsha said, "That is a relief for sure! I am using all the resources available to work on multiple options because I cannot go ahead with a single plan. Forget about all that, how was your first experience of a real battlefield?"

Durgavati said, "Words cannot explain the thrill of an actual confrontation. I learned so many things including being calm when the situation is tense."

"You were a lioness in the battlefield today, a sight to behold," said Harsha, admiringly.

Durgavati's face lit up with a smile.

Just then Daksh stepped out of the huddle and approached Harsha.

"Come, Prince Harsha! Join us."

"No, not tonight. I am not in the right frame of mind."

Daksh pulled the prince by his hands, "Come with us and believe me, you will feel better."

Harsha joined them reluctantly, but later spent a sleepless night plotting the next course of action. Precious time had passed in trying to regain control of his kingdom and thwart the takeover attempt by the Hunas. Some difficult choices awaited Harsha—whether to take a big risk or to go the more practical way.

Next morning, when Bhandi woke up, he saw Harsha sitting on a wooden chair in front of him.

"You are up pretty early."

"I didn't get much sleep last night. Come with me for a stroll in the garden," said Harsha.

It was foggy and the mist had just settled on the green grass. An attendant came in and handed them copper cups of hot milk with ground jaggery and nuts.

"A full-scale war will lead to a loss of lives and resources. We can handle this current situation through a covert mission," said Harsha.

"My view is that it is too much of a risk," commented Bhandi.

"I have asked our dear King Bhaskaravarman to help and he has sent in a team led by a trusted deputy named Hamsavega. They are already there," said Harsha.

"Let's hope that luck favours them," remarked Bhandi, taking a sip from his cup.

"I just got a message from them about a certain possibility. I am going in also," said Harsha.

Bhandi's eyes widened and he stopped walking, "No, Harsha! It's an irrational decision, don't do it."

"Hear me out! I have too much at stake here. I don't want to put you or anybody close to me at risk. I still suffer from the guilt of not having opposed brother Rajyavardhan enough when he overruled me from going and went into the battle himself. I cannot live with any more regrets," said Harsha.

"I am coming with you," said Bhandi.

"No! I don't want a repeat of a treachery episode like we had because of Janardhan. Stay back, keep an eye on everything and everybody. As far as possible, people should not figure out that I am not around. I can trust only you for that," said Harsha.

"Harsha! I still don't think it's a good idea."

Harsha said, "Don't worry! I am just going to oversee what is being planned and suggest any ideas to improvise. By the time the mission actually happens, I would have returned safely inside our borders. I will be using safe routes used by our spies that are not patrolled. So, absolutely no risk at all."

"Where are you off to?"

"From what the spies tell us, it is a prison south-east of

Indraprastha in an area controlled by Visnugupta," said Harsha.

"By when are you likely to return?"

"I have memorised the map, directions and main mud roads. If all goes well and we have the horses, then on the fourth day, I will enter our border either near Haldaavni or Kanakapura," said Harsha.

"What if something goes wrong?"

Harsha sighed, "This is the part I want you to hear carefully. If I don't return on the fourth day, on the sixth morning you should quietly sneak out of the palace with a few trusted soldiers without telling anybody other than old Avanti. Cross the border between us and Gauda through a route which our spies confirm is not heavily patrolled."

"Where to?"

Harsha handed a scroll to Bhandi. "Here! I have marked the route and destination. It is a peculiar hill with a bald top of rocks called Shivaganga Hill with a stream that circumnavigates it."

"Is the Parashuram Vatika around this hill?"

"Exactly! Stay there for exactly one day. I will be there."

Harsha was going to take a leap of faith. Bhandi could not understand his reluctance for a full-scale war. Harsha had two reasons—the disruption and loss of lives for soldiers and civilians that a war causes and, something else that he did not want to admit. The resistance against the Hunas was in home territory which Harsha was familiar with. A lot of factors were under his control. To wage a successful army campaign against a formidable adversary in no man's land was a different challenge altogether. Harsha lacked the confidence at this moment for something of that scale. In his mind, he feared that a failure would shake the confidence of the people who were now aligned to him.

thirty-one

Rescue Plan

It was a tedious journey through barren ravines and forests. At one point, Harsha wondered whether it had been a bad idea, but with just 18 days left for his sister's execution, no option was worth discarding. Dressed as a villager, with concealed weapons, lots of coins and some gold, Harsha crossed over the Malava border. After a treacherous trek through the jungle, he reached the banks of the Adivarna River. Behind a large old banyan tree, a small group waited for him. It was early evening and the air was filled with the sounds of birds returning to their nests.

"Greetings! We finally meet, Hamsavega!" said Harsha, greeting the trusted deputy of King Bhaskaravarman of Kamarupa, his father's closest friend.

"Suswagatam! The pleasure is mine, lord of Sthaneshwar. You came at the right time," said Hamsavega. He had five soldiers with him from the rugged mountainous regions, very tough and physically fit. His Kamarupi Sanskrit accent was rushed, almost gobbling and slurring through parts of a sentence.

"How long have you been here?" asked Harsha.

Hamsavega replied, "We have been here for 14 days. We had done enough due diligence and checks before we sent a message to you. We didn't expect you to come all the way here."

"I wanted to personally ensure that we make the most of this chance. By the way, what are our chances?"

Hamsavega smiled before replying, "Initially, it looked grim. As conveyed to you, something has started happening recently which has opened up new opportunities for us."

As the skies embraced darkness and the breeze blew colder, the small group took different mud roads through forests and grasslands to finally reach their destination.

"There it is!" said Hamsavega, pointing to a big white structure ahead. It was a political prison where Visnugupta detained rebel senior officials or tribal leaders. The structure had three floors with open galleries.

"Where is Rajashri?" asked Harsha.

"First floor, middle cell. It's a long dash from either side of the gallery."

Harsha sighed, "So you initially thought of barging into this highly guarded compound!"

"Yes, we did evaluate that, but that plan was full of risks. Please follow me." Hamsavega and his men led Harsha down a mud road which went up a dune with dense vegetation to the other side, where he could hear the sound of water gushing.

"What is that smell?" asked Harsha.

Someone behind Hamsavega replied, "It's a wild berry which rots and creates a pungent smell." The path became rocky and steep, making the climb difficult. Another of Hamsavega's men appeared from the opposite side. "Are they already there?" Hamsavega asked him.

"Yes, they might leave in a short while."

Hamsavega turned towards Harsha, "That means only you and I should proceed further or else we will be spotted."

The two of them started to climb the rocky slope.

"Five days back, they started bringing her out in the open twice daily. We observed it and thought of informing you," said Hamsavega.

Panting, Harsha replied, "I felt it was a very good chance. The only chance. So I wanted to come here and personally evaluate our alternatives. I will be gone by the time you execute the rescue plan, but I will leave assured in my mind that we came up with the best possible course of action."

"We will! There is ample scope. They allow her to spend some time near the shallow stream. It's heavily guarded but we can plan something," said Hamsavega. By now, Harsha was feeling impatient to get a glimpse of his sister. When they reached the top of the slope, Hamsavega told Harsha to crouch. Harsha peeped through a row of bushes and saw a rock cliff ahead. It was an elevated view; a well-hidden vantage point.

A shallow gushing stream split the land midway, as if taunting the big rocks on either side. There were green trees and dense vegetation on both sides. Upstream, it appeared as if the brook had just magically appeared from the forest. Downstream, it seemed to be taking swift dangerous turns as if rushing towards a waterfall. A shiny green slimy coating was visible on all the rock faces. There, seated on a rocky platform between three boulders with soldiers a little behind her and another group across the stream, was Rajashri. She looked unwell, but it was the sadness in her eyes that was heart-breaking for Harsha.

Jayachandra, the court poet of Sthaneshwar, had once written about Krishna after the great war was over. His kingdom and the beautiful palace of Dwarka had been swallowed up by the rising sea. He lost every last one of his dear ones—his wife, children and extended family—in the natural disaster. He was all alone. The astute strategist of the Kurukshetra war was now a broken man. In grief, he wandered around the vast expanses of the northern plains finally deciding to go to where it all started—his native place of Vraja. Once he was there, he found out that a mass ritual was taking place with people taking a holy dip in a stream. Near the placid water body, after decades, he saw his childhood lover Radha. She was there along with her fellow villagers from Repalli. The poet described with intense melancholy a depressed and detached Radha. Her life had been slow death without her Krishna. The last time he had seen her, she was a young and cheerful girl. Time had withered her. Krishna looked at his own situation and her plight. He remembered the glorious past they shared in dark contrast to the grim present. Tears rolled down his face. So much so that in one heartbreaking verse, the poet says that Radha's glance flitted over Krishna and she looked away, not even recognising him. She was so consumed by grief. Such was her state of mind.

In Rajashri's face Harsha saw what the poet had described. Detachment, grief beyond relief and eternal gloom. His heart sank for a moment.

"Prince Harsha, please have a quick look at the whole terrain and be careful!" whispered Hamsavega from behind.

Harsha sighed. Craning his neck, he looked out from between the shrubs, "Can we go ahead a little, towards the right, for a better look?"

"No, I am afraid not, Prince Harsha! We risk being spotted at any other place."

"All right! Then let me see her for one last time," said Harsha as he leaned forward from between the shrubs. The look on Rajashri's face was as if she did not want to live. Harsha was sure that by now she knew that, along with her husband, she had lost her father, mother and brother. Harsha surveyed the landscape from end to end, evaluating all possibilities. For a moment it appeared as if Rajashri was looking in his direction, but it was highly improbable, considering the camouflage of the vegetation.

"Time to go!" whispered Hamsavega.

Later in the evening, Harsha, Hamsavega and his team stood in the forest discussing the way ahead. It had taken Harsha a while to pacify his emotions and switch to a clear frame of mind.

"I wonder why they are allowing her to go outside the prison twice daily. Most importantly, how many more days will this last?" said Harsha.

Hamsavega replied, "It could be as a goodwill gesture or because the princess is unwell."

"From what I hear about Visnugupta, compassionate gestures are not a part of his nature. I strongly feel we have only a few days left before he puts her into permanent lockdown," remarked Harsha.

"So, we have come up with plans but they all have flaws."

"Go on, Hamsavega."

"We evaluated many possibilities but one option looks practical. Like ambushing the soldiers on both sides while a raft comes from upstream to rescue the princess and she can escape downstream," said Hamsavega.

"I am afraid that might not work," said Harsha with a sigh. "The way the stream twists and turns, gushing forward at such ferocity, any raft will capsize. Then Rajashri and everyone else on the raft will need to be rescued."

"That can happen. You have any thoughts, Prince Harsha?"

"Ambushing from both sides simultaneously is a good idea. I am thinking about those three big rocks in the middle of the stream. Can we have people hiding there?" wondered Harsha.

"But it's filled with water. How will they breathe?"

"Maybe wooden snorkels, but considering the long waiting time, it is not practical," said Harsha.

Just then, one of Hamsavega's men came rushing and whispered something in his ears.

Hamsavega's expression changed as he spoke up, "I am afraid, prince, that one of our men was arrested by the guards on grounds of suspicion while loitering around the complex where the princess is imprisoned."

"That is the last thing we wanted."

Hamsavega said confidently, "I know him very well. He will not blurt out anything even if he is tortured. It will be just a matter of days before he is released."

"We cannot be sure about anybody's breaking point. It is difficult to predict when someone will snap," remarked Harsha.

"I agree, but he is tough."

Harsha said, "Anyway, I am afraid I can't be here for that long."

"No problem, prince! You proceed back to your kingdom. We will keep strict vigilance and at an opportune moment, rescue Princess Rajashri," said Hamsavega confidently.

thirty-two

Strange Places

On a street next to a dry well, Harsha saw a bunch of street dogs fighting over what looked like a bloody human leg. It seemed to be in shreds, in many hues of red and dark blue. They were fighting each other mercilessly for their bite of flesh. Harsha knew he was in hostile territory, where he needed to avoid being around for long, but his hunger was unbearable.

Indra Bhojanalaya stated the wooden etching on the board outside a remote eatery near the Gaya highway in the kingdom of Gauda. This place called Chattra was a lawless place famous for criminal activities, arson, robbery, murder and kidnapping. Hamsavega's man was being interrogated by the Malava army. In such a situation it was unsafe to remain in Malava-occupied territory. On his way back, riding on the best horse Hamsavega's team had, Harsha was spotted by a Malava army patrol. He was not sure whether they recognised him but when they chased him, Harsha galloped on his big brown stallion across jungle mud roads to finally evade the soldiers. Harsha let go of the horse once out of the jungle, since one of its hind legs had been seriously injured during the chase. Now it was foolish to take the obvious routes from Malava back to his kingdom. So, Harsha did the unthinkable of going across the eastern border between

Malava and Gauda. From one enemy kingdom to another. This was the fall-back route to be taken in case of a 'distress scenario' which Harsha had explained to Bhandi. Harsha had to really hurry now and reach his capital. Durgashtami, the day they had planned to conduct the sacrificial ritual of Rajashri, was just 14 days away. At that moment, he was outside his kingdom and without any resources at his disposal.

As he ate the last morsel of thick milk porridge from his *patravali* plate, he saw groups of travellers flocking into the eatery from the highway. People moved in groups in these parts where straying alone meant inviting trouble. To travel at night was like embracing doom. The weather was humid and the air thick with dust. The loud barking of two dogs distracted Harsha as he peeped out of the eatery's window. Harsha realised that he had probably underestimated the cleverness of his enemies. The menacing twins he had encountered in the forest were right outside the eatery. From their gestures he could make out that they were asking the passers-by for directions. Were they looking for him? Had a palace staff member alerted rival spies about Harsha's absence? Had the Malava soldiers told their counterparts inside Gauda about this possibility? An army confrontation was coming up and spies of all three kingdoms were working hard to spread any useful information fast. Harsha's birthmark on his cheek was a bane for his safety, making him easily recognisable. He was in enemy territory under the constant fear of being recognised. The twins were holding on a metal leash two ferocious dogs with huge faces, sharp teeth, big reddened eyes and salivating mouths secured by metal jaw grilles. If the grille was removed, they could shred anyone to pieces within moments. These vicious animals were the reason why the passers-by were intimidated and avoided the twins. Harsha got up quietly when he felt that the gaze of the crippled twin had fallen on him. Within seconds, he had moved from the hustle and bustle within the eatery to the counter where its owner was seated. He placed two coins of the kingdom of Gauda on the counter, turned towards the kitchen and exited. Moments later, the twins came in.

"What happened?" asked Vamsi.

Vakul's eyes darted all over the place, "I thought I saw someone familiar."

A little away in the woods, Harsha waited to catch his breath. Holding his sack of belongings, he continued walking through the wilderness till late afternoon. He was tired and exhausted, but was sure that he was safe for the time being. He now needed to sort through his belongings in case he was caught with them. Under a banyan tree on the green grass, he unpacked his things to rearrange some and dispose of the rest. There were a lot of coins of Gauda and Malava, along with his gold ornaments and two big daggers. "I told Old Avanti and Bhandi to not load me with all these. All this wealth would just invite unnecessary trouble," he muttered. These were to be used in case of exigencies during the mission, but now that he was near the border of his kingdom, he could do away with them. Dressed as a commoner, he knew that he would be in grave danger if caught by criminals or arrested by soldiers for carrying these highly valuable articles across the border. Harsha had heard that in these parts, the soldiers were worse than criminals in their ways.

Just when Harsha was thinking about the various options, he felt something heavy land on the back of his head. His vision blurred as he became giddy, blinking at a hazy image of two soldiers. Struggling to get up, he swung a punch at one of them and missed. The other hit Harsha again on the back of his neck.

When he regained consciousness, Harsha found himself in a prison cell in what appeared to be a small *dandanayaka-karyalaya*, a law enforcement station, where suspects trying to smuggle goods across the borders, criminals and highway robbers were locked up after detention, till they were moved to the *nyayalaya* or main law enforcement complex in the nearest town. A large metal door separated the dingy lock-up section from the rest of the structure. There were four cells in this section. From the murmurs around, it looked like only the cell in front of Harsha was vacant. Harsha felt the back of his head; it was badly bruised. One of his eyes was swollen and partially closed. The game was over. His enemies had made the prize catch and it was only a matter of time before he would be transported to the capital town of Karnasuvarna. There the old treacherous King Shashank of Gauda would behead Harsha in the town square with fanfare. Once Visnugupta of Malava sacrifices Rajashri on the day of Durgashtami, the Pushyabhuti family would disappear into history forever.

Harsha looked around through partly-open eyes. The door of the cell had a metal frame and bars made of sturdy iron rusting in places. The light in the room came from a small window close to the ceiling, also covered with a metal grill. From the sound of birds and the breeze outside, Harsha could make out that this place was in the middle of the wilderness and not in some village.

A middle-aged guard with grey hair entered Harsha's section with a plate of millet flatbread and water in a metal cup. "You are awake! Here, eat this."

Harsha muttered, "What is this place?"

"Your home for now because the cart assigned to our station is being repaired. Otherwise, we would be at the court in Kashi town by evening," said the guard. Harsha looked at him thinking about what to say next.

"I think you have caught the wrong person."

The guard smirked, "We are cleverer than you assume. Take rest because tomorrow will be a long journey. Let me warn you that the mud roads to Kashi are in really bad shape and the journey will be tiring."

"We have been locked in here for two days now, how come he goes before us?" said a rough voice from the adjacent cell.

"What about me?" said another voice from its opposite cell.

"Stay quiet! We just feel the need to interrogate you people more," yelled the guard.

Harsha wondered why he was being taken to a court in Kashi and not the king's court in the capital.

"Look at you! Such a young man on the wrong side of law. How come you got into bad company?"

Harsha replied, "Bad company?"

"You tell me! We caught you with a fortune of coins from multiple kingdoms. The ones of Gauda were definitely fake. All that smuggled gold also. Why so much greed?" said the ageing guard.

Relief swept across Harsha's face. He pretended hard to conceal it. They had not identified him as the prince of Sthaneshwar, but assumed him to be a fake coin smuggler.

"You are mistaken! They are not fake coins. I work for a dairy product trader in Malava. We sell clarified butter," said Harsha.

"Where in Malava? Prove that with documents." Harsha was unable to respond. "See! Considering the number of coins we nabbed you with, you must be associated with some well-known trader. How come you were all alone? Don't lie! You are smuggling fake coins and you know the punishment in our kingdom for that."

"I know the punishment! You people chop off the hands of the culprit around the wrists," replied Harsha.

"Right, my boy! It's a little harsh, but we are having a lot of trouble with people like you smuggling in those cheap metal pieces from across the borders."

Harsha knew it was only a matter of time before someone identified him here or in Kashi, but he was not in as much trouble as he had previously imagined. If these guards knew who he was, he would have been dead by now.

Harsha looked around the cell. The walls were made of black stone blocks and the floor was layered with tiles which were old and cracking. There was a wooden bench with a broken leg, a mat and a wide flat-bottom metal drum filled one-fourth with water next to the wall.

"Hey boy! You there?" said a voice from the adjacent cell. Harsha did not reply; the tone had a certain unpolished, intimidating feel which discouraged him from being friendly with the prisoner.

He noticed that one of the metal rods on the window grill was bent. Maybe someone had tried to escape before, but it was too small for most people to pass through. He tried in vain to leap towards the window frame. On the wall, there were a few cracks, big and small. Taking off his footwear, Harsha stretched out his hands. He could touch the walls on either side. Hooking his bare toes in the cracks and using the wall for support, Harsha dragged himself upwards till he could get a firm hold on the window grill. Hanging on to one of the metal rods, he used his free hand to twist the one that was already loose. Unable to take the strain of his body weight on one hand, he dropped to the floor.

"What was that sound?" asked one of the inmates in the cell next to his.

Harsha crawled his way up to the window again. This time he suspended his weight on the loose metal rod and jumped to the floor along with it.

"Are you doing some jumping game, you worm?" asked a rough voice. Harsha did not bother to reply and looked at the rod. It was two palms' length and had a sharp edge. Just then the bolt of the big metal door leading to his section opened. Panicking, Harsha threw the metal piece into the water drum and sat eating his millet flatbread. Three guards came in. If they had keen eyes, they would have noticed that the window above him had one rod missing. Instead, they went ahead to the cells next to his.

"Come! Some people are here to meet you. We came to know why you were loitering in these parts," said one of the guards.

"What are you talking about?"

"Stop pretending! Now either you will tell us where you have hidden it or we will beat the last bit of life out of you," said a guard. Harsha listened with bated breath as the conversation turned more intense.

"We don't know what you are talking about."

"Let us talk about this outside," said the guard.

They opened the cells and dragged out the two inmates—who were already beaten, bruised and limping—across the section, beyond the metal door that the guards locked behind them.

Seeing this, Harsha wondered whether he would be next in line to be assaulted. He picked up the rod from the water drum and looked at it. *What could I possibly do with this?* He knew he had no answer. By venturing into enemy territory and exposing himself to the associated risks, he had jeopardised the future of his kingdom, his sister and his own life. *What if I am trapped here forever*? Harsha wondered. A loud crack of thunder distracted him from his thoughts.

thirty-three

Finding the Balance

In the royal court at Sthaneshwar, Bhandi sat on the chair of the erstwhile army chief Chakravarti. In front of him were the trusted commanders of the Yuva-Sena, the old strategist Avanti, Durgavati, her father Parikshit, Kuntala, Daksh and Simhananda.

"At some point of time, we might have a full-scale war. The good news is that the Sthaneshwar army has slowly reached more than half of its original strength after Janardhan's regime was toppled. These are ably supported by the full strength of the Yuva-Sena cadets. The bad news is that our numbers are much less compared to our rivals. We need to start preparing for war now," said Bhandi as he looked at the faces of everyone present. He was a man of few words, preferring to always remain in the background in large groups. The recent set of events had changed that. He knew that the situation demanded him to come to the forefront and use the power of the spoken word.

Simhananda said, "Our fighters are ready. Even if our numbers are less, we will finish the rival army."

"Sounds good when we say that nothing is impossible and nothing can stop us. The reality is that on the battleground, numbers matter," interrupted old Avanti.

Bhandi continued, "So let's divide the work. We all go out in various directions across the kingdom and recruit young men. We tell them that our kingdom and their families are in danger of being taken over by tyrants. It's time to save Sthaneshwar. Everyone needs to be part of our retaliation."

"And their training?" asked Durgavati.

"I suggest we quickly evaluate their skills—sword, spear, mace or bow and arrow—then put them through an intensive training for three days," said Bhandi.

"Should we also increase the number of horses and war elephants?" asked Kuntala.

"Horses are fine, but elephants are not required. Let's all put in our best efforts," said Bhandi.

"I am sure every family across our kingdom will volunteer its members and resources to support our army for this cause," commented Parikshit.

Simhananda asked, "Where is Prince Harsha? He has been missing for the past few days."

"He is into something important and could not be present here," said Bhandi.

"With the three kingdoms heading towards a major showdown, we need him here now!" exclaimed Daksh.

Bhandi took a deep breath and said, "I am sure he understands that we all are running against time and is putting his time to good use."

"We trust Prince Harsha's judgement," added old Avanti. The others started thinking about how they would go about their task of recruiting more people. Restlessness was evident on Daksh's face. Bhandi wondered what was bothering him.

"Anyway! Let's disperse in different directions and get back with motivated and skilled men from across our kingdom in the next few days. It's always better to be prepared for any eventuality," instructed Bhandi.

After everyone left, Bhandi sat wondering if they had a winning chance if Malava and Gauda attacked together. The past days had taken a toll on both him and Harsha. More than himself, he was worried for Harsha. Bhandi had started feeling that the young prince had taken a wrong path in leadership because of his initial success. Bhandi felt that Harsha had taken too much upon himself, compared to his age and experience. When they met again, he decided that he would advise him to be more prudent and less emotional. A leader should not be under stress to come up with the best ideas every time and then follow it closely all the way to closure. A leader should encourage the team to come up with good ideas and then trust them to take it to completion; checking only intermittently, keeping the overall authority but delegating to others who have demonstrated potential.

Unknown to Bhandi, the young prince was fighting the odds in a dingy prison cell inside the kingdom of Gauda.

thirty-four

Confinement in the Dark

The strong breeze was followed by flashes of lightning and the rumbling of thunder. Squatting in his cell, studying every part of it, Harsha did not allow self-doubt to numb his mind. Knowing that now he was all alone in this section of the prison, Harsha decided to make use of the metal rod. He had no idea how much time he had before they all came back again. There was a particular spot on the same wall as the window, a little towards the corner, which was difficult to spot from the other side of the door of his cell. Here, the stone block had cracks all around and the limestone plaster was chipping off at some places. Again, loud thunder boomed and rain started to fall. With his metal tool, Harsha started to the scrape the borders of the stone block, praying that the sound of the torrential rains would mute his gentle, gradual scraping. The cracks of this old structure made it easier for him to rupture the wall. He hoped that no guards were patrolling outside. If they were, his attempt to escape would be futile.

After what seemed like an eternity, the stone block started to wobble a little. In addition to his swollen eye and the pain at the back of his head, Harsha's hands were bruised with the effort. One push and the stone block would fall on the other side.

Harsha could then crawl through the wall. It was evening and it would be more sensible to attempt the escape in the dark. Also, the rain might have stopped by then. Just then, the bolt of the main metal door creaked. Pretending to be asleep on his mat, Harsha watched through half-closed eyes the two other inmates being dragged to their respective cells in a half-dead state. They were moaning in pain and left a trail of blood behind them.

"Let me wager with you—by tomorrow they will reveal the location," said one guard.

The other one replied, "They are tougher than that. Seasoned criminals like them are difficult to break."

Once the guards left, Harsha got up and started pushing the stone block through the wall. The cracks around it were widening. It fell out with a slight thud, leaving a gap. Harsha put his head through and scanned either side. No guards were patrolling this side of the structure. There was a boundary wall a little ahead leading into wilderness. It was twilight; the forest was calm. Harsha breathed deeply of the dusty air, had water from the metal drum and started on his enterprise again. The hole in the wall was of a peculiar oval shape. He put his head through, then a hand. Slanting his shoulder, he managed to get a portion of his torso through the wall. Gradually, he tried to push himself out. As he nervously looked around, he heard the faint sound of the bolt creaking as the main door opened. His body was now half in and half out of the cell. He quickly pulled himself back in, scratching his armpit and neck in the process. The pain was intense but he bit his tongue and dropped on his mat just in time, as the middle-aged guard entered the section. It was getting dark; he had come to light the fire torches fixed on the wall. Harsha was worried that if he came too close to his cell, he would spot the hole in the wall.

"Sleeping still!" the guard commented as he illuminated the section with his fire torch and threw two bananas into each cell. "Eat! This is your dinner." Harsha rubbed his eyes and thanked him with clasped palms.

Once the old guard left, Harsha tried to crawl through the wall again. The gradual push and pull continued. No matter how hard and whatever combination he tried, he was getting stuck in the hole and could not get across. It was a little too small for his waist. The other stone blocks around it were too big. It would take him more than a night to destabilise them. Frustrated, he sat on his mat sweating, bleeding. Time was running out and he needed to do something quickly. He drank some more water and evaluated all the possibilities. Near his feet he saw the cracks on the floor. Like branches of a tree leading to the trunk, they were increasing near the water drum. Harsha tiptoed to the corner where the water drum was, right in front of his cell door. He moved it a little and saw multiple cracks there. After placing his shoulder cloth on the surface, Harsha used his metal tool to strike hard on the floor, cracking it further. He threw the pieces of the tile out of the hole in the wall. There were stones and mud below. An idea suddenly occurred to him. He moved the metal drum from its position.

As the night progressed, Harsha started creating a hole in the floor, removing one stone after the other, digging out a handful of mud at a time and hurling it as far away from the wall as possible into the bushes nearby. It was a long and tedious process, but there was no choice. By midnight, the hole was longer in length and depth than his fully outstretched arm. As time went by, his fellow inmates slowly stopped groaning and fell asleep. The fire torches were extinguished due to the breeze coming in from the windows. It was pitch dark inside this section. Harsha was so exhausted that he collapsed and almost fell asleep.

He was woken up suddenly by loud curses from behind the metal door. Harsha crouched inside the hole, dragging the metal drum over him. The main door was flung open and the guards dragged in a violent prisoner. Harsha could hear the commotion, cuss words and sounds of struggling as the new inmate was thrown into the cell opposite his.

"Bastard! We finally managed to get our hands on you," said one of the guards.

"Let's see how long you are able to hold on to me!" came the reply in a baritone voice.

"The bounty on your head is for bringing you in dead or alive. We would not hesitate for a moment to kill you, but capturing you alive gives us more credit," said another guard.

There was a loud laugh in response, "Good work! Claim your bounty and credit!"

Harsha knew that it was a serious setback to his plan to have an inmate in the cell facing his.

Once they shut the door of that cell, the guards started inspecting each cell using their fire torches; first, the cells where the victims of their evening brutality had collapsed. Then Harsha heard footsteps near his cell, followed by absolute panic.

"The fake currency smuggler! He is not here!" Harsha heard the sound of his cell opening.

"It's unbelievable! He seems to have escaped from that hole in the wall."

"How did he do that?"

Harsha stopped breathing.

"Quick! Let's nab him before he goes out of our reach."

Crouching below the metal drum inside the hole he had dug, Harsha sighed with relief as they left with the door of his cell open. However, as expected, they locked the main metal door. Harsha took deep breaths. A little later, he heard faint conversations from the other side of the hole in the wall, which eventually subsided. The guards seemed to have gone in different directions searching for him.

Harsha knew he would have to wait till the inmate in the opposite cell fell asleep before he could sneak out to wait in the passage until the guard arrived in the morning. He waited. Sometime between midnight and dawn, when he was sure that there was no activity in the cell in front of him, Harsha quietly moved the drum a little to steal a glimpse. The rugged-looking prisoner was sound asleep. He moved the drum further and quietly stepped out of the hole. He tiptoed out of his cell, moving in the shadows as he pressed against the wall next to the new inmate's door.

"I saw you! You thought I was asleep, but I spotted you emerging like a snake crawling out of its hole," came the baritone voice of the inmate.

Harsha said, "So, now what?"

"I will yell out to the guards that you are right here."

"So why aren't you doing it already?" asked Harsha.

"I think we can work together on this. You break the lock of my cell and let me also escape with you," came the reply.

Harsha looked at the man. He was dirty and muscular, bearded with bloodshot eyes and a sly grin. Harsha's mind was racing. Could he trust this apparently dangerous person? His situation was precarious.

"Do it quickly," the man said, "or I will start yelling that the absconding prisoner is still inside."

Harsha stood without moving for a while. He had to go with his instincts.

The man was getting impatient, "Do it!"

Harsha stepped forward and started to strike the lock of the cell with his metal rod. Thinking that Harsha was finding it difficult to break the lock, the bearded man stepped up to the door to help. As soon as he came near, Harsha stabbed him across his cheek, smashing his jaw with the sharp part of the rod.

"Now you try yelling, you low life!" he said.

"Aaaah! Urrgh!" the bearded man cried out in pain, spitting blood. Harsha ran and hid behind the main door. Hearing the cries, two guards rushed in. Harsha pounced on them from behind, keeping his rod against the neck of one guard. In one swift move, he grabbed the guard's sword and placed it against the other's neck. "Drop your sword! Now!"

Holding the guards hostage, Harsha moved out of the main door and locked them inside. Outside, there were no guards; they had gone in search of the fake coin smuggler. Harsha disappeared into the darkness.

A little before dusk, as the guards of the law enforcement station sat in disgust evaluating the mess that had been created overnight, they had two visitors, representatives from the king's karyalaya.

"We heard you had a problem here last night," said the muscular twin.

"Yes, unfortunately we did," replied the middle-aged guard.

The twin with the crippled hand asked, "Can you describe the young man whom you had locked up here yesterday?"

thirty-five

A Traveller

It was difficult to guess on a map which *bhukti*, *visaya* or *pathaka* this hamlet belonged to. 12 huts stood in the middle of the wilderness surrounded by trees. The men of the village squatted on a burnt brick platform around the banyan tree, discussing their toils after a hard day at work. It was a village that seldom had visitors.

"Look! Someone is coming this way," said the blacksmith.

From a distance, it looked like an old man wrapped in a blanket, limping and with a stick in hand. As he came nearer, the villagers realised that it was a young man.

"What is your name? What happened to you?" asked the old headman.

"My name is Natha from Kannauj. A farm boy travelling to Gaya to see the Buddhist shrines. I was attacked by a wayward bull. I survived but was injured as I rolled down a slope," said Harsha, explaining the injury marks on his body. With killers on the lookout for a fit young prince, Harsha's disguise made him almost invisible. He had wrapped his sword in a cloth and strapped it to his back under the blanket.

"You look very tired. Sit here and rest for some time. Let me get you some water," said the potter, who went to his thatched roof hut and got a clay cup of water. Harsha drank and asked, "I think I have lost my way. Which place is this?"

"Our village is Sundaragram," replied the headman. Harsha's eyes narrowed as he tried to recollect the map but he had seen no village with a name like that. Maybe because it was a small hamlet, not worthy of being mentioned on maps.

"Where do you want to go?"

Harsha replied, "My village Madhurgaon is behind the Shivaganga hills." To this the villagers suggested that he head west to a small stream and follow it all the way to the bald hill of rocks. The only thing the villagers found strange in the young man with a red birthmark on his cheek was the tiger-claw pendant, chain and precious stone ring. Harsha explained that these were gifts from a rich silk merchant whom he had saved from robbers on the highway.

The sun was beginning to set in the west and the children of the hamlet returned from the fields after playing. The women who until now were cooking outside their huts received them and there was an elaborate cleaning ritual around the village well. It was well past dusk when Harsha bid adieu to the villagers and started to leave.

"You are our guest. Come eat with us, have a good sleep and then leave in the morning," suggested the headman.

"I need to reach my village by day after," said Harsha.

The blacksmith said, "It's not advisable to travel at night. If you are lucky, you might get a ride with a convoy of bullock carts carrying goods in the morning."

After much persuasion, Harsha agreed.

Every night, the villagers assembled outside the headman's hut and each family brought whatever they could for everyone else. Harsha watched as different families brought jaggery, milk, quail eggs, baked barley balls, millet flatcakes and bananas, each contributing to the community in their own way. Then they all said a prayer in praise of the sun, earth, fire, water and air, thanking the elements before starting to eat.

"We are very poor people, but we make the most of whatever we have," said the potter as he skinned a banana.

"Quite an unusual custom, this one," remarked Harsha about this daily community supper.

"Seven years back, during the summer, villages around us lost small children to hunger and malnutrition. That is when we decided that we are all in this together and no child in our village will die of hunger. It's fine if the administration does not do anything for us," said the headman.

"That is our story. In Gauda, we pay a big part of our produce to the king as taxes and very little is left. Every day is a struggle with lawlessness in our region and apathy from the people governing us," added the blacksmith.

"I have recently heard of rampant corruption by the administration," said Harsha.

"Just one of our many problems. Rains used to be too little and now it's too much, harming our crops. In between all this, we stick together for each other and survive. It's getting worse with time," said the headman who was a farmer by profession.

"Why such a grim outlook for the future?" asked Harsha.

The headman sighed, "Bharatvarsh is a land divided into a lot of small kingdoms and each king tries to show off his wealth to the other at the expense of the common man. There are rampant disputes between royal families. Most kingdoms have a failed administration. God forbid, if the barbaric tribes of the west or further north invade us, we have no single, powerful united front."

"I agree, we are not a united entity. Just a collection of weak kingdoms constantly in tussle with each other—Gauda, Malava, Sthaneshwar, Utkala, Kosala, Saurashtra, Kalachuris and Chalukyas. Each one for themselves," said Harsha.

"My grandfather used to say that this land and its people had seen so much welfare under great kings like Chandragupta Maurya, Asoka, Samudragupta and Vikramaditya. As I look around, we have no such ruler today!" said the headman.

"When we tell our children about the folklore and glory of those times, they ask why are things so bad now," smiled the potter.

The headman added, "We can't tell them that things might get worse. Our village gets all the news about various kingdoms from the network of newsmen. None of the ruling kings or their crown princes have the potential to salvage the situation and unify Bharatvarsh."

"There was one single ray of light in the darkness. Rajyavardhan of Sthaneshwar. A leader who was equally capable in administration and the battlefield. They got together and killed him," said the blacksmith. Harsha's expression changed.

That night, as Harsha lay on a mat outside the potter's house looking at the starlit sky, he was in deep thought. It was evident after observing this impoverished but blissful village that nature, if respected and shared, had enough to nurture every living being. All this helplessness and poverty was created by men. Men who drew boundaries in the soil. Men who staked claims or diverted water bodies to their advantage. Men who burnt down large stretches of forest lands carelessly to extend farms, for grazing and expansion of their towns. Men who nominated themselves to be agents of welfare of their people but could not look beyond their own gains. Men whose ego and lust for power killed their inner compassion. Harsha was deeply moved by the plight of these people and of so many others around Bharatvarsh whose voices were unheard. He realised the mistake he had made. He was not a prince any more but a representative of his people. Their hope. By venturing into enemy territory and risking his life driven by emotion, he had let his people down. Nobody would give Harsha any consideration for his young age. He was their leader and was expected to be more prudent. What if something happened to him? Sthaneshwar would plunge into turmoil. Kings like Shashank and Visnugupta would extend their control further and the misery of the common man would know no bounds. When his elder brother had said that his emotions needed to be his strength, not his weakness, this is what he had meant. Something Harsha did not follow because he didn't fully understand.

The last words his father had said, "Above everything, dedicate yourself for our people and motherland." This was not just a statement but a life mission for his children. Harsha knew that someone someday had to take control of the situation. Life was insignificant enough to disintegrate into soil one day and significant enough to positively affect the masses and generations. A motherland split into small kingdoms ruled by wayward kings intoxicated by power, ego and wealth could stand no chance against a mighty foreign invasion. In the near future, if he survived this current ordeal, he decided to work towards this bigger cause. Many people believed it was Rajyavardhan's fate to be the unifier of the land, but destiny had laid out that path for Harsha. Now he had to walk on that path. In the cool breeze of the silent secluded village, Harsha had the best sleep he had had for a long time.

When dawn arrived, the villagers realised that the visitor had left. In the afternoon, patrolling guards of the Gauda army rode into the hamlet on their horses.

"Did you people see a young man who had strayed into these parts?" asked the leader.

The villagers remained silent, wondering why the young man was being chased by the Gauda army.

"He is an enemy of the kingdom. Did anybody notice any traveller who looked suspicious?" repeated the soldier. The villagers had felt the previous night that their young visitor was a pleasant, well-mannered person. They chose to stay away from this situation and revealed nothing.

The guards galloped out of the village. In the fields, they saw some children playing with dried mud balls. A soldier dismounted and walked towards them.

"Did you boys see any visitor or stranger in your village in the past two days?"

"Yes!"

The soldier said, "Describe him to us."

thirty-six

Rabid Companions

Harsha woke up with a shudder, breaking into a cold sweat. Exhausted, he had fallen asleep under a berry tree in the middle of a grassland. Shedding the terror of his dream involving the mutilated body of his sister, he started walking again. After a treacherous hike through the forest, Harsha finally reached the stream which ran around the grey stone hill. Locals called it the Shivaganga Parvat since the bald hill and the stream encircling it looked like the aniconic representation of Lord Shiva. The light blue placid water was in contrast to the brown and grey rocky banks on either side. The land surrounding it was covered with all kinds of light green shrubs, thorny and leafy ones. A little ahead, it transformed into darker shades of green with floral plants. According to legend, after slaying numerous Kshatriyas to avenge his father's death, Parashuram, the incarnation of Lord Vishnu, arrived at this spot and was mesmerised by the natural beauty. These tranquil surroundings gave the warrior immense peace and he stayed here for a while before heading south. That stretch of greenery with its grass and flowers of all colours was also called Parashuram Vatika.

Harsha decided to rest for a while. The sun was yet to reach overhead. He placed the sword on a rock, the one he had snatched from the law enforcement post, and walked ahead into the stream. The first splash of water on his face and he felt refreshed beyond words. The water was like medicine that eased the fatigue in his body. One eye was still swollen, the back of his neck was bruised and the scratches all over his body ached. As he washed his face and arms half-submerged in the clear waters of the stream, he looked at the big boulders in front of him leading to the two hills. A large old tree had fallen in, disrupting the placid flow in the stream. The only sound in the entire stretch was the rippling of the water.

The sound of approaching chariots distracted Harsha as he looked to his right across the valley in hope. As he splashed a handful of cold water on his neck, he heard the loud and savage barking of dogs. He froze. This was the same petrifying sound he had heard across the forest on the night he had escaped out of the hunting mansion. Looking upstream, Harsha spotted his nemesis. The twins stood holding on to the leashes of their two huge and scary-looking dogs, one brown, the other black. Their faces were big, jaws bigger.

"See! I told you that our boy was here," said Vakul as he pointed to Harsha.

"I had to wait so much for this moment!" said Vamsi, a sadistic grin on his face.

Vakul took off the metal grills covering the jaws of the dogs who were roaring in rage by now. "Go!"

Unrestrained after a long time, they dashed towards their prey like arrows shot from a bow. Standing in the middle of the stream half submerged in water, Harsha panicked. It would be useless to dash backwards through the gravel to his sword on the rock. The dogs were rapidly closing in with every passing moment. Salivating and growling, they were near the stream in a flash. Harsha started to swim forward. The dogs followed him into the water. It took all of Harsha's strength to stay afloat and reach the other side. The dogs made the crossing look easy. Harsha turned back and saw the dogs closer than before. He needed time to think and evaluate his options. While sprinting on the rocky ground, Harsha slipped and fell. Looking back, he saw the dogs making aggressively for the shore. He got up and sprinted up a large rock, using its cracks for toeholds. Once he reached the top, he could see the stream, the broken tree towards his left and the twins grinning at his helplessness.

Harsha took up two big rocks, the only weapons available at the moment. The big black dog spotted the route Harsha had taken to the top of the rock and followed it. The brown one tried to make his way directly up the rock front. Harsha was looking around for a tree when suddenly the black dog pounced on him, biting into his thigh with its sharp teeth, its growling more intimidating than its bite. As a reaction to the sharp pain, Harsha used all his strength and smashed the canine's head between the two stones. The impact loosened the animal's jaws, thus disorienting it. He repeated the blow. The black dog collapsed, though still breathing. Within moments, the brown dog launched itself on Harsha, biting his left wrist and latching on to it, sending man and beast rolling down the slope and into the stream. The impact of falling into the water did not seem to affect the dog, which continued to cling on to Harsha's wrist. The sharp pain was unbearable. The water was streaked with red. Driven by the current, Harsha grabbed a branch of the fallen tree while the dog sunk its teeth deeper into his wrist. Harsha broke off a sharp shard of wood from the tree and stabbed the dog below its jaw. Its mouth opened in a sharp cry of pain and it was swept away downstream.

Exhausted and bleeding, Harsha tried to stay afloat. He was in that interlude of semi-consciousness until a pair of strong hands grabbed him, dragging him to the other side of the stream. The twins kicked Harsha at will, enjoying the torture. Harsha spat blood on the ground.

"Look at him, he is almost finished," sneered the muscular Vamsi.

Vakul said, "Let's just kill him right now. Or better still, let's present him alive to King Shashank. He will be happy to personally behead him, and put an end to the family feud."

"Maybe Shashank will gift him to Visnugupta of Malava. That man will torture this young bloke, shredding him to tiny pieces," remarked Vamsi.

"This young man is deceptive. Let's not delay and give him more chances. I suggest we kill him and present his dead body to King Shashank," said Vakul, drawing his sword.

Vamsi held Harsha, "Let's do it my way! Prince Harsha, ever imagined what it's like to have your skull crushed open?" Vamsi grabbed Harsha's throat with both hands, lifted him, and pressed his skull against a rock. Floating in mid-air, Harsha's eyes bulged as he felt the intense pressure that was about to crack his skull. Darkness descended and he started breathing slowly. Summoning all his strength, Harsha gave Vamsi a violent kick in the crotch. He lost his grip and let go of Harsha. Harsha leaped forward and headbutted Vakul, who fell, his nose bleeding, sword thrown out of his hand. Harsha kicked his face hard, knocking him senseless. Vamsi grabbed Harsha, and pressed him against the rock to crush his skull yet again, but Harsha dug his fingers into his eyes and freed himself. He rolled around, grabbed a rock and hurled it at Vamsi, but the latter dodged it.

Suddenly, a spear caught Vakul on his shoulder as many horses came galloping in their direction led by Bhandi. Bhandi swung his sword at the muscular Vamsi and slashed his neck, killing him instantly. The soldiers gathered around Harsha, who had fallen to the ground. Harsha looked at his cousin through half-open eyes and murmured, "You are late for your pick-up."

"You came early and this is a little away from the decided spot," said Bhandi as he dismounted and supported Harsha in getting up.

At that moment, Vakul, whom everybody had presumed dead, stood up. This was not the way he wanted things to end. He pulled out a dagger from his waistband and flung it at Harsha.

"Take this, you bastard!"

Bhandi's men quickly realised their mistake and one of them pounced on Vakul, stabbing him to death. The young man with the dagger wound on his back stood motionless. The dagger had hit Bhandi instead of Harsha. Harsha himself was barely able to stand erect. He saw Bhandi collapse like a log, his face pale, mouth open and in a pool of his own blood. Harsha's heart sank. He shook the cold body of his cousin. For once, Harsha felt he was indeed alone in this battle.

thirty-seven

Complications

As a last attempt to arrest the escalation of conflict between the kingdoms, Bhandi had sent a message of peace on behalf of Harsha to Shashank of Gauda. In the message it was stated that there was no need for a full-scale war between Sthaneshwar and the alliance of Gauda and Malava. Shashank was advised to use better judgement rather than plunge the region into instability. The onus was on Shashank to drive this point with Visnugupta. It was assured that if Rajashri was released unhurt, there would be no declaration of war from Harsha's side. If all the parties agreed, there could be peace for the foreseeable future.

Harsha's body was battered. His eyes were swollen, neck bruised, there were deep bites on his wrist and thigh, along with scratches all over his body. The wounds required time to heal, but Harsha had no time at hand. Durgashtami was seven days away, and his sister's life was in peril.

As the palace physician attended to his wounds, a messenger from Gauda entered, a tall lanky man in their saffron and brown uniform. He carried a scroll from his master.

Prince Harsha of Sthaneshwar,

I was surprised to get this message of peace from you. Your advisers must be telling you that buying time is the best way to manage the current situation. Rest assured, I will not be providing you the luxury of time. Your time is up, young man. Shashank of Gauda will not rest until each and every last one of you Vardhans perishes. I was a doting father who in good faith had got my young beautiful daughter married into your family. After the early death of my queen, I was father and mother to all my girls. What happened to Swaranya was not bad luck or a mishap. Her bad luck was to be a part of your family. To you it might not even sound like a reason, but I lost my little girl. God knows what excruciating grief I went through. I neglected food, medicines, fell ill and had a near-death experience. When I recovered, I wanted to get into an open conflict with your kingdom but my family stopped me and advised me to take my revenge in a more tactful manner. Also, I did not want the general public to think that I was dragging two kingdoms to war for personal reasons. I and my daughters, Sharada and Gautami, evaluated all the options. Sharada was never in love with you to start with; she played along and I set up a trap for you in the forest mansion. She thought I would imprison you but I wanted you dead, just like I cut short Rajyavardhan's life. You somehow escaped last time but you won't be lucky every time. My revenge ends with the death of you and Rajashri in the next few days.

We are all victims, crusaders against wrongs and the reincarnation of godly powers in our own stories. Let me not try to be a saint here or an aggrieved father out on a revenge trail, which, to be honest, is true only in parts. For long I have nurtured the dream of establishing myself as the single biggest power in the whole of Bharatvarsh. To be the Rajadhiraj, the king of kings. I had given up on that with time, but now when I look around it looks so achievable. Today, the Maukharis are heirless, Malava is my ally, the Kalachuris are recovering from the Chalukya onslaught. Kamarupa, Utkala, Dakshina Kosala and Saurashtra are in weak hands. This is my time to come to the forefront and I will grab it with both hands.

They say that there are no permanent friends or enemies in politics. Our situation is different and way too personal now for a truce to ever materialise. I cannot forget what happened to my daughter Swaranya and you can never forgive me for what happened to Rajyavardhan. At 17 years of age, you are too young to die but that is inevitable, considering the large army that I am commanding to your kingdom. Our military might is further enhanced by our allies and warlords. Prepare for war.

King Shashank of Gauda

The messenger's assistant handed over a covered tray to Harsha. When Harsha removed the silk cover, he saw that it was a broken piece of the family sword Asi. The one which Shashank had used to stab Rajyavardhan. Harsha recoiled in shock and for a while his gaze remained transfixed on the piece of metal. Harsha realised that Shashank had done this to emotionally destabilise him so that he would lose focus. Instead, Harsha chose to remain calm, control his emotions and be in the moment.

"Leave now and take that along with you!" he commanded.

Harsha was left deep in thought. The attendants brought turmeric milk, fruits and nuts but he did not even notice. *How things have changed*, he thought. When Rajyavardhan had married Swaranya, it looked as if eternal bliss was in store for the future. When less than a year later, Swaranya had conceived, the happiness of the families and subjects of the two kingdoms knew no bounds. At the same time, the families had decided on the marriage between Harsha and Shashank's younger daughter Sharada. The engagement between Harsha and Sharada was an elaborate ceremony full of pomp and grandeur held in Karnasuvarna palace in the capital of Gauda. The Vardhans left after 20 days, leaving Swaranya behind at Gauda palace. However, once they reached Sthaneshwar, the Vardhans did some rethinking. They felt that the first child in the royal family's next generation should be born in Thancsara palace and not outside the kingdom. The message was sent across to King Shashank who was not in agreement for this. Swaranya was midway through her pregnancy and like all doting fathers, Shashank was worried for her. Prabhakarvardhan and Yashomati were adamant. Rajyavardhan chose to support his parents on this issue. After some back and forth on this, Shashank finally succumbed to the family pressure from the Vardhans and agreed to personally drop his daughter at Thanesara palace. It was the peak of summer as their convoy of chariots took to the mud road connecting the capitals of the two kingdoms. A mishap followed as the chariot carrying Shashank and Swaranya cracked a wheel in a ditch and toppled. Father and daughter were violently thrown off the speeding chariot. On that hot summer afternoon, Shashank saw his pregnant daughter bleed to death on the rocky mud road in the middle of nowhere. Holding her cold dead body, he cried like a madman in the arid wilderness.

Harsha now knew that Shashank had never looked at that incident as a mishap. For him it was the royal ego of the Vardhans that brought about such a horrible end to his daughter's life, making revenge his single biggest objective. He still pretended to be on cordial terms with the Vardhans. Prabhakarvardhan, with his stature and allies, was not somebody with whom he could declare open enmity. Shashank's plan was to wait and eliminate the family when they were in a vulnerable situation.

Harsha knew that it was not their royal ego that had brought about this situation. It was an assertive want that spoils relationships. In his mind, he had begun to understand that most of the complications in the adult world are because people are fixated on things happening in a certain way. What follows are fixations achieved at the cost of relationships. It is a constant tussle where someone ends up playing a victim in their own mind. Love slowly starts to shrink while bitterness and resentment thrive. It happens between families, groups and nations. That fixation in the spur of the moment had caused immense damage to the Vardhan family. Who was right, the Vardhans or Shashank? Is there a single version of the truth? Harsha knew that like everything else, the one who eventually wins will be right. Success washes away a thousand wrongs and failure makes a thousand rights futile. All Harsha wanted to do in this complex situation was to save his sister who had nothing to do with this conflict.

Before leaving, the physician said, "It will take seven to ten days for your wounds to completely heal."

"I don't think I can afford to have that kind of relaxation. In three to four days, we go to war with Gauda and Malava. I hope to recover at least partially by then."

Harsha limped across the corridor to the chamber where Bhandi was being attended to by a team of physicians. He sat near him on the bed, his hands on his cousin's head. Bhandi lay on his stomach, eyes closed, skin pale. The wound caused by the dagger near his spine was coated with a yellow medicinal mix. After he was wounded, they had rushed him to Thanesara palace. He was attended by the chief physician and his nephew Anandam. As of now, it looked like their best ayurvedic treatment was still not enough. Harsha looked at the cold but still breathing body and pondered over the sad life his cousin had led. Harsha was faced with the grief of being orphaned only now. Bhandi had faced it as an eight-year-old child. Harsha experienced the feeling of being lonely in a crowd only now. Bhandi had experienced it forever. If Harsha had complaints about life, Bhandi had a lot more to complain about.

"How is he now?" asked Harsha, gently running his trembling fingers over Bhandi's head.

The chief physician said, "Bhandi has lost a lot of blood. Look at his skin; it's so pale. Our worry is that he has not regained consciousness."

"He is too young to die. Please do something!" requested Harsha with clasped hands.

"We are using all our skills and knowledge," Anandam consoled Harsha even as Bhandi moaned in agony.

"Anandam, is there anything we can do to improve his chances?"

"Already done that, Prince Harsha! I have sent out some riders for medicinal herbs from the Shivaliks. If they reach here on time, then it would be very helpful," said Anandam.

"I trust your judgement and skills. My cousin is a resilient man who has overcome so many obstacles in his life from the very beginning. He is a fighter and all we need to do is to give him a chance," said Harsha, his voice choking.

"It is evident from the scars on his body that he has survived major burn injuries in the past. He is indeed a fighter. I haven't slept since he was rushed into the palace. We are doing our best."

"I am grateful for that, Anandam."

The two things worse than physical pain are to see a loved one suffering and being distanced from a loved one. In the face of both these agonies, his physical pain seemed inconsequential. Harsha came out of the chamber with tears trickling down his face. He looked around and wiped them with his shoulder cloth, careful that no one saw him crying. It was part of the facade of looking in control of the situation for this 17-year-old leader. Hiding his tears from others was the most difficult part of his day. Nights were more compassionate since there was nobody around. Seeing Bhandi in this state was as if he was witnessing the death of Rajyavardhan play out in front of him. He felt a rush of rage against the people responsible for all this. For once, he was not worried about a full-scale war or its consequences. He limped back to the royal court, where shortly, all his close confidants and army commanders would be preparing the strategy for the impending war. He had a task at hand and the biggest challenge of his life was in front of him.

When he entered the court, Harsha saw a large wooden board on the ground over which a map was etched with clay models of the terrain. Durgavati, who was the only one present, was examining the display carefully. On seeing Harsha, she greeted him with a pleasant smile, "We are so glad to have you back here."

"Me too! I had some close brushes with death in the past few days. Looks like the prayers of our people saved me," commented Harsha.

"Everyone in Sthaneshwar is praying that these dark clouds of turmoil subside and we go back to living peacefully like we used to."

Harsha said, "Hope that comes true! I must tell you that having you lead the archers and your father helping with the archers on horseback is a big relief for me. I can focus on other things."

"I am glad to hear that, Prince Harsha," she said, beaming.

"I am just curious as to how you have become so mature beyond your age," Harsha said, as he occasionally glanced at the layout in front of them.

Durgavati paused for a moment before responding, "I think it came from a childhood of being deprived of things most people take for granted."

"Like what, Durgavati?"

"To start with, my mother passed away shortly after my birth. My father had to leave his job in the army and take up agriculture to look after me. We lived frugally. I was in bad health throughout my childhood. Missed out on a lot of things due to being bedridden all the time," she sighed and continued. "When I was 12, my father decided to put me through intense physical training to counter my bad health. I used to train along with his amateur students. My health and confidence improved because of the rigour. Since then I have always pushed my limits."

It only takes a heart-to-heart conversation to figure out that one is not alone in misery. A realisation that everyone is fighting their own series of battles.

Harsha said, "I think great things start by believing in yourself. You make all of us proud."

"Prince Harsha, at a personal level, I must tell you that the resilience you have shown against adversity in recent times is really commendable."

"I have no choice," said Harsha as he walked to the other side of the layout for a better look.

As Harsha's team of army commanders and confidants like the old strategist Avanti, Durgavati's father Parikshit, Kuntala and Simhananda entered, Durgavati became self-conscious and started studying the layout again.

"Where is Daksh?" asked Harsha.

"He said that he will be joining us a little later," said Kuntala.

"We are discussing the battle plan, which is a do or die situation for all of us. Every one of us should be here!" exclaimed Harsha.

Avanti intervened, "Let's just discuss the possibilities and finalise the plan once he joins us."

Harsha looked at the map and asked, "Where do you think the final face-off will happen?"

Pointing to the map, one of the commanders replied, "The armies of Malava and Gauda will merge somewhere here. Once they start moving, we can intercept them here, near the hills, or the plains or on the banks of the river."

"What are their numbers versus ours?" asked Harsha.

"Our numbers, after our soldiers rejoined along with the allied tribes, is 15,000, including foot soldiers and cavalry. Malava and Gauda will have a combined strength of 55,000 including war elephants, cavalry and foot soldiers," said Avanti.

Harsha paused and thought for a moment, "That is more than three times our size. Now, I suggest everyone just take a moment to think of the options available."

At that moment, Harsha's glance moved to Daksh and two of his men who appeared near the door, "Can I request Prince Harsha to join us for a word in private?"

Looking at his face, Harsha knew that something was wrong.

thirty-eight

Lost Worlds

The attendants were lighting the wall lamps that had been extinguished in the breeze. Harsha signalled to them to leave. Daksh and his clansmen were showing signs of hesitation before starting. Avanti stood behind Harsha, wondering what was brewing.

"As you know, we all hail from Kedarapura that is landlocked between Sthaneshwar, Kamarupa and Gauda. Our clan has inhabited the place for hundreds of years. It has our holy shrines and temples. Most importantly, our childhood memories dwell in every nook and corner of that area," said Daksh.

"I don't understand the relevance of this to our current situation," remarked Avanti.

"There is! Our villages were plagued by lawlessness after a local warlord called Sisupal murdered our king, a vassal of Kamarupa. Rival gangs of looters, smugglers and criminals also started to operate in our region. That is why we migrated to Sthaneshwar around nine years back and we thank you for welcoming us with open arms," said Daksh.

"That has been reciprocated. You have been our partner through some really difficult times recently, especially against the Hunas," said Harsha.

"Around the time of Princess Rajashri's wedding, the army of Gauda had encroached and captured our region, slaying Sisupal during the assault. So that puts us in a really difficult situation," said Daksh.

"What difficult situation?" asked Avanti.

"If King Shashank comes to know that we participated in this war with Sthaneshwar against Gauda, then he will never let us return to our villages. To return to our homeland is sacred for us and we hope for that in our lifetime," said Daksh, with deep feeling.

"Wait a moment!" Harsha thundered. "You have assumed that we will lose. If we defeat Gauda and Malava, then there are no further hurdles for you to return to your homeland."

Daksh fumbled with his words, "That is what we all want to believe. The truth is that our combined numbers are fewer than our enemy's. In a battle, we will most likely lose."

Harsha tried hard to control himself, "I am surprised by your lack of confidence! If you stand on the terrace of this very palace and look eastwards, you can see a place of great significance. The battlefield of Kurukshetra, where five brothers with a smaller army defeated 100 brothers with a much bigger army."

Daksh mumbled, "In the Mahabharata, Lord Krishna himself was with the Pandavas. Who will save us mortals from the wrath of the Gauda and Malava armies? We really don't know what to do."

Avanti intervened, "When you don't know which path to take, then do as Krishna said in the battlefield. Follow the path of righteousness and justice against tyrants. Do what is right."

"For us poor villagers, going back to our home is more important than the bigger right or wrong of the world," remarked Daksh.

"I am 17 years old and yet I have the courage to stand for what is right. You grown-up men showing such lack of courage appals me," said Harsha.

Avanti added, "We have a leader who is beyond his age. Trust his ability and stay with us."

"I haven't studied the Gita or the Vedas like you learned people. Even an illiterate like me knows about a 16-year-old in the Mahabharata who dared to venture into hostile territory. When luck was on his side, young Abhimanyu did get some success. But eventually, when his luck ran out, we all know what happened to him," said Daksh, lowering his gaze.

Avanti interrupted, "That is not a fair comparison." He looked at Harsha and could see that Daksh's words had pierced him. The line of argument was very vicious.

"This is not the time for debate! From what I can make out, you people have already made up your minds," Harsha paused for a moment. "You came here and stated your position frankly. I appreciate that and wish you people the very best."

Daksh apologised again and left.

Avanti looked at Harsha's mortified face for a long time. His eyes were red and he did not say a word.

"What happened?" asked Avanti.

"The more I interact with people, the more I realise that I should not trust them easily," said Harsha.

"Prince Harsha, it's not your fault. They have abruptly switched sides. My worry is that their deserting will have an impact on us. In our situation, each soldier counts."

Harsha said, "I am fine with fewer people than more of those who don't believe in our cause or are fending for themselves."

"Let's put this behind us. I am shocked with Daksh's use of harsh words just to get away from this situation."

Harsha sighed, "Like Abhimanyu, it might be my fate to be one of the many dead bodies in a battlefield. My only reassurance then will be that I would have died keeping the family's honour intact. Let's meet tomorrow a little before sunrise."

While everybody else had a sound sleep, Harsha sat on the grass covering the garden. Bhandi fighting for his life and Daksh's words had created a whirlwind of restlessness in his mind. Even the shining moon and the tranquil night were not able to pacify his anxiety. He remembered how in his childhood, during the peak of summer, the Vardhan family used to sleep on the terrace of the palace. It was memorable. The starlit sky, the breeze and the laughter. The children used to talk about all the things they planned to do when they grew up and their parents would tell them how it would be possible to achieve them. Where was that world? Where every morning did not start with a challenge. Where one's duties were not painfully carried forward from one day to the next. Where wants didn't send people on an endless chase. That world had disappeared along with its promises. Where was the future they had imagined? Where were those people who could listen and understand all this? That uncomplicated world had vanished along with its inhabitants. The palace towering behind Harsha in the dark remained silent.

The expectations of a young person starting life and the reality of where it eventually moves may be two separate directions, but acceptance is the first step towards healing. Harsha cursed himself to stop living in the past and focus on the present. Accept the present and do something about it. Well past midnight, Harsha fell asleep.

Just before dawn, old Avanti, Simhananda, Kuntala, Durgavati and Parikshit, along with the commanders and seconds-in-command of the Sthaneshwar army assembled again in the war chamber around the map and the models of the terrain. While heading for the chamber, Harsha glanced at the painting hanging on the corridor wall which depicted Rajyavardhan, Rajashri, Bhandi and Harsha in a joyful group embrace. It was gifted to them by their parents on the day Rajyavardhan was declared crown prince. Below, a wooden panel had an inscribed message from the erstwhile king and queen: "Our precious gems. Rajyavardhan, the future of our kingdom. Bhandi, our strength. Rajashri, our pride and happiness. Harsha, the light that will illuminate the world one day." Harsha stared at the last sentence for a while before entering the discussion chamber.

"We heard what happened with Daksh," remarked Kuntala.

Simhananda added, "It never occurred to us that someone from among us would desert us at this moment."

Harsha paused and sighed, "He did what he thought was right for his people. Time for us to discuss the battle plan! With the numbers clearly in the enemy's favour, they will be full of confidence. What are your views on intercepting them? Here, near the river or just behind these hills? Tell me, what exactly is there at this stretch on the map?"

Everyone assembled looked at one another till a commander from the back row spoke up, "I am a native of this region, let me have a look." He stepped forward, looked carefully for a long time at the map and said, "There are two or three small ponds here between vast grasslands."

"That is good! Our enemy has a huge cavalry and the stallions would love to graze in grasslands like these. What is the size of these ponds?" asked Harsha.

"Very small. Not sure if they have dried up by now."

Harsha sighed, "We need to take our chances."

"What is there in these parts?" asked Parikshit.

"There are twin villages here, Narigaon and Manjipura, separated by a man-made canal."

Durgavati commented, "Then I guess we should avoid this direction altogether for a confrontation with the rival army."

"What about this particular place?" asked Kuntala.

"These have four or five natural caves."

Kuntala was excited, "Can we hide some of our soldiers here to act as reinforcements?"

"I am afraid these will not be of much help since each can accommodate 30 to 50 soldiers only."

"That's of no use to us," sighed Avanti. Harsha walked around the map, observing it carefully from all sides.

"Prince Harsha, is it prudent to allow them to enter so deep into our territory?" asked Simhananda.

"Let's look at this as just one of the options. I welcome you all to present your ideas," said Harsha, like his father and brother used to do during discussions. The last time, when they had gathered together to plan how to counter the Huna invasion, Harsha had a good idea and had blurted it out. Only later did he realise that others could not contribute with their ideas because of his enthusiasm. They became mere followers. It worked once, but it was not the best path to take. Unlike other people who only evaluated failed campaigns and celebrated the successful ones, Harsha reviewed even successful endeavours to figure out the weak links. He had reflected on his mistake from the last time. A single individual, even if he is the leader, cannot have the best ideas all the time. All good ideas are scattered among the members and the leader brings them together, choosing the best. Also, it is unreasonable to expect a team to wholeheartedly own a plan in which they have little or no say. A true leader is not the one who speaks the most in any gathering. He is the one who says very little and speaks after everybody else, only after he has patiently listened to everyone. So, one by one, each person spoke and Harsha listened carefully.

Durgavati's father Parikshit felt that all the ideas were going in different directions. "I don't think we are getting anywhere."

"Don't worry! We are doing well. Respected Avanti, your suggestion?" asked Harsha.

Avanti said, "One of our strong points is that our enemy is not united. Shashank of Gauda and Visnugupta of Malava are both ambitious and egocentric individuals. They are together only to bring us down; otherwise they cannot see eye-to-eye."

"What you said is interesting and we should leverage that. One suggestion. Those boys we met at the Yuva-Sena Kendra just days before Rajashri's wedding. Badrinath and the one who was an expert in animals, I think his name was Radheya. Can they be summoned to the palace today?" Harsha asked.

"Yes! We will arrange that," offered Kuntala.

"I have already sent a convoy of chariots for my tribal friend Soma and men from his Koruwa tribe to be here with some material today. I had saved his life once, he reciprocated it and now his tribe will be doing another favour for all of us," said Harsha. "In the meanwhile, any suggestions for improvement in our weapons arsenal?"

"We have asked for bows made of *singpho* to be transported from Kamarupa by tomorrow for our archers. They give a much longer range," said Parikshit.

"Good! Near this river, which I am assuming is a tributary of the Ganga, we need a lot of large boats and assistance of the local fishermen," said Harsha. "If everyone has put forward their ideas, then let's formulate the final course of action."

Every eye in the war chamber was on the young prince,

who had, in a very short period of time, been able to muster so much courage and confidence despite having faced terrible difficulties. Only Harsha knew the turmoil inside him. One half of him had lost the will to live. Like Buddha, after watching so much of sickness, death and suffering, he was disillusioned by the world. It sucked out all the fear he had ever had, but made him stay afloat and gave him direction. His sister was the reason for him to be anchored to the shores of life. This strange mix of emotions was his driving force as he approached the biggest battle of his life.

thirty-nine

Battle of Pundravardhana

The armies of Malava and Gauda converged just short of the border of Sthaneshwar. The kings of both the kingdoms, seated atop their war elephants, came closer to discuss the situation. As per what some spies had communicated, there was supposed to be an ambush prior to their reaching the border, but there had been none.

"Greetings, Shashank of Gauda! You seem to be in high spirits."

"Maybe because I smell victory, Visnugupta."

"Even I do! It's too early in the morning. Should we not rest our armies before venturing inside enemy territory?" asked Visnugupta.

Shashank replied, "My scouts tell me that Harsha has positioned the Sthaneshwar army at a distance from the border, near the river. I see no harm in our moving a little ahead, then taking some rest."

Visnugupta said, "Then we are inside enemy territory. I don't feel that is a good idea."

"The last time you and your brother thought and planned something, I had to intervene. So, let me do the thinking this time around."

"Mistakes happen! Do you plan to launch the attack today itself?" asked Visnugupta, his expression changing momentarily.

Shashank replied, "Timing is key. Let's hunt down the Sthaneshwar army and eliminate them today. Then we should proceed to raid their main towns. I am told that Harsha is seriously injured and might not lead the army in the battlefield. Let's not give him time to recover and launch a planned attack on us."

"I agree. Let's put the boy out of his misery!" said Visnugupta. The way Shashank was trying to control the proceedings was irritating him, but he decided to let it be for now.

The armies proceeded inside Sthaneshwar, across the hill and around the small natural ponds. Once they were in sight of the vast stretches of grasslands, they stopped to rest till noon. The horses grazed the grasslands and drank from the three ponds. The elephants were given the rest they needed. The sun was slowly moving overhead, but the surroundings were pleasantly cool because of the cover of greenery. A little before noon, they were ready for the onslaught. A combined army of close to 55,000 covered the vast landscape for as far as the eye could see.

"That boy Harsha! The way he overthrew Janardhan's regime and defeated the Hunas, we should not underestimate him," commented Visnugupta. He and Shashank were having their meal together—jaggery milk porridge, along with dry fruits, nuts and banana crushed and mixed with milk.

Shashank smirked, "If you ask me, he is lucky. Both his achievements were just good luck, achieved in a place of familiarity, his own palace. An open battle at this scale will expose the shortcomings in his leadership."

"So, what after we defeat him?" asked Visnugupta, studying the expression on Shashank's face closely.

"I wonder why you are asking this again and again. You already control most of Kannauj, so Sthaneshwar should largely come to us."

Shashank had not even completed his sentence when Visnugupta interrupted assertively, "Kannauj was won solely with the tact and efforts of my brother, so that has nothing to do with our deal. We should split Sthaneshwar into equal halves between us."

"You forget things so easily, so let me jog your memory. Remember that after your brother was slain and you were on the run between the ravines, I gave away my own son-in-law Rajyavardhan to you people. I don't think you have any bargaining power considering that I saved you from that precarious situation."

After a brief pause, Visnugupta said, "Let's leave this negotiation for another day. Today is not the right time and it is diverting our focus."

"I agree. Looks like we have to sort out a lot of things after this is over," said Shashank.

A little later, the armies got ready and started to move in the direction where the scouts had spotted the Sthaneshwar army. Shashank and Visnugupta were excited. The time they had been waiting for had finally arrived. Moving a little ahead, they saw the Sthaneshwar army. Towards their left was the tributary where a few fishing vessels could be seen anchored to the river bank and towards the right were the flat-top hills. Harsha's army was stationed right ahead of a stretch of dense vegetation and tall trees.

"Their numbers look much smaller than I had anticipated. A part of their army might be stationed outside their capital to protect the royal palace," yelled Shashank from the top of his war elephant to Visnugupta.

"To me their numbers look to be around 7,000. Not a single war elephant. My spies were right when they said that most of Sthaneshwar's army has absconded due to a lack of confidence in their leadership. Are you able to spot Harsha?" asked Visnugupta at the top of his voice.

"There he is! Wearing a helmet with a white mane, on top of the white and brown horse," shouted back Shashank.

Suddenly, a row of archers came out of nowhere in front of Harsha's army and showered arrows at the enemy. It was as if the sky was covered by the lethal projectiles. The armies of Malava and Gauda took out their shields and efficiently blocked the arrows coming their way.

"This is what happens when you put an immature boy in command of an army. Let's finish Harsha and his men forever! Attack!" yelled Visnugupta.

"Attack!" Shashank gave out the war cry.

Gauda and Malava's foot soldiers and cavalry charged at the Sthaneshwar army. Absolute commotion followed. There were sounds of metal clashing against metal, horses neighing loudly, soldiers screaming war cries or crying out with pain. Shashank and Visnugupta were unable to see anything because the dry stretch of terrain was covered by clouds of dust.

"I hate engaging in warfare on such terrain where after a point nothing is visible," muttered Shashank.

Then followed loud chants of "Harsha is dead! Harsha is dead!"

Shashank and Visnugupta smiled. The soldiers and their commanders returned from the cloud of dust, their swords held high and their horses galloping fast. To one of his returning commanders Shashank asked, "What just happened over there?"

"Looks like one of our spears got their leader Harsha. It went straight through his chest. The Sthaneshwar soldiers have started to flee the battlefield."

"Bring me Harsha's dead body," ordered Shashank.

"They managed to carry their injured leader to the fishing boats anchored on the river bank. You see those boats moving right there? They are attempting to save their leader. No use, Harsha was already dead in the battlefield, from what we could see," explained the commander.

Shashank was delighted at having eliminated the heir to the Sthaneshwar throne. He asked a messenger to go back and inform his daughter Sharada whose convoy was trailing her father's army at a safe distance from the battlefield. She was waiting impatiently to hear from him.

"Tell Sharada that it is safe to move forward into Sthaneshwar and join us." Father and daughter had devised a plan to make their victorious entry into Thanesara palace together. A long-cherished moment.

Shashank glanced at Visnugupta who was already in a celebratory mood and was preparing to finish this conquest in the next two days to return to his capital. After the ceremony, he could finally get his hands on Rajashri for a night before she went to the sacrificial altar the next morning. Without giving his ally any time to think, Shashank quickly put forward his interest. "Visnugupta, I think it's a little premature to celebrate. Let's complete the annexation," yelled Shashank from his war elephant, "Let's split from here. You proceed to towns north of

Indraprastha and we move ahead to Thanesara. Let's eliminate all the threats."

Visnugupta's expression changed, "Wait! Let's make it the other way round. We move to Thanesara and you take a detour to the north of Indraprastha."

"I told you our understanding was that since Kannauj is already yours, most of Sthaneshwar will come to us. You can take a few towns north of Indraprastha, but that's it!" Shashank was losing his patience.

"You treat us like dogs, giving us leftovers! Kannauj was conquered due to the brilliant timing of my brother. We are collaborating in this invasion of Sthaneshwar. So, nothing less than half of the territory, including Thanesara town, belongs to us!" exclaimed Visnugupta.

"These things are not to be discussed in a battlefield but over a negotiation table," said Shashank, but he was interrupted by Visnugupta. "No better place than this and no better time than now!"

"You are so unpredictable! I think I should have let both of you brothers die at the hands of Rajyavardhan and not intervened at all," Shashank shouted in rage.

Visnugupta smirked, "Too late for a reconsideration!"

"Then I will correct the mistakes of the past!" said Shashank. The allies had swiftly turned into enemies, their armies broke their formations and tore into each other. Shashank and Visnugupta drove their war elephants to either side of the battlefield. Mayhem followed. There was no strategy or plan, just brutal, mindless violence. Both sides suffered casualties, losing more than half their strength by late afternoon. At this point, first the Malava army played their war trumpet which was shortly followed by the Gauda army. It was a declaration of stoppage of battle from both sides. This kind of impulsive confrontation seemed unnecessary, but it had taken everybody a while to realise it. There was an uneasy silence as Shashank and Visnugupta tried to move closer to each other to have a word. Every soldier waited for what was about to transpire.

While the friends-turned-foes were busy fighting, something else was also taking place in the battlefield. The cavalry had a strange problem on their hands. Their horses had suddenly become unresponsive; some were frothing at the mouth while others simply collapsed, falling face first to the ground. 8,000 horses behaving erratically had sent the soldiers into panic.

What happened suddenly? wondered Shashank. Visnugupta gaped at the scene before them.

As Shashank and Visnugupta watched, a human chain appeared from between the rows of trees far ahead of them. They were carrying something in their hands along with fire torches. As the chain came forward, Shashank and Visnugupta noticed that right in the middle was Harsha. At that moment, in the fishing boat on the other side of the river, Badrinath of Jantiya village, with his striking resemblance to Harsha, took off the fake spear attached on either side of his armour to seem as if it had passed through his body, removed his helmet and wiped off the fake blood.

In the battlefield, standing next to Harsha in the human chain was Radheya, the village boy who knew all about wild fruits, berries and tribal poisons. His poisonous fruit had been mashed in large quantities, mixed in tanks of water and drained into all the three ponds a little ahead of the battlefield. As anticipated, the armies of Malava and Gauda had taken rest at the same place just before the battle. Their horses had grazed the grasslands and drank from the pond, as a consequence of which the invader's horses were now sick. The men in the chain were carrying big balls made of wild creepers and herbs. Shashank and Visnugupta watched as they set the balls on fire and hurled them forward. All across the battlefield the fireballs rolled forward in rows, emitting large volumes of smoke. The soldiers surviving the confrontation between the Malava and Gauda armies stopped and wondered what was coming their way. Worried that the fumes were poisonous, they tied their turban cloths around their faces. All that the fumes did was to irritate their eyes, but the 1,000 war elephants went berserk, throwing off their mahouts and riders, and stampeding across the battlefield, trampling the soldiers and unresponsive horses along the way as they ran amok. The men of Soma's Koruwa tribe had worked sleeplessly for the last few days, to create these fuming balls of mayhem. It was elephant pandemonium as the Malava and Gauda generals stood clueless. They realised that they had more dead bodies on the ground than standing soldiers.

Ahead of them, from behind the stretch of trees appeared more Sthaneshwar soldiers. The Malava and Gauda armies saw their rivals getting into war formation. Unlike his brother Rajyavardhan, who had a preference for the *deva-vyuha* or inverted arrowhead formation, Harsha had a preference for the *asura-vyuha* or pointed triangle formation. Here, he had made a variant of it, where the foot soldiers formed a triangle with archers in the middle and near the tip on either side were smaller triangles of cavalrymen. Like a jungle boar with tusks on both sides of its mouth, this was the wild boar formation.

"Har Har Mahadev!" Harsha gave out the war cry. "Har Har Mahadev!" his men yelled. "Jai Sthaneshwar!" as the wild boar formation charged like a rampaging storm into the enemies.

The soldiers of Gauda and Malava, already in shock because of their internal conflict, their horses and elephants going berserk, did not know what hit them.

Harsha sliced through the rival generals with his sword. Shashank and Visnugupta quickly crawled down from their war elephants. It was evident that their otherwise hefty and strong bull elephants were slowly becoming agitated because of the fumes. The strong breeze had now spread the deadly fumes all across the battlefield. Once on his horse, Shashank saw Harsha charging towards him and started to retreat.

Seeing Harsha chase Shashank, four of Shashank's bodyguards intercepted him on their horses. Harsha responded immediately. He steered his horse between two of them and holding his shield near his face, charged into them, making two clean swipes of his sword on either side. The bodyguards did not get time to raise their weapons as Harsha's sword sliced through one's stomach and hit the other's arm almost simultaneously. The horses of the other two bodyguards were behind Harsha. He reined his mount, making it rear, then took a sudden turn and stabbed one of the soldiers in the chest. At the same time, he smashed his shield into the other bodyguard, dislodging him from his horse. Having taken care of the bodyguards, Harsha galloped towards the escaping Shashank. From the corner of his eye, he saw Durgavati and one of her archers riding to intercept Shashank from the east. In a quick move, Durgavati and her archer sheathed their swords, took out their bows and aimed. A strong breeze was blowing across the battlefield. Shashank whipped his horse to gallop as fast as it could. This stretch of terrain was rather uneven, shaking the riders with unexpected jolts. As Harsha watched, Shashank increased the distance between them at a rapid pace. Harsha knew that the breeze and the terrain could still be to Shashank's advantage. As he watched, Durgavati and the archer paused for a moment, then let loose their arrows.

Two arrows were shot at the same time. Harsha's heart almost stopped beating. His eyes darted between Shashank and Durgavati.

"Nice!" said Harsha, as the arrows hit Shashank on his back and shoulder. The old king continued to ride on in spite of the bleeding. They saw him half dangling from his horse and disappearing over the horizon. Harsha rode close to Durgavati and her archer.

"Poison-tipped arrows?" he asked.

"Yes. There is only a small chance that he might survive. Even if he does, he will have permanent damage to his eyesight and mobility," said Durgavati.

"I want him to live," Harsha said, his voice hard and cold. "Death is a lesser punishment. I want Shashank of Gauda to die every single day. Live the rest of his life as a bedridden, sick old man, clinging on to whatever little territory he has. He should shed tears every day thinking about his shattered dream of world domination and repenting his deeds."

Behind them, there was commotion. Harsha turned his horse. Most of the Gauda and Malava soldiers had escaped or died in the battlefield. Harsha's soldiers had formed a circle and in the middle was the king of Malava, Visnugupta. Dislodged from his horse, sword and helmet snatched from him by Harsha's men, he was on his knees. A spear had gone through his shoulder and he was bleeding profusely.

"Ah, you! Dismount your horse and fight me like a man, Harsha," he yelled.

Harsha replied, "I won't fight an injured man, Visnugupta."

"Then go ahead and kill me like a warrior!"

Harsha smiled, "You are no warrior. You are a demented beast. I don't need to kill you because the way you are bleeding, death is not far away."

"Just kill me and let's finish this!"

Harsha thought for a moment and looked up into the sky, "No! No way. For the peace of Rajyavardhan and Grihavarman's souls, I will not give you such an easy death."

By now, Visnugupta was rambling, speaking gibberish. Harsha glanced at the sky again as he started to walk away, instructing his men, "Encircle him and let him bleed. The other bodies should be respectfully cremated or buried. Let the eagles and vultures have this bastard alive."

forty

Scarred Survivors

A distinct smell similar to a citrus orchard pervaded these parts of the forest. In this season, the colour of the leaves ranged from light yellow to dark brown. As the caravan moved uphill, crossing the border into the kingdom of Kamarupa, Rajashri should have felt a soothing sense of relief after a long time, but she did not. Instead, her anxiety peaked with suffocating intensity.

"Finally, we are inside our border. Good work, team!" exclaimed Hamsavega who was leading the row of chariots on his horse. He and his team had stayed back after Harsha had escaped from enemy territory. They kept a close watch daily on the proceedings inside the prison complex. The resourceful Hamsavega had forged an alliance with two local clans led by chiefs Vyaghraketu and Bhukampa. King Visnugupta instructed his army chief to move Rajashri to a makeshift prison inside his main palace complex to prevent any attempts to rescue her. Vyaghraketu's informants had passed on the news to Hamsavega. That night, when the Malava soldiers were trying to relocate Rajashri, Hamsavega and his team ambushed the convoy near the Vidisha farmers' market. Rajashri escaped during the fighting to a nearby forest where Hamsavega managed to trace her after two days. Today, his face was brimming with the pride of his victorious mission.

The convoy moved up the slope for a long time. When the chariots finally stopped, Rajashri, teary-eyed and anxious, saw someone familiar. Her father's friend King Bhaskaravarman of Kamarupa had come personally to welcome her.

"Come here, my child! I can't tell you how worried we were for your safety all along," said the old man whose grey hair and beard fluttered in the breeze as he cupped the young princess's face in his palms like a doting father, "Your brother and we worked relentlessly for this moment of your freedom. I can't believe we finally have you here."

"I am thankful to you all, especially Hamsavega and his men. They showed extraordinary valour to save me."

"I am glad that they were of help. We all believed that Hamsavega was the man for the job," said Bhaskar as he placed his hand on Hamsavega's shoulder, who bowed in respect in front of his king. "Why do you have tears in your eyes?" the king asked Rajashri.

"On the way here, I overheard two soldiers in the convoy saying that the news from the battlefield between Sthaneshwar and the combined forces of Gauda and Malava is not encouraging. That rival soldiers were celebrating joyfully, saying that Harsha is finished," she wept and her voice quivered as she mumbled, "These are just rumours, right? You are like a father figure, tell me the truth of what happened."

"I think Harsha is fine."

Rajashri studied the expression on the old man's face carefully, "The way you are saying it, it's not very convincing."

Bhaskaravarman sighed and said gently, "My little princess! Don't put me in this difficult situation. From what I hear from my messengers, nothing can be said for certain."

"Is my brother alive?"

"We are hearing all kinds of things from the battlefield. It is difficult to say," said Bhaskar.

Rajashri had got her answer and she turned and walked away.

"Where are you going my child?"

She walked towards the edge of the cliff and said, "I am feeling breathless, I need some fresh air." She could not come to terms with the fact that she was in all probability alone in this world now. The erstwhile queen, the Maharani of Kannauj, had lost everything. She was not scared of death today. She was scared of life. From a pampered princess surrounded by loved ones, she was now suddenly thrust into a lonely inconsequential grief-ridden existence. Bhaskar wondered what he could say to alleviate Rajashri's grief. She was indeed an unfortunate young girl who was just about to start her life when suddenly, everything had been snatched from her. Like a solitary tree at the edge of a jungle, unharmed by a forest fire, which had seen everything around it turn to ashes.

She stood closer to the edge of the cliff with her hair fluttering in the wind. Then she closed her eyes and took a deep breath as tears rolled down her cheeks. When she opened her eyes, she saw a small convoy pass right below the cliff in the middle of the forest. Leading the convoy was a young man on a white stallion.

"My brother!" she shouted as she started running in his direction. It was as if she'd had a new burst of life. Her brother rode the stallion up the slope and they met midway. Harsha dismounted and they hugged each other. Finally united in their bliss of reunion and in their grief of having lost their whole family.

"It looked as if an era of suffering had separated us, but we are finally here, my sister," said Harsha, fighting hard to control his tears. His voice had acquired a strange stoic tone to it.

Rajashri broke down. "The thought of being left alone in this world terrified me. I don't want a life where I have nobody; I can't take any more loss. I am so glad that you made it through all this. Where is cousin Bhandi?"

Harsha sighed, "When I left our palace, he was fighting life and death. On our way here, the palace messenger caught up with us. He informed us that Bhandi is weak but regained consciousness yesterday. That is a good sign. Our young palace physician Anandam has worked day and night for his recovery."

"Endless misery came upon all of us! I wonder why we were subject to so much suffering in the past few months," cried Rajashri as tears flowed uncontrollably from her eyes.

"That is probably the way the world works, my little sister. Nobody is spared from the balancing forces that run our world, that's what a wise monk told me recently," said Harsha. Rajashri saw the deep wound on Harsha's wrist and cried out, "What happened to your wrist, your eyes, your neck?"

Harsha smiled, "You have no idea how many more wounds I have under the battle armour, you just can't see them. There are more scars inside me than outside on my body." It was evident to Harsha that getting wounds and continuing with those scars was part of life. When life puts people through toil, they emerge as scarred survivors. Nobody is spared, not even gods in their human form. Ram himself had a lifetime of tragedies in the forest, during the war with Lanka and later inside the Ayodhya palace until he walked deep into the Sarayu River to disappear forever. Krishna wandered the earth heartbroken after having lost his kingdom, his palace at Dwarka and all his loved ones. A glorious life culminating in an even greater tragedy until the hunter's arrow finally got to him in the forest. They were both remembered for their days of glory and heroics, but the years of agony find no mention. Suffering is a human condition, but even the gods carried the scars of the battles they had fought. Harsha remembered his father saying that most beautiful and the most dangerous people in the world, both have numerous scars inside them. What they became was due to the path they took when these scars were being inflicted on them. Harsha now understood the true meaning of those words. He was fed so much poison in the last few months, it almost felt as if the poison had been transformed into the elixir of clarity in purpose. Like a scorpion's poison, the venom became burden and strength. A poison that made him more alive. It had transformed him from a young prince horrified by the battlefield into a leader who commanded his army to famous victories against formidable adversaries. Harsha went to Bhaskar, hands clasped, and bowed respectfully in front of him.

"Today is the day to rejoice. To have defeated a rival army three times your number is an achievement unheard of in these parts for decades. My friend Prabhakarvardhan will be brimming with pride in heaven today. Your resilience calls for a celebration, young man," said Bhaskar.

"More than celebrations, I want some days of complete peace for now," said Harsha.

They waved at the convoy below and Rajashri remarked, "Who is that confident woman leading the soldiers next to the old man?"

"Her name is Durgavati. I have made a lot of new friends during the past turbulent days. Let me introduce you to them," said Harsha.

They proceeded down the slope to meet everyone. As they reached the foot of the slope, a messenger came galloping and presented himself to Harsha. Harsha and Rajashri looked at each other wondering if it was good news or bad. It was difficult for Harsha to take any more bad news.

"Master! You will not believe whose convoy walked into our territory. Our soldiers spotted a troop of soldiers holding the Gauda flag. We encircled them and unexpectedly nabbed Princess Sharada of Gauda. She is in our custody now," said the messenger.

Harsha could sense that the soldiers behind him were in high spirits after hearing this. Sharada had led Harsha into a trap at the hunting mansion. The murmur behind Harsha was that this was a great opportunity. He took a while to think through this new development.

"That's a tough decision to make. To be honest, we don't know her part of the story," said Harsha.

Bhaskar said, "It's a difficult decision."

"She made her choice and I am making mine. It's un-warrior-like to mistreat a woman or use her as a bait to get Shashank," Harsha said as he took off his ring with the rare garnet gemstone and handed it over to the messenger. "Set her free and give this to her. I don't need it any more. Tell her that I was not looking for gifts but genuine affection. I wish the very best for her."

After spending some days in Kamarupa, Harsha and Rajashri went back to their palace at Thanesara. Ten days later, Harsha was crowned king of Sthaneshwar. That evening, clad in a white *angavastram,* he went alone to the Hillock of Gods to offer flowers at the place where his father was cremated and his mother had sacrificed herself. It took a great deal of courage for Harsha to come to this place where the turbulent episode of his life had started. He sat there the whole night, shedding tears before planning his way ahead. The next day, he left for Haridwar to immerse the urns with the mortal remains of his parents into the holy river. To overcome his grief and trauma, he occupied himself with matters of the state. Harsha was broken inside to the extent that he thought he might never be healed. Some wounds don't heal; they remain open and continue to bleed. Harsha constantly felt the piercing shards of the broken pieces inside him. He believed that the cracks inside him were beautiful, depending on how one looked at it. He was damaged brutally for a purpose. His guiding principle was the last words spoken by his father, that above everything, dedicate your life fully to your people and motherland. Harsha aimed to make the whole Bharatvarsh a welfare state under a unified leadership. His mission distracted him from the excruciating memories, those images of pain, treachery and suffering. Like his family deity Lord Shiva, Harsha had to drink the most lethal of poisons and move ahead as if nothing had happened. The happiness and prosperity of his land became his life's mission.

He chose to live the kind of life that his brother Rajyavardhan believed in, a life defined not by what one received from the world but by what one gave to the world. The sequence of tragic events after his parents' deaths had shaped Harsha's personality forever. In his literary works where he was god, the endings were happy. He used to call himself the more *lenient* god. In his mind he believed that in real life there were no happy endings, only mixed endings. An ending where one walks around with their wounds with a smile. For a long time, this dark episode from his past prevented the smile on Harsha's face. However, there were some dark nights when deep in his sleep his face had a slight, pleasant smile when he experienced the lost world. Covered in a dreamy haze he would see his father King Prabhakarvardhan, mother Yashomati, brother Rajyavardhan and his noble wife Swaranya. Even if it was for a few moments, time shifted back to when things were good. Times when he used to look forward to his day when his eyes opened in the morning. Back when life felt great and every day was a celebration. When they had a blissful home and everyone was a part of it. A world where eternal sunshine bounces on green grasslands to light up the many smiling faces. In that world, among Rajashri, Bhandi and all the people who were long gone, Harsha, like the meaning of his name, was happy.

Harshavardhan went on to become one of the greatest kings of India with an empire covering most of northern India. His reign was a golden period in Indian history where the country was ruled by three great kings: Harsha in the north and Pulakeshin-II, shortly followed by Narasimhavaraman in the south. Harsha's reign was a period of prosperity, benevolence to all religions, promotion of arts and welfare for the common man. Even the Chinese travellers were in awe of the prosperity and welfare enjoyed by the common man during his reign. Harsha married Durgavati and ruled for 41 years. Bhandi remained his trusted associate and his army chief. Somewhere towards the middle of his reign, Harsha took up Buddhism. A prolific writer, Harsha is believed to be the author of famous works of literature in Sanskrit namely *Ratnavali*, *Nagananda* and *Priyadarsika*. The remains of his palace in the northern part of India are today known as 'Harsh ka Tila'.

Acknowledgements

My wife Priya for being my partner in everything and inspiring so many people around with her courage. My parents Muraleedharan, Padmaja Pillai and grandma Ambika Devi for shaping me to become the person I am. Their sacrifices have been my motivation always. My brother Sumit for being my best friend and partner in so many endeavours.

This book is dedicated to the two little ones who bring purpose to my life, Atharv and Advika. You are everything for me.

A big thanks to my manuscript consultant and editor, Sucharita Dutta-Asane, for being my trusted partner in this third novel together. We share a great understanding, and the perspectives we bring to the table while collaborating take a manuscript many notches ahead. The depth of her involvement with this story was very reassuring. I always look forward to working with her.

A big shout-out to my colleague and friend Ved Lal for always putting forward the best advice and pointing out gaps in a story, a rare quality. Special thanks to him. Also, thanking Arun R for being my oldest friend and telling me point blank what is good and what is not. Special thanks to the team at

Jaico for believing in this manuscript; the efforts undertaken in editing, proofreading and cover design. It was a great experience working with them.

This book is inspired by Banabhatta's original work *Harshacharita* and accounts of Chinese travellers during that period. It is only partly fictionalised; most of the characters and events are aligned with actual historical records.

About the Author

Born in Thiruvananthapuram, Rajat spent most of his early years in Delhi and later in Kerala. He did his MBA from IMI-Delhi and ESC-France. While working as a software program manager in the financial services sector, he wrote his first novel *Chandragupta* which became a national bestseller and was translated into regional languages. *Chandragupta's* motion picture rights were acquired in 2017 by a global production house. Rajat's second book *Dead Woman Writing* was a top-selling psychological thriller in 2014. His third book *Yoddha*, a work of historical fiction, was released in early 2018 to critical acclaim by major national publications. This is only his fourth book in 11 years. You can connect with him on Facebook (Rajat Pillai – Author) or Instagram (@pillairajat).

JAICO PUBLISHING HOUSE

Elevate Your Life. Transform Your World.

ESTABLISHED IN 1946, Jaico Publishing House is home to world-transforming authors such as Sri Sri Paramahansa Yogananda, Osho, The Dalai Lama, Sri Sri Ravi Shankar, Sadhguru, Robin Sharma, Deepak Chopra, Jack Canfield, Eknath Easwaran, Devdutt Pattanaik, Khushwant Singh, John Maxwell, Brian Tracy and Stephen Hawking.

Our late founder Mr. Jaman Shah first established Jaico as a book distribution company. Sensing that independence was around the corner, he aptly named his company Jaico ('Jai' means victory in Hindi). In order to service the significant demand for affordable books in a developing nation, Mr. Shah initiated Jaico's own publications. Jaico was India's first publisher of paperback books in the English language.

While self-help, religion and philosophy, mind/body/spirit, and business titles form the cornerstone of our non-fiction list, we publish an exciting range of travel, current affairs, biography, and popular science books as well. Our renewed focus on popular fiction is evident in our new titles by a host of fresh young talent from India and abroad. Jaico's recently established Translations Division translates selected English content into nine regional languages.

In addition to being a publisher and distributor of its own titles, Jaico is a major national distributor of books of leading international and Indian publishers. With its headquarters in Mumbai, Jaico has branches and sales offices in Ahmedabad, Bangalore, Bhopal, Chennai, Delhi, Hyderabad, Kolkata and Lucknow.

SINCE 1946